A DAY FOR DYING

An Inspector Luke Thanet Novel

DOROTHY SIMPSON

SCRIBNER

SCRIBNER
1230 Avenue of the Americas
New York, NY 10020

This book is a work of fiction. Names, characters,
places, and incidents either are products of the author's
imagination or are used fictitiously. Any resemblance to
actual events or locales or persons, living or
dead, is entirely coincidental.

Originally published in Great Britain by
Michael Joseph Ltd

SCRIBNER and design are registered trademarks of
Simon & Schuster Inc.

Manufactured in the United States of America

ISBN 978-1-5011-5376-1

To my niece, Alison, with love and gratitude

ONE

It was on a Saturday evening in late March that Ben dropped his bombshell.

Thanet and Joan had had a quiet evening at home. They'd eaten supper off trays in front of the television set and were now discussing their holiday plans before going to bed.

'Didn't you say the Dracos went Greek-island-hopping last summer?' said Joan.

'Yes. They had a marvellous time. The Super came back looking so relaxed we could hardly believe it was the same man. Of course, it was partly huge relief that Angharad was still in the clear.'

Angharad Draco, wife of the Superintendent of Sturren-den Divisional Police Headquarters, where Thanet worked, had been diagnosed as suffering from acute myeloid leukaemia four years ago. So far, she had been one of the lucky ones. The average outlook is only two years of life from diagnosis and there had been general rejoicing when she had passed this milestone and begun to put on weight, regain her spectacular good looks. Now, with every month that went by, the hope grew stronger that the danger really was over.

'I ran into her in the town the other day,' said Joan, 'and she looks wonderful.'

'I haven't seen her for ages.'

'Well, you will at the party.'

They both glanced at the invitation card on the mantelpiece.

Thanet grinned. 'There are all sorts of rumours flying around . . . marquee, top-notch band, caterers, the lot.'

'Well, you can't blame him for wanting to celebrate. Her birthday must mean something pretty special these days.'

The front door slammed and they glanced at the clock. It was only 10.30. They raised eyebrows at each other.

'Hi!' said Ben, poking his head into the room.

'You're early!' they said.

'I wanted to catch you before you went to bed. I'll just . . .'

'. . . get a snack,' they chorused, smiling. Their son's snacks were a family joke.

He gave a sheepish grin and disappeared.

'Sounds ominous,' said Thanet.

'Certainly does. Must be important. Ten-thirty on a Saturday night? Unheard of!'

'Perhaps he's finally made up his mind at last.'

'Let's hope so!'

It was decision time for Ben. He was bright enough to have been offered a place at both Bristol and Durham Universities, and had been trying to decide which was his first choice. There had been endless family discussions on the respective advantages and disadvantages and they had all reached the stage where it would be a relief when the decision was made.

Ben came in carrying his 'snack' – a triple-decker sandwich flanked by an apple and a banana.

2

'So,' said Thanet when Ben was settled. 'What did you want to talk about?'

Ben had taken a huge bite out of his sandwich and finished masticating before saying, 'I've made up my mind what I want to do.' He cast a swift, assessing glance at his parents before taking another bite.

Thanet felt the first stirring of unease. 'And?'

Another pause. Ben swallowed, then put his plate carefully down on the table beside his chair before saying, 'I've decided not to choose either.'

'Ah.' Taken aback, Thanet didn't quite know how to react. He sensed a crisis looming.

'What d'you mean, exactly?' said Joan. Her tone was strained. She was trying, but just failing, to conceal her dismay.

Ben sat back, folding his arms across his chest as if to defend himself from the attack he was sure would come. 'I've decided not to go to university at all.'

Thanet knew his face must be betraying something of the disappointment which welled up in him, and was helpless to prevent it. Not having been to university himself and having always regretted it, he had pinned his hopes on Ben. Bridget had not been academic and he had been happy to encourage her in her chosen career, admired the success she had made of it. But Ben . . . Ben was bright, had sailed through his exams with ease. What a waste it would be, not to take up this unique opportunity to enlarge his mind, his experience, his knowledge. Careful, he told himself. We must be careful. He glanced at Joan and could see her thinking the same thing. Safer to say as little as possible, make sure that no bridges were burned.

'At all?' he said, echoing Ben's last words.

Ben nodded.

3

'You mean, you want to defer taking up your place?' said Joan. 'Have a year out?'

Thanet could hear the hope in her voice. That could be it, of course. So many young people these days did just that after taking their A levels, eager to see something of the world before they settled down to three or four years of further study. Having missed out earlier, Bridget was travelling at the moment. Perhaps that was it. Perhaps Ben had been made to feel restless by the postcards which had been arriving from the Far East and, of late, New Zealand and Australia?

But Ben was shaking his head. 'I've made up my mind what I want to do, and I can't really see the point of wasting three years going to university.'

'What do you want to do?' said Thanet. Ben had always said he couldn't make up his mind.

Ben raised his chin and looked straight at his father. 'I want to go into the police.'

Silence.

Thanet didn't know what to say. This was the last thing he had expected and his reaction was mixed. He was touched, proud, yes, that his son was choosing to follow him. But he was, above all, dismayed. Apart from the tragedy it would be for Ben to throw away this chance, life in the force was not what it had once been. Over the last decade the problems of law and order had proliferated, slowly seeping out into the rural areas from the cities. He loved his work, had never regretted his choice of career, but of late had often wondered if, had he been starting again, he would have thought more than twice about it.

'I see. I assume this isn't a sudden decision?'

Ben shook his head. 'I've been thinking about it for ages. But I knew you'd both be disappointed if I didn't go to university, so I kept on putting off telling –'

4

The telephone rang and Thanet went to answer it, not sure whether to be glad or sorry that their discussion had been interrupted. He hoped it might be Bridget but it was Pater, the Station Officer.

'Sorry to disturb you, sir . . .'

'It's all right, it's too early for me to be enjoying my beauty sleep. What's the problem?'

'Report of a suspicious death just come in, sir. Out at Donnington. Body of a young man found in a swimming pool. There was a party going on.'

'Sounds as though he might have had too much to drink. Have you notified the Super?'

'He's out. I left a message on his answerphone, then rang you.'

'I'll leave right away. What's the address?' Thanet scribbled directions and put the phone down. No need to tell Pater what to do, the sergeant knew the routine off by heart. He returned to the sitting room.

Joan stood up as he came in. 'We heard.'

'Yes, sorry, Ben. This is important to you, I know.'

Ben shook his head. 'It's OK, Dad, I understand. We can talk about it some other time.'

'Yes, of course.' And it was probably best that way, thought Thanet. It'll give Joan and me time to discuss how best to react.

Outside the air was fresh and cool after the warmth of the house. A light breeze had sprung up, chasing away the ragged clouds which from time to time had obscured the sun throughout the day. The sky was clear and the street and driveway were bathed in the silvery light of a moon that was almost full.

Thanet shivered and turned up the collar of his coat. Donnington wasn't far, only a couple of miles from Sturrenden on the other side of the river. At this time of night it shouldn't take more than ten minutes or so to get there. A party, he thought gloomily. The place would be crawling with potential suspects.

He found the house without difficulty. It was in a country lane leading out of the village, one of several properties standing well back from the road. There was a big bunch of balloons tied to the gatepost and a patrol car parked on the verge outside. A uniformed officer waved him down as he slowed.

'Sorry, sir, there's no room to park inside at the moment, drive's crammed with cars already. There was a party going on.'

'What sort of party, do we know?'

'Engagement party for the daughter of the house. The dead man was her fiancé.'

Poor girl, thought Thanet as he parked his car. What a way for the night to end.

As he got out another car could be heard approaching along the lane and he saw with satisfaction that it was Lineham's Escort. He waited for the sergeant to join him and told him what little he knew as they walked to the entrance to the drive. Then they paused for a few moments to look around.

The wrought-iron gates, hung on brick pillars, stood wide open. Just inside them the driveway forked, the narrower arm leading off to the right in the direction of a bungalow where lights still burned. A gardener's cottage, perhaps? The grounds of the house were sufficiently extensive to warrant one; the drive was a couple of hundred yards long and the moonlight revealed wide lawns spreading away on either side, bisected by flower borders and flanked by stands of mature trees. Cars were parked nose to tail all the way along the drive and in the big parking area in front of the house. This was ablaze with light, a long, low, sprawling structure, 1930s stock-brokers' Tudor by the look of it, built at a time when domestic help was still readily available. At one end, projecting forwards at right angles to the main house, was a single storey building and as he and Lineham drew nearer Thanet could see it was a separate structure, a block of garages. Somewhere behind the house a dog was barking, a big one, by the sound of it. It had probably been chained up for the evening.

'Let's hope things haven't been disturbed too much,' he said. 'Looks as though there's quite a crowd here tonight.'

But predictably Lineham was too busy taking in the general air of affluence to respond. 'Four garages!' he said. 'Not exactly paupers, are they?'

Thanet grinned. Lineham's stock reaction to any property larger than the average never failed to amuse him. 'Fancy the place, do you, Mike? You'll have to ask for a rise.'

'Ha, ha. Very funny.'

Thanet could hear more cars arriving in the lane behind them. The SOCOs, perhaps, and Doc Mallard. 'Come on, let's get a move on, find out what's what.'

They quickened their pace. The curtains had not been drawn and they glimpsed people standing around or sitting huddled in small groups. Even from outside the air of shock was evident.

Almost before the reverberations of Lineham's knock had died away the door opened.

The woman was in her late thirties, with fashionably tousled long dark curly hair, deep-set brown eyes and a pointed nose. Her careful make-up could not disguise the hint of ill humour in the set of her mouth, the frown lines scored between the heavy brows. Her simple black dress

7

looked expensive and she was wearing a chunky gold necklace and earrings. The 'lady' of the house, Thanet assumed. But he was wrong. She introduced herself as the housekeeper, Barbara Mallis, and gestured them into a large, square hall with panelled walls and a wide oak staircase. The subdued murmur of conversation emanating from the rooms on either side died away as people craned to catch a glimpse of them.

'I'll let Mr Sylvester know you're here.'

But there was no need. A man emerged from the room to the left.

'Ah, there he is,' she said.

Sylvester was casually but expensively dressed in cashmere sweater and soft silky cords. He was around fifty, Thanet guessed, with thinning hair and the pock-marked skin of a former acne sufferer. He looked distinctly unhealthy. Heavy jowls and a protruding belly betrayed a penchant for too much rich food and the skin of his face was the colour of uncooked dough.

He acknowledged Thanet's introductions with a tense nod. 'This way.'

Sylvester obviously didn't believe in wasting time on social niceties, thought Thanet as he and Lineham followed him across the hall and along a corridor at the back leading off to the left. They were presumably going to the swimming pool.

'I gather it was you who found him, sir,' said Thanet.

'Yes.'

'And he was your daughter's fiancé, I believe?'

Sylvester nodded, tight-lipped. He had stopped in front of the door at the end of the corridor and was fishing a key out of his pocket. 'I made sure it was locked before we left.'

Thanet's heart sank. 'We?'

Sylvester's shoulders twitched impatiently. 'Oh, I know, I know, I've seen the films, I'm aware that you shouldn't disturb anything and looking back I can see I should have kept everyone out, but at the time ... You're just not thinking straight. You can understand that, surely.'

'Only too well. Unfortunately it does make our job more difficult.' It also ensured that if Sylvester himself had helped the unfortunate young man on his way, it would be more difficult to isolate scientific evidence against him.

Sylvester merely grunted and turned the key in the lock. Warm moist air and a smell of chlorine rushed out to greet them. Thanet caught a brief glimpse of dark water shimmering in the moonlight before Sylvester flooded the room with light.

Thanet caught Lineham's admiring glance and knew what the sergeant was thinking. *They really must be loaded.* The pool house was indeed unashamed luxury. It must have been around twenty-five metres long and was built entirely of glass, and double glazed, too, for there was no sign of condensation on the windows or roof. Of irregular shape, the pool itself was deep enough to sport a diving board at the nearer end. Comfortable *chaises-longues* with yellow-and-white-striped cushions which would bring a hint of sunshine to the gloomiest of days were interspersed with groups of exotic potted plants, some of which were as tall as young trees. It would be a real pleasure to relax here after a hard day's work – a pleasure which from now on would no doubt be blighted by the memory of what had happened tonight.

The body lay at the far end of the pool and as they approached it Sylvester was explaining that the only way he could get it out was to tow it to the shallow end. He

9

had found that it was impossible to lift a dead weight out of deep water without help.

'You went in after him yourself?' said Lineham.

'Yes.' Sylvester glanced down at his clothes. 'I had to go and change.'

Thanet was scarcely listening. He was bracing himself for his private purgatory, that first close look at the corpse. By now he was resigned to the fact that he was never going to overcome this weakness of his and that all he could do was grit his teeth until it was over.

And here it came.

This time it wasn't as bad as he had expected, perhaps because apart from a bruise on one temple there were no outward signs of violence. The young man lay on his back in a puddle of water near the steps leading down into the shallow end, limbs neatly arranged, eyes closed as if he were asleep. He had been in his late twenties, Thanet guessed, well built and handsome, with the sort of looks a male model would envy. His dark hair was still wet, sleeked back from his forehead, his expensive suede trousers and silk shirt sodden.

'What was his name?' Thanet asked.

'Max Jeopard.'

Max Jeopard. Thanet repeated the name in his head. Over the next days, weeks, perhaps months, he would come to know Jeopard in a way that no one else could possibly have known him. Thanet was aware that our view of the people in our lives is subjective, coloured by our own thoughts, attitudes, prejudices, life experience, and rarely do we learn what others truly think of us. But in a murder case the investigating officer is in the unique position of gathering together many different views of one person so that, gradually, a composite picture begins to emerge. Often it is only then that the true cause of the tragedy can be understood.

Thanet glanced around. There was no sign of a break-in. 'Are the doors to the garden kept locked?'

'Yes. Locked, bolted and morticed.'

Lineham was already checking. He nodded confirmation.

So, if Jeopard had indeed been murdered there was no question here of an intruder. Someone he knew, probably someone he knew well, had felt that life would be intolerable if Jeopard continued to walk the earth. Thanet shivered as the familiar *frisson* of excitement trickled down his spine. It was as if he had caught the first scent of his quarry.

He had to put another obvious question, even though he was sure of the answer he would get. 'Could he swim?'

Sylvester compressed his lips. 'Like a fish.'

There was a knock at the door and Barbara Mallis put her head in. 'Inspector,' she said, raising her voice to be heard across the intervening space, 'the police doctor has arrived. And some more of your men.'

'Right. Thank you. Show him in, would you? And the Scenes-of-Crime Officers too, if they're there. Tell the others I'll be out in a moment.' Thanet turned back to Sylvester. 'As soon as I've got things organised I'd like to talk to you again, get a little more detail. Er . . . is there a Mrs Sylvester?'

'She's with Tess, our daughter. The doctor's with them. I believe he's giving her a sedative – Tess, I mean. Naturally she's in a terrible state. Anyway . . .' Sylvester glanced at Doc Mallard, who was now approaching, accompanied by the SOCOs. 'I'll be around when you want me. But my guests – when will they be able to go home?'

'I'll be out to talk to them shortly. Perhaps you could assemble them all in one room?'

'Of course.' Sylvester hurried off.

Mallard nodded a greeting, holding back for the photographer to take shots of the body. Then he squatted down, peering at the bruise on the temple. 'Nasty contusion here.'

'He could swim like a fish, apparently,' said Thanet. 'So the question is, was he dead or unconscious when he went into the water? I don't suppose you'll be able to tell until the post-mortem.'

Mallard glanced up at Thanet over his half-moons. 'Quite.'

'Anyway,' Lineham said to Thanet while they waited for Mallard to finish his examination, 'looks as though it's a suspicious death, all right.'

'He could have been drunk, slipped, banged his head.'

'When he was all alone? At his own engagement party? You don't really believe that, sir.'

Thanet didn't. 'Unlikely, I agree. Still, we'll see.'

Mallard held out a hand. 'Give me a heave up, will you? Must be getting old.'

Thanet obliged. 'So, what's the verdict, Doc? How long has he been dead?'

'Well,' said Mallard, 'you know how I hate committing myself . . . and it's tricky because it's so warm in here . . . but I think it would probably be safe to say some time in the last three hours.'

Thanet glanced at his watch. Eleven-forty. And the phone call had summoned him at around eleven. So, some time between 8.30 and 11, then. Not much help, really. 'Right, thanks, Doc.' He glanced at the SOCOs. 'We'll leave you to it, then.'

Sylvester was waiting in the hall with DCs Bentley and

Wakeham. He looked relieved to see Thanet. 'It's a bit of a crush but I've got everyone together in the lounge.'

Mallard glanced at Thanet. 'Don't bother to see me out. I'll be in touch.'

Thanet nodded and followed Sylvester. He saw at a glance that the man had not been exaggerating. There must have been a hundred people crammed into the room, mostly standing. A few were sitting on the floor or perched on the arms of chairs. Right at the front were seated two elderly women, one of them in a wheelchair. The subdued hubbub of conversation died away and a sea of faces swung expectantly in his direction as he entered.

Thanet introduced himself. 'I'm sure you are all aware by now of the tragedy which has taken place here tonight. You must be anxious to leave but we'd be grateful if you could be patient just a little longer . . . Then, after giving your names and addresses, you can all go home. But before you do so we should be grateful if you would think hard and see if you heard or noticed anything, anything at all, which could be even remotely connected with Mr Jeopard's death. I'm afraid that at the moment I can't respond to any questions because almost certainly I wouldn't know the answers. That's all. Thank you.'

He was turning away when a young man darted forward. 'Inspector . . .?'

'This is Hartley Jeopard, Max's brother,' said Sylvester.

'A terrible business, Mr Jeopard,' said Thanet. A platitude, but what else could he say? Hartley Jeopard was a couple of years younger than his brother, Thanet guessed, and resembled him not at all. He was much taller and thinner, for a start, with the apologetic hunch adopted by so many of those who are of above average height. His clothes were nondescript, brown trousers and fawn crew-necked lambswool sweater, and he lacked his brother's striking good looks. Hazel eyes beneath floppy brown hair looked anxiously down at Thanet from a narrow undistinguished face.

'Inspector, I'm worried about my mother.' He glanced at the woman in the wheelchair. 'It's been such a terrible shock for her . . . Would it be possible to take her and my aunt home right away?'

'I didn't realise she was here. Yes, of course. I can come and see you tomorrow morning. Give Sergeant Lineham your address, will you, while I have a word with her?'

Jeopard's mother did indeed look ill. Her pallor was alarming and she was gripping the arms of her chair as if to prevent herself from sagging forward. What on earth was Sylvester thinking of, Thanet thought angrily, to have herded her in here like this? But the man had only been obeying instructions. Perhaps, before that, the two women had been given some space and privacy. Thanet hoped so, anyway. As he murmured condolences and apologies for holding them there his genuine concern must have shown because Mrs Jeopard's expression lightened a little and her sister gave a little exclamation of relief when he said that Hartley could take them home immediately. 'I will need to talk to you, though. Between 10 and 10.30 tomorrow morning?'

'Yes, of course. Thank you.' Mrs Jeopard was controlling herself with difficulty. Her lower lip trembled as she spoke and Thanet was glad that Hartley arrived at that moment to take charge of her wheelchair. Her sister, he saw when she stood up, was almost as tall as her nephew. Genes were responsible for some curious family quirks.

A buzz of conversation broke out behind him as he left

the room. A man and a woman were just coming down the stairs: Mrs Sylvester and the family doctor, Thanet guessed. He was right. Tess was under sedation, he learned, and shouldn't be disturbed. The doctor left and Thanet told the Sylvesters that as soon as he had got his men organised he would like to interview them first. 'Have you got a room we could use?'

Sylvester frowned, thinking. 'Most of them are being used for the party. There's the den, I suppose . . .' He glanced at his wife as if seeking approval or suggestions.

But Mrs Sylvester wasn't really listening. She was looking put out. 'I wanted to go back up to sit with Tess. Just in case she wakes up.' She was a little younger than her husband, in her late forties, with a floaty mane of streaked blonde hair, bright blue eye shadow and a lipstick that was far too harsh for her skin colour. She was wearing a tight sequin-covered black lace dress which revealed every curve and shimmered as she moved. And she was, Thanet realised, saying one thing to her husband and trying to communicate another. The look she was giving him was fierce in its intensity, pregnant with words unspoken.

Sylvester frowned at her. Either he couldn't work out what she was trying to tell him or he was deliberately choosing to ignore it; Thanet couldn't make up his mind which.

'Perhaps a friend could sit with her for a little while?' suggested Thanet.

'Yes. How about Anthea?' said Sylvester.

For some reason this suggestion upset Mrs Sylvester even more. 'What, after –?' She glanced at Thanet and broke off.

Interesting, he thought. What was going on here? But perhaps he was misreading her. Perhaps she was simply reluctant to relinquish her role to someone else and was angry that Sylvester had suggested an alternative.

She compressed her lips. 'All right,' she said grudgingly. Then to Thanet, 'I hope this won't take long . . .'

Thanet wasn't going to be forced into giving a promise he might not be able to keep. How could he possibly tell, at this stage, how long the interview might be? 'Thank you.'

'I'll see if I can find her,' said Sylvester. He disappeared into the sitting room, returning a few moments later with an exotic creature in a scarlet satin cheongsam. Her long dark hair had been put up in a knot secured by a long wooden pin, enhancing the chinese effect, but the matching heavy make-up was streaked and blotchy, her eyes swollen with tears shed and unshed. Here, apparently, was someone who really did mourn Max Jeopard's passing.

'Are you sure you'll be all right?' Sylvester was saying.

The girl gave a determined nod. 'I'll be glad of a bit of peace and quiet.' She gave Mrs Sylvester, whose face was stony, a somewhat shamefaced look before going upstairs.

Thanet watched her go. No doubt about it, there were interesting undercurrents here. He glanced at Lineham and could see that the sergeant was thinking the same thing.

Sylvester patted his wife's shoulder. 'Don't worry,' he said reassuringly. 'Tess'll be all right with her.' He turned to Thanet. 'They've been friends for years.'

Five minutes later the Sylvesters were leading the way to the 'den'. Thanet followed with Lineham on his heels, aware of a sense of rising anticipation. This was the part of his work that he enjoyed most of all, the interviewing of suspects. It was where he would begin to understand the complex web of relationships which surrounded the dead man, the point at which, for Thanet, Max Jeopard would start to live and breathe again.

He was eager for the process to begin.

TWO

The den turned out to be a small square sitting room equipped with a huge television set and saggy leather armchairs from which it would clearly be a struggle to get up. Impossible to conduct an interview from their depths; Thanet elected to lean against the windowsill, Lineham to sit sidesaddle on the broad arm of one of the chairs. Despite their apparent disharmony of a short while ago the Sylvesters presented a united front and chose to share one, she perched on the edge of the seat, tugging down the skirt of her tight black dress which had ridden halfway up her thighs, her husband sitting on the arm beside her, one hand resting on her shoulder. They watched apprehensively as Lineham took out his notebook and flicked it open.

'Right, well, perhaps you could fill us in on this evening,' said Thanet.

The Sylvesters stared at him. It was interesting that they didn't look at each other, Thanet thought. It was, he felt, almost as if they were afraid to. If so, why?

Mrs Sylvester put her hand on her husband's knee, her painted fingernails standing out like drops of blood against the pale velvety cords.

'Where . . .' Sylvester cleared his throat, tried again. 'Where d'you want us to begin?'

Alarm bells were definitely ringing in Thanet's mind. He was becoming convinced that the Sylvesters were not simply suffering a natural distress engendered by the events of the evening. They were frightened. It showed in the sheen of perspiration beginning to appear on Sylvester's forehead, the whiteness of Mrs Sylvester's fingertips where they gripped her husband's knee with excessive force. Was one of them responsible for Jeopard's death? Or did each suspect that the other might be? He refrained from the obvious response. 'What time were people invited for?'

Mrs Sylvester visibly braced herself, removing her hand and straightening her back. 'Eight o'clock,' she said. 'But they didn't start arriving until around a quarter past.'

'And Mr Jeopard?'

'A little earlier,' said her husband. 'Around a quarter to eight, I should think.'

His wife was nodding. She was being as matter of fact as possible, but the fear still lurked at the back of her eyes. 'Must've been. I was still getting ready.' She put up a hand to fluff out her hair, unconsciously miming what she had been doing at the time.

'He lives locally, I gather.'

'Yes,' said Sylvester. 'At least, that is, his family home is here. But he and Hartley both have flats in London. Hartley came down last night, I believe, so that he could drive his mother and aunt to the party tonight, but Max drove down from town this evening.'

'How was he?'

'His usual self,' said Mrs Sylvester. Her tone was tart and she cast an uneasy glance at her husband, conscious of having betrayed rather more than she would have wished.

19

'Which was . . .?'

'Full of himself,' said Sylvester shortly. 'Look, Inspector, there's no point in pretending. We weren't too keen on Tess's choice of a husband. But not, I assure you, to the extent of pushing him into the swimming pool to make sure she didn't marry him!'

Even if someone else did. The unspoken words hovered in the air and Thanet allowed a brief, uncomfortable silence before he nodded, content to accept the statement at face value for the moment. Time would tell whether or not it were true. 'So,' he said. 'Mr Jeopard was in a good mood – why shouldn't he be? After all, it was a special occasion for him. In your opinion, then, there's no question of it being suicide?'

'Suicide! Good God, no!' Sylvester had relaxed sufficiently to appear amused rather than shocked at the suggestion. 'Max was the last person in the world to want to kill himself. He enjoyed life far too much.'

'Then could it have been an accident, d'you think?'

'Difficult to see how,' said Sylvester reluctantly.

'Oh I don't know, Ralph,' his wife protested, a hint of desperation in her tone. 'He could have slipped, hit his head on the side as he went in.'

'Oh come on, darl! Those tiles are all special non-slip, you know that. Cost us a bomb. And we know he wasn't drunk, we were talking to him in the supper queue just before he disappeared. What the hell was he doing in the pool house, that's what I want to know. He was only supposed to have gone for a pee!'

'I know that, but . . .'

'I'm sorry,' interrupted Thanet. 'Let's go back to what we were saying, shall we? So in your opinion at least, Mr Sylvester, it couldn't have been an accident, either. We won't close our minds to the possibility of course,

20

but meanwhile we have to look closely at our third option.'

There was a brief silence. Mrs Sylvester was staring at Thanet as if mesmerised, clearly terrified of what was coming. Without looking at her husband she put up her hand to feel for his, which closed over it, gave it a reassuring squeeze. 'No point in pussy-footing around, is there?' Sylvester said. 'We all know what we're talking about, don't we? Murder.'

His wife made a little moaning sound and he leaned forward to put his free arm around her shoulders. 'It's all right, darl,' he murmured into her hair. 'Don't worry.'

She jerked away from him, twisting to look directly into his face. 'How can you say that, Ralph? Someone is deliberately killed, under our own roof, and you say don't *worry*?' Her voice went up, almost out of control, and Thanet could tell from her expression that once again she was willing Sylvester to hear what she was not saying aloud.

Thanet found himself leaning forward as if to catch those unspoken words. What was it that she was trying to communicate to her husband?

'We don't *know* that it was deliberate yet, do we?' said Sylvester.

'It's what you just said!'

'Not exactly. I said that's what we were talking about.'

'What's the difference? You're just splitting hairs! I don't –'

'There's a big difference darl, surely you must see that? Someone might have killed him, yes, but not because he intended to. It could have been murder by accident, sort of, if you see what I mean.'

Now he was doing it too, staring intently into his wife's eyes as if to convey an unspoken message. And it seemed to work because after a moment Mrs Sylvester relaxed a fraction and looked at Thanet. 'Would that be possible, Inspector?'

'Possible, yes. How likely, we don't yet know. It's all speculation at the moment. We won't get anywhere until we've established the facts, so if we could go back to what we were saying . . .? Mr Jeopard was in a good mood earlier in the evening, you say. Did you see any sign of problems with any of your guests?'

They were shaking their heads.

And they were lying, Thanet was sure of it. He could tell by the way they still studiously avoided looking at each other and by the glazing of their eyes as they strove to conceal the truth.

'We weren't exactly keeping an eye on him,' said Sylvester. 'I was moving around all the time, topping up people's drinks. And you were busy circulating, weren't you, darl?'

Mrs Sylvester was nodding. 'People were spread out through all the downstairs rooms.'

'Including the pool house?'

Again the head-shaking double act.

'No. Just in case anyone had one over the eight and fell in,' said Sylvester.

'You know what young people are,' said his wife with a false little laugh. 'Sometimes they get carried away, even jump in with their clothes on. We didn't want to risk any accidents. And even if they all behave perfectly there's always the chance of a glass or a bottle getting broken and that's dangerous where people walk around in bare feet.'

'So we locked the door and left the lights off, to show it was out of bounds, so to speak.'

'And the key?'

'Always hung on a hook beside the door.' Sylvester

shifted uncomfortably. 'Looking back, I suppose it would have been sensible to take it away altogether, but we never do. The place is only ever locked for extra security. And tonight, well, it never occurred to me to do anything else. After all, you'd have to be pretty brazen, as a guest, to ignore a hint like a locked door with the key removed.'

'Right. So you both saw Jeopard from time to time, but neither of you noticed any sign of a scene, a quarrel or disagreement of any kind?'

Once again the shutters came down. 'No.'

Thanet didn't press the point. No doubt the truth would emerge eventually. 'So how did you come to find him in the pool house, Mr Sylvester?'

Sylvester hesitated a moment, as if uncertain where to start. 'As it was an engagement party, it was arranged that the two families would sit together at supper – that is, Max, his mother and aunt, Tess, my wife and myself.'

'We had one table set aside for us,' said his wife, 'specially laid and decorated. Just to mark the occasion. It was Tess's idea.'

'So when it got to time for supper –'

'Sorry to interrupt,' said Thanet. 'But, just to be clear on this, did you have caterers in?'

Sylvester glanced at his wife. *Your province.*

'Yes,' she said. 'It was a buffet meal. Just before it was served they set up a number of small tables, in the various rooms, so people could eat in comfort.'

'Can't stand eating off my knee,' said Sylvester. 'Hopeless if it's a knife and fork job.'

'And what time was supper served?'

'Nine-thirty,' said his wife. She paused in case Thanet had any further questions before continuing. 'We all collected our food from the buffet, then found somewhere to sit. Afterwards the caterers cleared everything away, including the tables. We've done it like that before and it works very well.'

'So the six of you queued up for your food with everyone else and took it to your table?'

'Yes,' said Sylvester. 'Well, sort of. Mrs Jeopard is in a wheelchair, as you saw, so she and her sister chose what they wanted to eat, then Tess carried their plates and Max pushed his mother's chair to our table, got her and his aunt settled. Then he and Tess went back to collect their own food. About five minutes later Tess got back and sat down. We all assumed Max would join us shortly and it must have been a good ten minutes before his mother said she wondered where he'd got to.'

'That's right,' agreed Mrs Sylvester. 'We didn't pay any attention at first. Like my husband said, we assumed he'd gone to the loo – which was, in fact, what Tess told us. When Max's mother said she wondered where he was, I mean.'

'What time would that have been?' said Lineham.

'Well,' said Sylvester, working it out. 'Supper was arranged for 9.30, and I think it was on time, wasn't it, darl?' He waited for his wife's nod. 'Then it would have taken us about ten minutes to get settled. Usually, at parties, we serve ourselves last, but on this occasion there was a bit of fuss made about the special table and so on, and everyone waved us to the front of the queue.'

'So you sat down about twenty to ten?'

'Thereabouts, I should think. Then it was another ten minutes or so, like I said, before any comment was made about Max not having come back yet, and it must have been a further five or ten before I went to look for him.'

'Around ten o'clock, then?'

24

'It must've been about then,' said Mrs Sylvester. 'Tess had been getting restless and I think by then she felt we'd all waited long enough, so she said she'd go and see if she could find him. But my husband said no, she was to stay and enjoy her supper and he'd go instead.'

'So I did,' said Sylvester. 'Trouble was, there were so many places to look – a cloakroom and two bathrooms for a start, then tables had been set up everywhere, like we said – hall, lounge, dining room, conservatory, and quite a few of the young people had settled down on the stairs and the upstairs landing. And everywhere I went people kept on delaying me – saying what a great party it was and so on, and I had to keep stopping to chat. I even went into the bedrooms, to make sure he hadn't crashed out on one of the beds, unlikely as that seemed.'

'Did you ask people if they'd seen him, as you went around?' asked Thanet.

'No. What was the point? If he'd been there I'd have spotted him. I was sure I'd find him somewhere, talking to somebody. I just thought he'd probably got engrossed in a conversation and hadn't noticed how time was slipping away.'

'Max was like that if he was really interested in what someone was saying,' said Mrs Sylvester. 'Sort of intense.'

'Anyway,' said her husband, 'he was nowhere to be seen. The only place left to look was the kitchen and it was on way my back from there that I thought of the pool house – it's at the other end of the corridor which leads to the kitchen, you see. I didn't expect to find him there but as I got nearer the door I could see the key wasn't hanging on its hook, it was in the lock. And even when I switched the lights on in there, at first I thought the place was empty. I didn't go right in, there seemed no point, just glanced quickly around. But as you saw, the deep end is nearest to the door and the diving board obscures your view of the pool, so it was only as I swung around to turn away that I glimpsed something dark in the water. When I moved for a better view I saw that there was a body floating on the surface. I kicked off my shoes, tore off my jacket and dived straight in. I suppose I must have realised it was Max, but I wasn't sure until I got him out, and that was a real struggle, I can tell you. I don't know if you've ever tried to get a dead weight out of water, but in the deep end it is absolutely impossible – if you try to push it up on to the side you just go under. So I towed him to the shallow end and even then I had problems getting him up the steps, it was like heaving a couple of sacks of potatoes.'

'Ralph!' protested his wife.

'Sorry, darl, but that's the way it was. Anyway, I could see right away that he was dead, and it was hopeless, but I knew I mustn't take that for granted, I'd still have to make an effort to revive him. I also knew that every second counted, that I couldn't delay by going to fetch help. God, I was wishing I'd taken first-aid classes, I can tell you. I felt absolutely useless. I put him on his stomach for a few minutes first, tried to pump some water out of him, then rolled him over and tried to give him the kiss of life – to the best of my ability anyway. I'd only ever seen it done on television.' Sylvester shook his head, his face screwed up in distaste. 'Not an experience I would wish to repeat. But after a few minutes I could see I wasn't getting anywhere so I rushed back to the party, asking if anyone knew about resuscitation.' He shook his head again. 'I'm sorry. I can see now that this will make things difficult for you, but at the time . . .'

'A natural thing to do in the circumstances,' said

Thanet. 'I'd probably have done the same myself. So how many people went to see if they could help?'

'We all poured in,' said Mrs Sylvester. 'It was awful. Tess had hysterics, as you can imagine . . .'

'But nothing could be done,' said her husband heavily. 'So we got everyone back out as soon as we could. Then we rang the police.'

But by then irreparable damage would have been done as far as finding any useful scientific evidence was concerned, thought Thanet ruefully. Well, it was pointless to bemoan the fact. 'What time was it when you found the body?'

Sylvester rubbed his bald pate in a polishing movement while he worked it out. 'Around 10.30?'

'Right. Now, let me make sure I have this absolutely straight. Living in this house are the two of you and your daughter Tess. Anyone else?'

Thanet thought it an innocuous question but suddenly the atmosphere was strained again, the fear back in their eyes. The answer to his question was obviously yes, but neither of them responded.

'Is there?'

'We have a housekeeper,' said Mrs Sylvester. 'Barbara Mallis.'

'Yes, Barbara,' echoed her husband.

'She's been with you long?'

'Must be four years now,' said Sylvester. 'That's right, isn't it, darl?'

'Yes.'

'And a gardener, Ron Fielding,' said Sylvester. 'Though he's not exactly one of the household. He and his wife and daughter live in the bungalow near the gates.'

'And that's the lot?'

There was a brief silence. Sylvester's hand closed over

27

his wife's shoulder again and she put hers up to clutch at it, twisting her head to look at him. They exchanged a despairing glance. *We'll have to tell them.*

Thanet glanced at Lineham. The sergeant raised his eyebrows. *What now?*

'And there's our son, Carey,' said Sylvester at last, capitulating.

'Your son?' Thanet did not try to hide his surprise. Why no mention of him till now? Perhaps the lad was a late child, too young to attend the party? But if so, why all this reluctance? 'How old is he?'

'Twenty-eight,' said Sylvester with resignation. 'He's ill, so his nurse lives in the house too. Michael Roper.'

So why all the mystery? Thanet wondered. Unless it was an illness which the Sylvesters were reluctant to admit to, like AIDS. But if so, and the young man was ill enough to warrant a full-time nurse, this still didn't explain why they should be afraid, as opposed to embarrassed. Unless . . . Yes, that could be it. 'What, exactly, is wrong with your son?'

Mrs Sylvester bit her lip and her grip on her husband's hand tightened. Sylvester gave a resigned sigh. 'He's schizophrenic.'

Thanet had guessed correctly. 'I see.' And he did. This, then, was the root of the Sylvesters' fear: they were afraid that their son was responsible for Jeopard's death. Schizophrenics were notoriously unpredictable. They were not all violent or dangerous, by any means, but many were.

'How serious is his illness?' said Thanet, aware that the severity of this particular condition can vary enormously.

'Pretty serious,' said Sylvester. 'Carey doesn't go anywhere without Michael, and they spend quite a lot of time in his rooms. The doors are kept locked.'

28

'And tonight? Did they come to the party?'

Sylvester shook his head. 'We were afraid the noise and the numbers of people might be too much for Carey to cope with. They stayed upstairs.'

So what was the problem? It was time to bring the matter out into the open. 'Look, Mr Sylvester, Mrs Sylvester, it's been obvious to me ever since we started talking that you are both very worried about something and from your reluctance to tell me about him I imagine that you're afraid your son might be involved in Mr Jeopard's death. But if he was safely locked up in his room with his nurse . . .'

They stared at him and Thanet saw the tears begin to well up in Mrs Sylvester's eyes. Her lower lip began to tremble and then, suddenly, the vestiges of her control snapped and she began to weep, turning her head away and pressing her face into her husband's thigh.

Sylvester looked down helplessly at her and began to stroke her hair. 'Darl, don't,' he pleaded. 'I can't bear it. Don't!' Then he glanced at Thanet. 'Carey got out this evening,' he said, wearily, the words barely audible above the sounds of his wife's distress. 'And he's still missing.'

THREE

Thanet and Lineham exchanged a glance. *Not surprising they're worried!* 'I see,' said Thanet. 'How long has he been missing?'

Sylvester ran a hand over the top of his head. 'I'm not sure. Oh, I know that might sound crazy, but everything's been in such a turmoil since I found Max in the pool. I didn't even know Carey was missing until my wife told me, did I, darl?'

She shook her head.

'So when did you find out, Mrs Sylvester?'

'Shortly after Ralph went off to look for Max.'

'Can you be a little more precise? It could be important.'

She frowned, screwing up her face as she tried to work it out. 'Say, a quarter past ten?'

And Max Jeopard had died between twenty to ten and half-past, when Sylvester had found him. 'And who told you?'

'Michael, of course. His nurse. He was very upset, as you can imagine.' Now that the matter was out in the open Mrs Sylvester couldn't wait to unburden herself and the words came tumbling out. 'He and Carey had supper much earlier than us, about 7.30, in Carey's sitting room.

But about twenty to ten Carey said he'd like a cup of coffee, so Michael came down to fetch one. There was a lot of activity in the kitchen and he didn't want to get in the way so it took him a bit longer than usual to make it. When he got back upstairs he found the door unlocked and Carey gone.' Mrs Sylvester glanced at her husband. 'He thinks someone who'd had a drop too much must have been looking for the bathroom, turned the key without thinking it odd that the door was locked from the outside, realised he'd got the wrong room, but didn't relock the door again. And Carey . . .' Mrs Sylvester's tone became despairing. 'Well, Carey regards it as a sort of game, to escape whenever he can. He hates . . .' Her voice shook and the tears spilled over again. 'He really hates being locked in.' She shook her head. 'Oh God, you must think us absolute monsters, locking our own son up like that, but you have no idea, you can't imagine –'

'It's the bloody Government that's to blame!' exploded Sylvester. 'And their sodding Mental Health Act! Closing all the mental hospitals and dumping these sick people either on their families or on the streets! Community Care! It's a joke, a bloody joke, that's what it is, and a sick one, at that.'

Sylvester was well launched into what was obviously a long-held grievance and there was no stopping him. Not that Thanet particularly wanted to. He agreed with practically every word the man was saying. There was no doubt that in the past there had been cases where people had been wrongly locked away, sometimes for many, many years, but the Government had now gone too far the other way. Thanet had seen some of the pathetic creatures turfed out to fend for themselves, perhaps for the first time in their lives, and completely unable to cope. Only recently he'd come across the case of a man

31

who had been supplied with money and a room of his own and who had been found virtually starving, having no idea how to budget or to prepare food for himself. Others either slept rough or persistently committed criminal offences in order to get themselves put in prison; incapable of organising themselves they were only too happy for others to do it for them. A roof over their heads, food on the table and a modicum of warmth was all they asked of life.

'They have no idea,' said Sylvester, 'they can't begin to realise what it's like to have a relative who has schizophrenia. I'd like to see Mrs oh-so-sweet Bottomley with all those statistics she reels off so pat trying to cope if *she* had a son or daughter who was a schizophrenic! We tried to manage by ourselves at first, didn't we, darl, but it was impossible. Marion was at the end of her tether, weren't you? So in the end we decided to get a full-time nurse to look after Carey. It still isn't easy, but at least now we can live something resembling a normal life and it's taken the pressure off Marion a bit. But we're lucky, we can afford to pay for a nurse. What about all those poor sods who can't, that's what I'd like to know?'

'I do understand . . .'

'Don't say you understand!' said Sylvester savagely. 'No one can understand, unless they've been through it themselves! No one! You can't begin to imagine what hell it was for Marion. She could never go out because she never knew what Carey would get up to if he was left alone. Once he slashed his wrists and she came home to find him bleeding to death on the kitchen table. Another time she found him unconscious. D'you know what he'd done? He'd stuck his tongue into an electric socket! His voices had told him to, he said! And what did the bloody doctors say? That we must make sure he took his medication! You try making a grown man take pills if he doesn't want to!'

'He hates taking them,' said Marion. 'Says they turn his mind inside out. But Michael seems to have the knack. Carey will accept things from him he won't accept from us.'

'If he's still missing, I assume someone is looking for him?' said Thanet.

'Yes. Michael is,' said Sylvester. 'And Ron. The gardener. They know most of the places he likes to hide. Fortunately he doesn't usually stray too far. But this time . . .' He glanced at his watch. 'Oh God, it's gone half past twelve. It's been more than two and a half hours now!'

No wonder Mrs Sylvester looked frantic, thought Thanet. What a disaster of an evening it had turned out to be for them. He stood up. 'You must be wanting to join the search. I'll arrange for some of my men to help you.'

Sylvester jumped up. 'No! He'll be frightened if . . . Oh, but then, I suppose . . .'

'I think it would be advisable,' said Thanet gently. 'But we'll be careful, I promise.' He glanced at Lineham. *Fix it, will you, Mike?* Lineham nodded and left the room.

Anxious to go, the Sylvesters were already at the door. Thanet raised his voice. 'Would you send Mrs Mallis in next, please?' In the course of her duties the housekeeper would have been better placed than anyone to have an overall view of what had gone on this evening.

Sylvester spoke over his shoulder. 'Right.'

While he waited, Thanet thought. Almost certainly, this was murder. But what had Jeopard been doing in the pool house? Had he arranged to meet someone there? Unlikely that he would have wandered in there alone. Thanet said so to Lineham who was soon back.

33

'I agree. He must have been meeting someone. But who?'

'I expect we'll find out sooner or later.'

'You didn't ask the Sylvesters why they didn't like him.'

'I was going to get around to that last of all. I thought if I asked early on they might clam up. Then when they dropped that minor bombshell . . .'

'Think their son did it, sir?'

'It's an easy conclusion to jump to. And for that reason I think we ought to be wary of doing so. It's not as though he's a homicidal maniac. How are the others getting on?'

'I put Bentley in charge of the search for Carey. Most of the guests have gone, there're just a few stragglers left and Wakeham is seeing to them.'

'Good.'

There was a knock at the door. Thanet raised his voice. 'Come in.' And then, to Lineham, 'You take this one, Mike.'

'OK.' Lineham stepped forward. 'Come in, Mrs Mallis. Sit down.' This time he leaned against the windowsill and Thanet sat on the arm of a chair.

It was interesting, Thanet thought, that Mrs Mallis chose to do likewise. She obviously didn't wish to confer a moral advantage by having to look up at them. Which perhaps meant that she had reason to be cautious. He folded his arms and studied her, remembering his initial impression that she was the 'lady' of the house. Yes, both clothes and jewellery were expensive, but if she had no family responsibilities there was no reason why she shouldn't indulge herself. She obviously cared a great deal about her appearance. Time, as well as money, had been spent on it. Her make-up was skilful and it must take hours to coax her hair into those deceptively casual tousled curls. There had been no mention of a Mr. Mallis so she must be a widow or a divorcee – the latter, he guessed, noting again the impression of bad temper conveyed by a mouth which turned down at the corners, the calculating look with which she was watching Lineham. Perhaps he was being unfair. Perhaps life had treated her badly. She caught his eye and he smiled at her, disarmingly, he hoped, and was disconcerted when she responded by giving him a flirtatious glance and running her tongue slowly over her upper lip. Good grief! Did she think he was making a pass at her? Glancing at Lineham he was irritated to catch a glint of quickly suppressed amusement in the sergeant's eye.

'We think you might be in a unique position to help us, Mrs Mallis,' said Lineham.

Very neat, Mike. A hint of flattery should go down well here.

But she was wary. 'Oh?'

'You've had quite a bit of time to think about Mr Jeopard's death, and you'll understand that unless and until we can prove otherwise, we have to treat it as suspicious. In which case, whether it was deliberate or accidental, we must assume that someone here tonight was on bad terms with him. Now, you are in the position of being in the family, so to speak, but not one of them. We're hoping you'll be able to put us in the picture.'

'I've been asked to do many things in my time,' and again she flicked a glance at Thanet, 'but never before to be a police informant.' She smiled to take the sting out of her words.

It hadn't registered when she met them at the door, but her voice was husky, gravelly, almost. Thanet guessed

35

she was a smoker and almost as if she had picked up what he was thinking she reached into a side pocket and pulled out a pack of cigarettes.

'D'you mind?'

Lineham would, Thanet knew, but the sergeant shook his head. 'Go ahead.'

She fished out a lighter – gold, by the look of it – and lit up, inhaling deeply. 'That's better.'

Lineham looked at the long plume of smoke curling towards him and Thanet could see the sergeant willing himself not to duck or wave it away.

'In a murder case we need all the help we can get,' Thanet said.

She drew on her cigarette, inhaled, blew out smoke again. 'I imagine the Sylvesters didn't say a word about Gerald Argent?'

'No,' said Lineham. 'Why?'

'They wouldn't. He's their blue-eyed boy. Until recently he was engaged to their daughter.'

'To Tess Sylvester?'

She nodded, looked around for an ashtray.

Lineham fetched one for her. 'So what happened?'

She tapped the ash off her cigarette before answering. 'Max was an old flame of Tess's, I believe, but he's been away a lot, travelling. He's a travel writer, I don't know if you knew that. Anyway, Tess and Gerald got engaged last autumn and they were planning to get married this summer. Then at Christmas Max comes back from a really long trip to South America. He'd been away about two years. When he found Tess was engaged he went all out to get her back from Gerald. And believe me, when I say all out, I mean all out – he positively showered her with flowers, presents, letters, the works. I should be so lucky! At first she wasn't having any but in the end she gave in, broke off with Gerald and got engaged to Max. Of course, you have to make wedding arrangements ages ahead these days, to book up the church, the reception and so on, so what does she do? Decide to use the ones she'd already made with Gerald, that's all! She was even going to use the same wedding dress – well, she was having it specially made, but even so it's a bit much, wouldn't you agree?'

Her attitude left a nasty taste in the mouth, thought Thanet. Where was her loyalty to her employers? Had the Sylvesters done something to set her against them? And if she didn't like it here, why stay? Competent housekeepers are at a premium these days.

'So, this Gerald,' said Lineham. 'Was he here tonight?'

'He was invited,' she said, stubbing out her cigarette. 'But he refused.' She paused, for effect. 'Originally, that is. He obviously changed his mind. Yes, he was here. But they weren't on speaking terms.'

'He and Max Jeopard, you mean?'

'That's right. In fact, I saw him deliberately snub Max.'

'What happened?'

'I wasn't right next to them, so I didn't hear what was said. But I saw Max speak to him and hold out his hand. Gerald didn't say a word, just turned away.'

'What did Max do?'

'Just shrugged and laughed it off. What else could he do?'

'Did you see either of them during the supper interval, before Mr Sylvester raised the alarm?'

'Not that I can recall. I was too busy collecting up dirty glasses to notice anyone, really.'

'Well, if you do remember, perhaps you could let us know.'

37

'There's more, if you're interested.'

'Please.' Lineham waved a hand. 'Go ahead.'

'Everyone will tell you that Max was a terrible flirt. The type who couldn't keep his hands off an attractive female.' Again that sideways glance from beneath her lashes at Thanet. 'You know what I mean?'

Was she implying Jeopard had made a pass at her?

'You're saying he was fooling around at his own engagement party?' said Lineham.

'I was moving around a lot, naturally, making sure that everything was running smoothly, and I saw him make a pass at least twice during the evening.'

'Was Tess around? Did she see him?'

'Once she did, certainly.'

'How did she react?'

'How d'you think? A face like thunder. But he got around her. He always could, I imagine. He had a lot of charm. But more to the point, I think his fun and games got him into some kind of trouble.'

'With the boyfriend of one of the girls he made a pass at?'

'No. With a woman. Unfortunately I didn't actually see what happened. I was in the next room, just heard this brief commotion, voices raised in anger, then an unmistakable sound.' She paused. She evidently enjoyed a little drama.

'Of?' said Lineham.

'Flesh meeting flesh,' she said with evident satisfaction. 'Then there was a brief silence before everyone started talking twice as loudly to cover up their embarrassment, if you know what I mean?'

'So what, exactly, had happened? Do you know?'

'Some woman had given the prospective bridegroom a good slap across the face, apparently. It took a while for the marks to fade.'

'So who was the woman?'

She shrugged. 'No idea. Someone he'd been playing around with, no doubt. Hell hath no fury and all that.'

She had nothing else to tell them for the moment and they let her go.

'Nice woman,' commented Lineham sarcastically.

'Ha, ha!'

'She certainly fancied you, sir!'

'You must curb that imagination of yours, Mike. More to the point, it looks as though –'

A knock at the door interrupted him. It was Bentley.

'Just to let you know we've found the Sylvester lad, sir.'

'Where was he?'

Bentley's mouth tugged down at the corners. 'In the dog kennel, with the dog.'

FOUR

'In the dog kennel!' echoed Lineham.

Bentley's face told them that this was no joke and Thanet experienced an uprush of sympathy for a fellow human being driven to take refuge in so unlikely a place. 'Think he had anything to do with Jeopard's death?'

Bentley shook his head. 'Impossible to tell. But he's pretty pathetic, I can tell you.'

'Where is he now?'

'His nurse has taken him up to his room.'

'What d'you think, John? D'you think we ought to interview him tonight?' Thanet trusted Bentley's judgement.

'To be honest, I shouldn't think there's much point. He's obviously in a bit of a state. By tomorrow he might have calmed down. And he's not going anywhere, is he?'

'We'll leave it then.' Thanet glanced at his watch. One-twenty-five. 'In fact, I think we'll call it a day.'

He got into his car carefully, conscious of his aching back, which always played up when he was tired. Lately it had been troubling him more and more and he had even begun to experience pain in his right hip. Over the years he had seen an orthopaedic specialist more than once and had undergone several courses of physiotherapy, but nothing had really worked. Lately, alarmed by the possibility that his back problem might now be affecting his hip, Joan had been urging him to see a chiropractor. Some people swore by them, she said. Tired of trying various treatments and convinced that nothing was going to do any good, Thanet had resisted. But Joan had refused to give up and finally he had been driven to make the fatal mistake of moving from outright refusal to argument.

'Do you realise just how many charlatans there are around? Anyone can put up a board and set up a practice as a chiropractor, did you know that?'

'Luke, for heaven's sake, I'm not a complete dimwit! Of course I know that! The simple answer is to make sure you find one that *is* registered.'

'There might not even be one, locally.'

They both knew that by now he was putting up only a token resistance. Joan had got out the yellow pages and plonked the book in front of him.

'"Let your fingers do the walking,"' she had quoted.

And so it was that, just to keep her quiet, he had capitulated. His first appointment was to be on Monday afternoon. Perhaps, he thought as he started the car, he would now be able to cry off, pleading pressure of work with this new case. No, there was no point. Once Joan made up her mind about something like this he might as well bow to the inevitable.

Next morning he ate a solitary breakfast and took Joan up a cup of tea before leaving for work.

She was awake. 'Oh, lovely, darling. Thank you.'

'I should have a lie-in if I were you.' Thanet sat down on the bed to be companionable for a few minutes.

'I'll see. What time did you get in? I didn't hear you.'

'A quarter to two.'

She gave a sympathetic groan. 'What did you think of Ben's little announcement last night?'

'Much the same as you, I imagine. We'll have to see what we can do to get him to change his mind.'

'The trouble is, you know what they're like at his age. Put up any opposition and it'll only make him more determined.'

'I know. We'll just have to be careful. But we must try, don't you agree?'

Joan sighed. 'There always seems to be some problem . . .'

'Bridget didn't ring last night?'

'No. I really am getting worried. She should have arrived in Adelaide by now.'

Bridget was travelling with the Experiment for International Living, an excellent organisation which arranges homestays for young people in most countries of the world, in the cause of international understanding. Bridget had heard about it through a friend. Thanet and Joan, alarmed at the idea of her travelling alone, had been happy to know that she would be moving from one family to another and that someone would be around to help her if she ran into difficulties. So far the trip had gone smoothly. Each time she arrived in a new place she had made a brief phone call to tell them of her arrival. She had stayed in both North and South Islands in New Zealand and was now in Australia. The day before yesterday she should have arrived in Adelaide but so far there had been no word. Fearsome stories of young women raped, mugged or even murdered in Australia during recent years had constantly been in Thanet and Joan's minds and now, once again, they tried to reassure each other by suggesting all the possible reasons for the delay. Finally Thanet glanced at his watch. 'Sorry, love. I really must go.'

Joan put up her face for his kiss. 'Hope it goes well today.' She knew how hectic the first full day of a new case could be.

Outside it was a beautiful day, warm and sunny, the clouds of blossom on the spring-flowering trees lighting up the quiet Sunday-morning streets. Thanet put behind him regrets that he couldn't spend the day with Joan and began to plan his priorities. By the time he reached the office he had them clear in his mind.

Lineham was already engrossed in reports of interviews with last night's party guests. He waved a sheaf at Thanet. 'Bentley and Wakeham must have sat up half the night to do these.'

'I thought I told them to go home!'

'You know what they're like.'

Thanet did: Bentley reliable and conscientious, Wakeham as keen as mustard. He shouldn't be surprised, really. 'Anything interesting?'

'Couple of things. You know what the housekeeper said about Jeopard being slapped on the face? That was a girl called Anthea Greenway, apparently. I was wondering . . . Wasn't the girl Mr Sylvester sent up to sit with his daughter called Anthea?'

'Yes, she was. The one in the Chinese outfit. She and Tess have known each other for years, he said. Does anyone know why she slapped Jeopard?'

'Not what actually precipitated it. But it seems to be common knowledge that she was his girlfriend at one time.'

Thanet frowned. 'I wonder when. According to the housekeeper, it was Tess he used to go out with before he

43

went to South America and Tess he made a dead set at when he came back at Christmas.'

'She certainly gave the impression that he launched straight into trying to get Tess back from Argent. So if it's true he used to go out with Anthea it must have been before he left.'

'But in that case . . . A bit odd, isn't it, Mike? Not only that she should still be angry with him, after so long, but that she should have saved up demonstrating it until his engagement party?'

'No use expecting logic where women are concerned. More to the point, I wonder if she was angry enough to have shoved him into the swimming pool later on.'

'He'd hardly agree to meet her after she slapped his face, surely. But I agree, it'll have to be looked into. Anything else?'

'A couple of people mention him making passes at other women, like the housekeeper said.'

'Any jealous boyfriends or husbands hovering in the background?'

'If there were, nobody's saying so.'

'That it, then?' Lineham had a tendency always to save the best news to last and Thanet suspected that the glint in the sergeant's eye denoted an interesting titbit yet to come.

'At least three people mention the fact that around nineish a note was handed to Jeopard. He glanced at it, then shoved it in his pocket.' Lineham made the statement with an air of triumph, like a dog laying a particularly juicy bone at his master's feet.

'Really? Now that *is* interesting. An assignation, you think? Meet me in the pool house during the supper interval, that sort of thing?'

'Highly likely, I should think.'

'We didn't find any note in his pockets, did we?'

Lineham shook his head.

'So what became of it, I wonder. Who delivered it?'

'One of the waitresses.'

Thanet glanced at his watch. Time for the specially called morning meeting. 'Get Wakeham to try and track her down, will you, find out who gave it to her. And get him to double-check Jeopard's clothes, make sure that it wasn't in any of his pockets. I suppose it's possible that we could have missed it. It might have been soaked and stuck to the lining. Anything else I need to know before I go down?'

'Only that accounts of Jeopard's movements at supper agree, so far as we can tell, with what the Sylvesters told us. Several people saw him wheel his mother to their table, then leave her. Tess followed him.'

'Did she, now? Let's hope she's recovered enough to talk this morning. We'll go out there after seeing the Jeopards, as arranged.'

Downstairs he followed the usual routine. Arriving outside Draco's door two minutes ahead of time he waited for his long-time friend and colleague Inspector Boon of the uniformed branch to join him, glad that Boon was on duty this weekend. Draco was a stickler for punctuality and recently Thanet and Boon had evolved their own little ritual to lighten their day. It was childish, they knew, but they both enjoyed it.

Boon joined him and they stood with wristwatches poised. A glance around to make sure that no one was watching and at ten seconds before one minute to, they began to chant quietly, in unison, 'Ten, nine, eight, seven, six, five, four, three, two, one . . .'

It was Boon's turn to open the door and he did so, bowing Thanet in ahead of him.

45

The ritual continued, though Draco was unaware that he was participating. Seated behind a desk which was a model of order and implied efficiency he glanced at the clock to check that they were not late, cleared his throat and said, 'Ah, Thanet, Boon, just in time,' and waved at them to sit down. He made a minute adjustment to the position of the pen on the blotter in front of him and sat back. 'If you're ready, then, Thanet?'

The morning meeting, one of many reforms introduced by Draco when he arrived several years ago, was an exercise designed to keep him in touch with everything that was going on in his subdivision and to ensure that each section knew what the others were up to. In Draco's view, good communications were of fundamental importance and Thanet had to concede that, as usual, the Superintendent was right. To begin with everyone had grumbled at the fiery little Welshman's crusade for greater efficiency but before long they were admitting that it had paid off. Morale had improved and the crime detection rate had shown a marked increase. At times the Superintendent had driven his staff to distraction but gradually his idiosyncracies had come to be regarded with an indulgent amusement and his staff had grown to respect him, become fond of him, even. They had all watched with dismay as Draco, who adored his wife, had struggled to keep his spirits up during her lengthy fight against leukaemia, and had rejoiced with him when, little by little, the tide had turned in her favour. Now it was hard to believe that the man who sat behind the desk, black eyes glittering like new-cut anthracite, body tense with suppressed energy, could ever have been so demoralised as to have barely been able to display even a minimal interest in his work.

He listened carefully to Thanet's report and as usual

Thanet was aware that the intensity of Draco's interest was forcing him to express himself as clearly and grammatically as possible, to present the facts as succinctly and comprehensively as he could. There was something about the man that made you want to meet the rigorous standards he imposed.

A few pertinent questions when Thanet had finished and then, 'Sylvester . . .' Draco mused. 'Sounds familiar.'

Thanet was tempted to say, 'Victor?', but restrained himself. If Draco had a failing it was that he lacked a sense of humour where work was concerned.

'Motorway construction!' said Boon triumphantly.

Draco snapped his fingers. 'That's right! On the trucks and diggers.'

'Probably has a plant-hire business,' Boon added.

'Something like that, I imagine,' said Draco. 'Right, well, I think that's it for today. We'll look forward to hearing how things develop, Thanet. Sounds as though it's the sort of thing that's right up your street.'

As they left the room he had already picked up a piece of paper from his in-tray and was reaching for the phone.

'What did he mean by that?' said Thanet to Boon when they were outside.

'Right up your street, you mean? Messy, I should think.' Boon's hands described knots in the air. 'Tangled family relationships.'

And Draco was right, of course, thought Thanet as he hurried back up to his office. As usual.

Lineham had got everything organised in his absence and was ready to leave. It was a pleasure, outside, to drive through empty streets instead of sitting in the traffic jams which invariably built up in Sturrenden during the week.

'Hope you hadn't planned anything special with the

children today,' said Thanet as they passed a family piling into an ancient Vauxhall which looked as though it might just make it to the end of the road.

'Not really. We were going to the in-laws for lunch, that's all. Louise'll still take the kids.'

'Talking about Richard, how did you get on at that demonstration on Friday evening?'

Lineham's son Richard was now a bright, lively nine-year-old. A couple of years ago, after considerable learning and behavioural difficulties at school, he had been diagnosed dyslexic. When the problem had been identified Lineham and Louise had had high hopes that now, at last, something could be done to deal with it. The difficulty was that although, theoretically, help was available, in practice specialist teachers were so thin on the ground that Richard had been receiving only twenty minutes special tuition a week. Consequently he had fallen further and further behind in his schoolwork and had become more and more convinced that he was incapable of learning. Lineham and Louise had made every possible effort on his behalf, but had got nowhere. Recently, however, Louise had read an article about the Denner system, a computer-based teaching method which was said to achieve astonishing results. On Friday the Linehams had gone to a demonstration in Folkestone.

Lineham's face lit up. 'Of course, I haven't had a chance to tell you. It was fantastic!'

'Really? You think it might be of some use?'

'Oh, definitely. In fact, Louise was so impressed – well, we both were, but this will show you how keen she was – she's thinking of doing a course and setting up a unit.'

'So what was so impressive about it?'

'The results it achieves! They claim – and there's loads of documentary evidence from delighted parents that the system really does work – they claim that on average a young pupil will catch up three to four months for every one month of study and once he has finished the course he doesn't slip back but keeps pace with his class!'

'That sounds amazing! So how does it work?'

'Well, the children work alone with a talking computer, using multi-sensory principles – touch, sight and hearing are all involved. They talk into a microphone, a voice answers, and they learn to touch-type commands. The software is individually designed for each pupil. Once they are happy about spelling – which sounds absolutely astounding, doesn't it? Imagine Richard, happy about spelling! Anyway, the claim is that their confidence then spills over into using a pen. Honestly, sir, for the first time we really do feel there's a ray of hope!'

'No snags?'

'Well, there is one – the cost. The Denners have set up a centre in Devon, but across the country the way the system works is to set up small units which have to be individually funded – you have to buy the computer and the software, for a start. We're hoping to get together with some of the other parents to set one up but if we can't, as I say, Louise is seriously considering doing it herself. It would be worth it, to be able to help Richard after all this time, and we're sure people will be clamouring to use it once the good news gets around.'

'I'm delighted, Mike, I really am.' If this system really worked, as it apparently did, it would be a major advance in an area which until now had proved an intractable problem for hundreds of thousands of frustrated parents and children.

'It just goes to show you should never give up, doesn't it?' said Lineham. 'We almost had, you know.'

'Do parents ever?' said Thanet.

The Jeopards lived a mile so beyond Donnington and Thanet and Lineham were out in the countryside now, driving through lanes where a haze of green was misting the hawthorn hedges and young lambs bounced about as if on trampolines. At times like this Thanet wondered why on earth he lived in the town.

Suddenly trees closed in on either side and a stone wall appeared on the left. Lineham was peering ahead. 'This is it, I think. The entrance is just along here, I've passed it before. Ah, yes. Here we are.'

He signalled and turned in between two tall stone pillars linked by a stone archway. Inside the drive swung sharply to the left and Lineham drew up in a gravelled parking area in front of an ancient wooden barn which was obviously used as a garage; the tall doors were open and there were a couple of cars parked inside, a newish Volkswagen Golf and an F-registration Vauxhall Astra.

'I expect the Golf is Hartley Jeopard's,' said Lineham as they got out. He was always interested in cars. 'And the Vauxhall is probably his aunt's.'

They walked back to the path which led up to the front door, a wide path of massive stone slabs flanked by narrow beds which in summer were no doubt ablaze with colour. Halfway along they paused to admire the beauty of the old house which slumbered before them, its Tudor façade of ancient beams, leaded windows and cream-washed plaster complacent in the spring sunshine. The place had a very different atmosphere from the Sylvesters' house – old money as opposed to new. Thanet wondered what Mrs Jeopard had thought of her son's proposed marriage.

Lineham inhaled deeply as they approached the massive front door, as if he could smell the affluence in the air. 'Oh yes, ve-ry nice,' he said.

50

There was no doorbell, only a heavy cast-iron knocker in the form of a twisted rope. Lineham let it drop twice, the sound unnaturally loud in the hush which lay over both house and garden.

'Should be someone in,' he muttered, 'with two cars in the garage.' He knocked again.

At last brisk footsteps could be heard approaching and the door opened.

'Ah, Inspector.' Hartley Jeopard loomed over them, a mournful heron in jeans and sweatshirt. 'Good morning.' He stepped back. 'Come in.'

FIVE

Inside the house it was cool and dark after the warmth and brightness outside and it took a few moments for Thanet's eyes to adjust. They were in a broad stone-flagged passage and Hartley led them through a door on the left into a square, spacious hall which stretched right up into the exposed roof rafters. A staircase led up to a railed gallery which ran around three sides at first-floor level. Heavy linen curtains in a jacobean design hung at the windows and there were comfortable chairs and sofas and a couple of really beautiful pieces of antique oak furniture glowing with the patina of centuries of polishing. The wide oak floorboards were bare of either rugs or carpet, Thanet noticed, probably to facilitate the movement of Mrs Jeopard's wheelchair.

Hartley waved them into armchairs but remained standing. 'Sorry I had to duck out last night, but I felt I really had to get my mother home.'

'We quite understood. How is she this morning?'

'Pretty well devastated, as you might imagine. And she looks very tired, I don't think she slept too well. But she's bearing up. She's always been fairly tough. Anyway, she insists that if you want to see her, you can.' He raised his eyebrows.

Thanet nodded. 'We would like to, if she's up to it.'

'Right. I'll just go and make sure she knows you're here. Do sit down.' He left the room through a door beneath the gallery.

'I imagine her room's on the ground floor,' said Lineham. 'It'd be difficult to install a lift in a house like this.'

In a minute or two Hartley was back and this time he sat down too, stretching out his long legs and steepling his fingers beneath his chin. 'I'm afraid she'll be at least another twenty minutes or so yet.'

'Fine,' said Thanet. 'Meanwhile, is there anything you can tell us about the party last night which might help us?'

'Such as?'

'Anything at all. Did you, for instance, notice any unusual incident involving your brother? Any quarrel or disagreement?'

There was something, obviously. The expression in Hartley's eyes had immediately become guarded and he lowered his hands and looked down at them, began to massage one thumb with the other. Then he glanced up. 'Do I gather that you have decided my brother's death was not an accident?'

'It's very difficult to see how it could have been. So at the moment, yes, we have to treat the death as suspicious.'

'You mean ... murder.' He blurted the word out as indeed most people do, when referring to the death of someone close to them. It is incredibly difficult to relate such an appalling crime to a husband, wife, brother, sister, or child, and putting it into words is a stumbling block which many find impossible.

Thanet nodded. 'I'm sorry.'

Hartley was shaking his head. 'It's all right. We – my

53

mother, my aunt and I – have already discussed this. And we agreed it was extremely unlikely that it could have been an accident. Even if he had fallen in, he could swim like a fish, did you know that?'

'Yes. Mr Sylvester told us.'

'I suppose there is just the remotest possibility that he could have slipped, or tripped, banging his head and knocking himself out as he fell in, but we all thought it extremely unlikely. It wasn't as though he was drunk, and there was nothing to trip over, or to slip on, for that matter. And what was he doing in the pool house in the first place? That's what we'd like to know.'

'And so would we,' said Thanet. 'In fact, these are all questions we are asking ourselves. Which is why I'm also asking if you noticed your brother having any argument or disagreement with anyone last night.'

Once again Hartley's eyes fell away from Thanet's, and again he failed to respond. He obviously wasn't going to volunteer the information.

'For instance, we understand there was an incident involving a friend of Miss Jeopard, a Miss Greenway,' said Thanet.

Hartley sighed and pulled a face. 'I suppose it was unrealistic to suppose you wouldn't hear about that. Yes, it's true. I wasn't going to say anything because I genuinely do not believe that Anthea – Anthea Greenway – could possibly have had anything to do with Max's death.'

'She slapped his face, I understand. In public.'

Hartley nodded.

'Why, do you know?'

A shake of the head this time. 'No. I was across the other side of the room.'

'She used to go out with your brother, I understand.'

A flash of fierce emotion, so quickly suppressed that Thanet might almost have imagined it. But he hadn't, he was sure.

'That was years ago!'

'When, exactly? Can you remember?'

'The summer of '92, as I recall.'

The answer had come immediately, which was astonishing. How many people have precise and instant recall of dates, especially if they are two or three years ago? Unless, of course, they have a personal reason for remembering. By now Thanet had a strong suspicion that Hartley was keen on Anthea himself.

'Before your brother went away on his last trip, in fact?'

'That's right. He came home in May of that year, for the publication of his first book. And he went away again in October.'

Hartley's tone was neutral but again Thanet had the feeling that he was keeping his real emotions well out of sight. 'I see.'

Max, Thanet learned, had always had itchy feet, ever since, in his gap year between school and university, he had spent the time back-packing alone around the Far East – chiefly in Thailand.

'Before he went away he was like the rest of us – didn't have a clue what he wanted to do for a living. It was more or less taken for granted that if we could get into university we'd go, but Max was determined to do some travelling first. And by the time he came back he'd made up his mind he wanted to be a travel writer. He was all for throwing in his place at Oxford but Ma somehow managed to talk him around, God knows how. Probably by offering to finance more travel during the vacations and even afterwards, for all I know. Anyway, he was always taking off somewhere and the minute he finished at university he left for China, this time with the specific purpose of gathering material for a book. He was dead lucky in a way, in that he arrived there at a very interesting time, in the aftermath of the Tiananmen Square massacre.'

'That would have been in – let me see – 1989, then?'

'That's right. The Western world was very keen to find out what was going on over there and don't ask me how, but Max managed to interest one of the national dailies in what he had to say. Before we knew where we were we were reading his reports over our toast and marmalade. They were very good, really gave you the feel of what it was like to be caught up in it all, and more importantly for him, they got his name known. As a result, he managed to interest a publisher in his book well before he'd even finished writing it.'

'How long was he away?'

'Almost eighteen months. He got back a few weeks before Christmas the following year, and spent the rest of the winter holed up here, writing.'

'As a matter of interest, what was the book called?'

'*Peephole into China*.'

Thanet made a mental note to try and get hold of it. Books reveal much about their writers and travel books more than most, relying as they do on the author's quirks, attitudes and viewpoint to give them their individuality. 'Was it successful?'

'Oh yes, very. Astonishingly so.'

'Enough to buy him a flat in London, I assume? That's where he now lived, I understand.'

'Yes. But the flat was actually bought with money Max inherited from Dad. It had been held in trust until he was twenty-five.'

And the same applied to Hartley, Thanet discovered. He worked as an accountant with a firm in the city, but often came down to Kent at weekends.

Max, he learned, had finished the book in June '91 and almost at once was off on his travels again, this time to South America, returning for its publication the following May.

'That was presumably when he started going out with Miss Greenway?'

Again the shutter came down. 'That's right.'

Thanet probed a little deeper. 'Was this a long-running affair? Had he been out with her before?'

'Oh no. Until then it had always been Tess. But she got fed up with him always taking off at every possible opportunity.'

'So on this occasion, the summer of '92, when he came home Miss Jeopard didn't want to have anything to do with him?'

Hartley was shaking his head. 'She was away herself, then. I imagine she thought it might teach him a lesson, if she wasn't always here waiting for him every time he came back.'

'Where was she?'

'In the States, I believe. Look, Inspector, I'm sure you know what you're doing, but is all this relevant? What possible connection can there be between Tess's trip to the United States and Max's death?'

'I'm not saying there is one. But one thing that experience has taught me is that you can never judge any piece of information irrelevant until the case is over. You simply never know what is going to prove significant and what is not, and you therefore have to try and gather in as much as you possibly can. As his brother you must know more about his life than most and know him better personally, too. So bear with me, will you?'

Hartley shrugged. 'If it'll help.'

'Anyway, perhaps we could now go back to the party last night. I believe there are some questions Sergeant Lineham wants to ask you about that.'

This was prearranged and Lineham took over smoothly. 'It's merely a question of trying to place people, sir. You'll appreciate that with so many guests present it's rather difficult to get a clear picture of who was where and when. Now so far the last sighting we have of your brother is at twenty to ten. Apparently he and Tess settled your mother and aunt at their table and then went back for their own food. That was the last anyone saw of him. According to Tess he said he was going to the toilet. Did you see him after that, by any chance?'

Hartley was shaking his head. 'I'm afraid not.'

'You weren't sitting at the family table?'

'No. It was just Tess, Max and the parents. My aunt was included, of course, but I had supper with Anthea and another friend of ours.'

'Would that have been Mr Gerald Argent, by any chance?' asked Lineham innocently. 'Miss Jeopard's former fiancé?'

A gleam of reluctant admiration appeared in Hartley's eyes. 'You don't waste much time, do you? Yes, that's right.'

An uncomfortable trio, thought Thanet. If he was right, they had a lot in common: unrequited love – Hartley carrying a torch for Anthea Greenway, Gerald for Tess and Anthea herself perhaps for Max. Very interesting.

'So you all queued up together, collected your food and sat down to eat it?'

Hartley shifted uncomfortably. 'More or less.'

58

Lineham raised his eyebrows.

'While we were queuing Anthea went off to the loo.'

'How long was she away?'

He raised his shoulders. 'I wasn't timing her, Sergeant!'

'Approximately, then?'

'Gerald and I were halfway through our first course when she joined us, so it must have been, let me see, about ten o'clock.'

'And she had left at . . .?'

'Around twenty to, I suppose. She said she'd had to queue for the loo. And she'd had to collect her supper too, of course.'

'But you and Mr Argent stayed together?'

'Well no, not for the whole time. I went off to the loo as well.'

A general exodus, thought Thanet. But understandable. Everyone stands around talking and drinking, not wanting to break up conversations, and then supper is announced, people queue up and some of them, seeing that they'll have to wait to collect their food, decide to go to the lavatory – where they also find queues, of course.

'And what time did you rejoin Mr Argent?' said Lineham.

'Ten minutes later, or thereabouts.'

'Around five to ten, then?'

Hartley nodded.

'And you're sure you didn't see your brother? That was where he said he was going, too, at around the same time.'

'No. I told you.' A hint of impatience there. 'He may have gone to a different one.'

'So in fact, at suppertime each of the three of you was alone for at least ten minutes, longer in the case of Miss

Greenway?' *At around the time your brother disappeared.* The words hung on the air, unspoken but implicit in what Lineham was saying.

Hartley sat up with a jerk and a quick, sideways glance at Thanet. 'Hang on a minute. What, exactly, are you implying, Sergeant?'

'I'm simply trying to get the facts straight, sir.'

'Oh come on! I'm not an idiot, you know! You're saying you suspect one of us, aren't you?'

'Not at all. We don't suspect anyone at this point. That's right, sir, isn't it?' Lineham glanced at Thanet.

Thanet nodded. 'Much too soon.'

It was clear that Hartley didn't believe them. 'Well, to answer your question, each of us was alone in the sense that we weren't with the other two, but each of us was emphatically not alone in the literal sense of the word. I'm sure that when you check you'll be able to find other people who can vouch for us.'

Lineham nodded, as if to accept this statement at its face value. 'To go back a little, did you by any chance see anyone hand a note to your brother, earlier in the evening?'

'Definitely not.'

'Have you any idea what it could have been about?'

'Not the faintest, I'm afraid.'

'Just one more question then, Mr Argent. How upset was he when Miss Sylvester broke off their engagement and became engaged to your brother instead?'

Thanet noticed that the door to Mrs Jeopard's quarters was opening. Hartley, seated with his back to it and intent upon the conversation, remained unaware.

'Well a bit upset, naturally. You don't ask a girl to marry you unless you're in love with her. But if you're suggesting Gerald could have had anything to do with

60

Max's death, you're out of your mind. He wouldn't hurt a fly!'

'You're being ridiculously naïve, as usual, dear.' The incisive voice sliced into the conversation.

This was a very different woman from the pathetic figure in the wheelchair last night. This morning Mrs Jeopard's back was ramrod straight and she had armoured herself against the world's pity in an elegant black silk dress. She was immaculately groomed, her greying hair framing her face in soft curls, her make-up discreet, her long, delicately-boned hands heavy with rings. Last night Thanet had put her in her early seventies but today he saw that she was considerably younger – mid-sixties, perhaps. He wondered what illness or accident had put her in a wheelchair.

Her sister was also dressed in black, though less expensively. They were really very alike, he realised, and wondered which was the older. It was difficult to tell. He soon found out.

Mrs Jeopard held out her hand. 'I don't believe we were properly introduced last night, Inspector. I am Eleanor Jeopard and this is my twin sister Louisa Burke.'

Non-identical twins, obviously, thought Thanet as he responded. Even seated it was evident that Mrs Jeopard was much the shorter of the two.

'I'm afraid you have to take everything my son says about Gerald Argent with a pinch of salt.' Mrs Jeopard gave Hartley what could only be described as a frosty smile. 'They're practically inseparable. "A bit upset", indeed! The fact of the matter is, Gerald has always been a fool over that girl. He couldn't believe his luck when she actually agreed to marry him so you can imagine how he felt when she threw him over.'

SIX

Hartley was driven to protest. 'Mother, really! You simply cannot go around saying things like that!'

'Why not, if they're true?' She turned her cool blue gaze upon Thanet. 'I assume you have come to the conclusion that my son's death was no accident?'

'Well, I . . .'

'I agree, there is no other possible explanation. Louisa, do stop hovering and sit down. I can't think with you looming over me like that!'

Louisa sat.

No doubt about who was in control in this house, thought Thanet.

Mrs Jeopard fastened her attention upon him again. 'There's no doubt in my mind. Someone must have pushed him in deliberately. Probably hit him over the head first. In fact, they must have done, or he'd have managed to get out. I'm sure that's what you'll find, when you do the post . . . post-mortem.' For the first time there was a tremor in her voice, but she recovered immediately. 'So naturally I have spent most of the night thinking who it could be. I assume you'd like to hear my conclusions?'

'Yes, of –'

'The trouble is, Inspector, everyone was jealous of Max, weren't they, Louisa?' The merest flick of a glance in Hartley's direction hinted – perhaps unconsciously, Thanet thought – that even her other son was not excluded from this accusation. 'He had everything, you see. He was handsome, intelligent, athletic, and creative, too, a most gifted writer. Have you read his book?'

'No, but –'

'I brought this for you.' Draped across her knees was a mohair travelling rug in a beautiful range of blues and greens and now she put one hand beneath it and pulled out a paperback, held it out to Thanet. *Peephole into China*. 'More than anything it will show you the sort of man he was.'

Thanet took it from her. 'Thank you.' The jacket design was striking, a typical two-dimensional Chinese landscape of high rounded mountains, misty gorges and stylised trees, glimpsed through a huge keyhole. He turned it over and Max Jeopard's face grinned up at him, assured, confident of his charm and ability to cope with any and every situation. Perhaps on that last, fatal occasion it was over-confidence that had brought about his downfall. Perhaps he had made the mistake of underestimating the strength and determination of someone known to him but to whom he had felt superior.

Mrs Jeopard was watching him and now she gave a nod, as if satisfied that Thanet's interest was sufficiently aroused for him to follow her instructions.

'That girl, of course, was besotted with him.'

'Miss Sylvester?' Thanet wondered how Mr Sylvester would have felt at hearing his daughter referred to as 'that girl'.

'Yes. We always knew it would never work with Gerald, didn't we, Louisa?' Once again Mrs Jeopard did

63

not wait for a reply, apparently taking her sister's agreement for granted. She cast a scornful glance at Hartley,
as if he, not his friend, had been the inferior suitor. 'We
knew that if Max came back before they were actually
married, she'd leave Gerald like a shot. I prayed he
wouldn't, I can tell you.'

'You didn't approve of your son marrying Miss
Sylvester?'

'I most certainly did not!'

Louisa Burke had made an involuntary movement of
protest and now Eleanor Jeopard snapped, 'Oh, for
heaven's sake, Louisa, why bother to pretend any more?
You see, Inspector, while Max was ... There was no
point in opposing Max's wishes. He was such a determined person he always got what he wanted in the end
and I'm afraid that what he wanted was Tess. The
trouble was, she couldn't accept that she had to come
second, after his work. She got tired of him going off on
his travels. I think she thought it was pure self-indulgence
on his part. She seemed incapable of understanding that
if he didn't have the material to write about he couldn't
make a living! She wanted first and exclusive rights in
him and Max felt he absolutely could not be tied down
like that.'

'Was that your only reason for disapproving of her?'

'Not at all. My reasons, as one might say, were many
and various.'

'Mother, really! How do you think Tess would feel if
she could hear you talking about her like this?'

'To be honest, I don't care a jot what Tess feels.'

'I thought you liked her,' said Hartley. 'You always
made her welcome and –'

'Hartley. I sometimes think you're an even greater
ninny than you look. Of course I made her welcome. She

64

was Max's choice, wasn't she, and I accepted her for his sake. If I hadn't, it would have driven him away, can't you see that?'

Hartley jumped out of his seat and stood looking out of the window, jingling the change in his pocket, his frustration revealed in hunched shoulders and rigidity of stance.

Thanet wondered what it must have been like for him, being Max's younger brother, probably overshadowed at school, always second in his mother's affections.

'But really, dear,' Mrs Jeopard's tone had changed. Now she was trying to coax him into agreement. 'You must admit the Sylvesters are not exactly our sort of people.' Somehow she embued the words with capital letters.

Hartley swung around. 'In your view, very few people are.'

'Well, even you will agree that it's not exactly a promising prospect, to know your son is marrying a girl with a brother who is insane!' Mrs Jeopard switched her attention to Thanet again. 'You have heard about him, I suppose, Inspector?'

'Yes, Mr Syl –'

'And they did tell you he was actually on the loose last night?' Mrs Jeopard twitched angrily at the rug on her knees. 'How irresponsible can you get?'

Thanet wondered if he would ever be allowed to finish a sentence. He was running out of patience. He caught the glint of amusement in Lineham's eye and decided that the time had come for him to assert himself.

He opened his mouth to speak but Hartley got in first. 'Mother, they did explain that it was one of the guests who –'

'I don't care what they explained, the fact remains that

65

Carey was roaming about last night and he's always been jealous of Max, as you very well know. He was furious when Max got into Oxford and he didn't. And he resented the fact that Max had so often made Tess miserable by going off on his travels again. He was always trying to persuade her to break away from him. You told me that yourself, years ago.'

Right, thought Thanet. He cut in, quickly. 'Do I gather that Carey Sylvester has only recently become schizophrenic?'

Mrs Jeopard was about to reply but this time Hartley pre-empted her, returning to his seat as if to re-establish his right to participate in the conversation. 'Carey was fine until halfway through his second year at university. He was taking a degree in Urban Land Management at Reading. Then suddenly he just . . . fell apart.'

Mrs Jeopard didn't like being ousted from centre stage. 'He went into a mental hospital for six months or so and he's been in and out of them ever since. Until that absurd Mental Health Act, in fact, when he was forced to stay out permanently. I don't know what the Government was thinking of, turning all those madmen out into the streets. Really, it's enough to make one think of resigning from the Conservative Party!'

'The Sylvesters,' said Hartley with a reproachful glance at his mother, 'have had a rotten time of it. In the end they hired a nurse for Carey. And I think it's downright unkind of you, Mother, to call them irresponsible. They've done everything they can to –'

'Maybe they have. But it still doesn't alter the fact that last night that maniac got out. Nor the fact that your brother was found dead in their swimming pool.'

'We don't know that there's any connection!'

'I'm not saying there is. I'm just saying that there's a

66

distinct possibility there might be! Anyway, that's not exactly what the Inspector was asking. He was asking for the reasons why I disapproved of Tess Sylvester as a wife for Max. And I'm simply saying that madness in the family was one, and one that I certainly consider valid, as I'm sure most people would. Have you got any children, Inspector?'

'Two,' said Thanet.

'Then I'm sure you'll know what I mean.'

And she was right, of course. But he wasn't going to give her the satisfaction of admitting it.

'And last but not least,' said Mrs Jeopard, 'I didn't like the idea of Max marrying a girl whose father didn't appreciate him.'

'In what way?' said Thanet.

She waved a vague hand. 'I suspect Ralph Sylvester didn't like the competition. That man absolutely dotes on Tess and he would, I'm sure, have preferred someone more ... malleable, like Gerald, as a husband for her. Someone local, who wouldn't be liable to whisk her off to the other side of the world at the drop of a hat. Someone with a nice steady boring job who'd settle down a couple of miles away and present the Sylvesters with a couple of grandchildren in the not too distant future. Max was altogether too unpredictable, too unconventional for his taste.'

'Your son didn't get on with his prospective father-in-law?'

'It depends what you mean by get on. Louisa, do you mind? This cushion . . .'

Her sister sprang to adjust the offending article. So far she had not, Thanet realised, contributed a single syllable to the conversation, and was unlikely to have the opportunity to do so in the presence of Mrs Jeopard. He

67

wondered how he could manoeuvre an opportunity to speak to her alone. In his experience the quiet ones often noticed far more than those who were too busy projecting their chosen image to be aware of the nuances of other people's behaviour.

'They obviously didn't get on in the sense of having much common ground or enjoying each other's company,' she went on. 'But if you're asking if there was any overt antagonism between them then no, there wasn't. Like me, Ralph Sylvester was making the best of a bad job. He didn't want to risk alienating his daughter by open disapproval. All the same, I'd be willing to wager that in private he'll be rubbing his hands together with glee this morning.'

Hartley was again driven to protest. 'Mother!'

'Don't "Mother!" me,' she said furiously. 'What is the point of pretending? Nothing will convince me that Ralph Sylvester isn't secretly delighted that Max is dead.'

Delighted enough to have helped him on his way was the implication.

From the moment she entered the room she had dominated the conversation but now, suddenly, her vitality seemed to fade away. That last spurt of anger seemed to have depleted her. The colour had drained out of her face and the skin of her forehead glistened. She produced a dainty lace-bordered handkerchief and dabbed at her upper lip. Hartley jumped up and bent over her solicitously. 'Mother . . . are you all right?'

For the first time she managed a faint smile, gave his arm a reassuring pat. 'Yes, of course, dear. Perhaps a glass of water . . .?'

He hurried off at her bidding. It was time to bring this interview to a close, thought Thanet. He wondered again what was the matter with her and wondered too how much it had cost her, just how far she had had to draw upon her evidently meagre reserves, to give the performance they had just witnessed.

'Well, you've certainly given us food for thought, Mrs Jeopard,' he said. 'And if you could just bear with me for a few moments longer while I check one or two facts, we'll leave you in peace.'

She inclined her head. 'Of course.'

Hartley returned with a cut-glass tumbler of water and she took it, sipped from it gratefully before returning it to him. She verified that yes, she had last seen Max when he had escorted her to their table at about 9.40, and that it must have been around ten when Tess announced that she was going to look for him and Ralph Sylvester went instead. She had no knowledge, she said, of any note handed to Max earlier in the evening.

'One last question, then,' said Thanet. 'There was an incident before supper involving some kind of argument between your son and a friend of Tess Sylvester, Anthea Greenway. Do you know anything about that?'

When Anthea's name was mentioned there had been an immediate flicker of comprehension in her eyes, quickly suppressed. She shook her head. 'I'm afraid not,' she said.

No doubt about it, she was lying. But why? Whatever the reason, questioning her about it would have to wait. She was clearly exhausted. Thanet stood up and thanked her.

Louisa Burke rose also and spoke for the first time. 'I'll see you out.'

Thanet was pleased. The opportunity to speak to her alone had unexpectedly been handed to him on a plate.

SEVEN

Thanet suspected that there was something specific Louisa
Burke wanted to say to him, but that she would be
frightened off by too direct an approach. In the hall he
said conversationally, 'Have you lived here long, Miss
Burke?'

She plucked at her black cotton skirt, as if to gather up
courage. 'Ever since my sister's marriage.'

'Beautiful house,' said Lineham, playing along.

'I don't actually live in the house. There's a little flat
over the stables . . . It used to be the chauffeur's, in the
days when people had chauffeurs. Eleanor's husband very
kindly did it up for me. It's nice to be independent.'

Thanet wondered how much independence she actually
had. 'Your sister is very fortunate, to have you to look
after her.'

She gave an embarrassed little laugh, as if unused to
compliments. 'I don't do it alone, you know. The district
nurse comes in regularly to bathe her and of course we
have help in the house.'

Thanet felt like telling her not to undervalue what she
did. Eleanor Jeopard couldn't be the easiest of patients
and there was little doubt that without her sister's help
she would either have had to employ a full-time nurse

or go into a nursing home. 'How long has your sister been' – how should he put it? – 'incapacitated?'

'Ever since the car crash in which her husband was killed, when Max was thirteen, so it must be . . . let me see . . . sixteen years now. Actually, that was what I wanted to say to you, Inspector. My sister . . . she's in constant pain, you know, and life is not easy for her. She was always such an active woman, with so many interests. So now, sometimes she . . . well, she tends to come across as much, well, harsher than she really is. I'm just saying that we have to make allowances for that in what she says.'

They had reached the front door now and they all stepped outside, automatically gravitating towards the sunshine.

Thanet paused, turning to face her. 'Are you saying that what she told us was a . . . shall we say an exaggeration of the truth?'

'Well, no, not exactly. It's just that I wouldn't want you to think less of her because she expressed her opinions so strongly. Max, you see, was always the apple of her eye. The only way she can begin to cope with what has happened is to turn her anger on to other people.'

'Yes, I do understand that.'

For the first time she met his gaze directly. 'Yes, I believe you do.' Already, her mission accomplished, she was turning back towards the house.

'Miss Burke . . .' He mustn't miss the opportunity. 'If I could just check one or two points?' But he learned nothing new and was interested to note that she, too, was reluctant to talk about the incident between Anthea Greenway and Max. She admitted having witnessed it from across the room.

71

'Do you know what might have prompted her to slap him across the face in public like that?'

She shifted uncomfortably from one foot to the other and glanced at the hall windows to her right. 'No idea. I'm sorry.'

Following her gaze Thanet saw that Mrs Jeopard had been watching them. She couldn't possibly hear what they were saying but Louisa Burke was behaving as if she could, edging unobtrusively back towards the haven of the front door. Reluctantly, he let her go.

'What was all that about?' said Lineham as they returned to the car.

'No idea.'

'I mean, why clam up about Anthea Greenway like that?'

'The only reason I can think of,' said Thanet as he got in and wound the window down, 'is that I suspect Hartley Jeopard is in love with Anthea and his mother is following the same policy as she did with Max, in trying not to alienate him by criticising his girl friend.'

'D'you think she might have been more open if he hadn't been there?' Lineham made a minute adjustment to the rear-view mirror before starting the car. He was somewhat obsessive about checking that everything was properly in order before moving off.

'I don't know. I doubt it, actually. I imagine family loyalty ranks pretty high with her and now that she's lost one son she's not going to risk losing the other.'

'You could have fooled me, the way she treated him! If you ask me she's an autocratic old so-and-so.' Lineham's own mother had always been something of a problem and his hackles invariably rose at the first signs of maternal domination.

'She did come over like that, I agree. But I'm not sure

how much of it was an act put on for our benefit. Or if, as her sister says, it's the only way she could cope. Didn't you notice how exhausted she was by the end of the interview?'

'Maybe. But if you ask me, there's no doubt who rules the roost. I felt sorry for the sister.'

'She can't have much of a life,' Thanet agreed.

They had reached the gates and Lineham leaned forward to check that the road was clear before moving out. 'Anyway,' he said, 'I suppose we're a bit further forward.'

'Depends what you mean by further forward. Our list of suspects is getting longer by the minute, true.'

'It certainly is! Gerald Argent sounds the most likely candidate, wouldn't you agree? He must have been really miffed at having Tess snatched away from him practically at the altar, especially if, as Mrs Jeopard claims, he's been mad about her for years. He's obviously still pretty fed up about it if, as the housekeeper told us, he originally refused the invitation to the engagement party. I wonder how she knew that, by the way.'

'I should think not much goes on in that house that she doesn't know.'

'Anyway, Gerald obviously changed his mind and went, but she did say that he deliberately snubbed Max. Not surprising, if you ask me. Did you notice, by the way, that Hartley was anxious to play down Gerald's involvement with Tess?'

'Yes. I'd guess that he and Gerald are pretty close friends.'

'But you agree, sir, that Gerald has a pretty strong motive?'

'So have a number of other people.'

'True. There's Hartley himself, for that matter. I

wouldn't mind betting that Max played the same trick on him as he did on Gerald, filching his girlfriend from under his nose. But for no better reason than that his own wasn't available at the time!'

'Possibly. Tess was away in the States, wasn't she?'

'That's what Hartley said. Anyway, it couldn't have been easy, having Max Jeopard as an older brother. I imagine he outshone Hartley at most things. And he was obviously his mother's favourite. I'd guess that's why Hartley is as he is.'

'Diffident, you mean?'

'Yes. Looking as though he's apologising for his existence. And we all know how dangerous the quiet ones can be, how the worm can turn.'

'But if that is so, why wait until last night? If Hartley was going to snap over Max taking Anthea away from him, surely he'd have done that when it actually happened? After all, Max has been away for a couple of years, until Christmas, in fact, and it sounds as though the minute he got home and found Tess engaged to Gerald Argent he went all out to get her back.'

'And I wonder how Anthea felt about that. I suppose we shouldn't rule her out, either. What if she'd been expecting him to take up where they left off, when he got home? And then he makes a dead set for Tess instead. It's interesting that both she and Max excused themselves from the people they were with at the same time, twenty to ten. D'you think they might have arranged to meet? That's a point, sir! That could be it!' Lineham flashed Thanet a delighted grin.

'Well? Go on!'

'I'm trying to think what time the face-slapping incident took place. Was it before or after nine o'clock, that's the point?'

'Ah. You mean that the note could have been from Anthea, apologising for the scene she made and begging him to meet her in the supper interval . . . to . . . what?'

'Apologise properly? And promising something, anything, so long as she could see him alone for a few moments.'

'Do you think he'd have gone along with that?'

'No idea. It's possible. If only to tell her that it was pointless to go on hoping he'd come back to her. Then she loses her temper, gives him a shove, he hits his head on something as he falls into the pool and she just walks out.'

'Leaving him to drown. When she's supposed to be in love with him?'

'It could have happened like that.'

'I agree. It could. But there's the same objection as there is to Hartley having done it. Why wait until now? If she were going to take any kind of revenge, surely it would have been at Christmas, when she found he wasn't coming back to her?'

'Oh, I don't know. She could have kept on hoping and hoping but then, when he finally got engaged . . . Anyway, you have to admit that to make that sort of scene in public she must still feel pretty strongly about him.'

'I suppose so. But let's face it, Mike. Some people enjoy making a spectacle of themselves, and Anthea looked a pretty colourful character to me.'

'You mean the way she was dressed?'

'It was fairly flamboyant, wouldn't you agree? In fact, I wouldn't have thought she was Hartley's type. I'd have thought he'd go for someone altogether quieter, more subdued. Still, all the signs are that he did, and if so then I agree, we have to consider him a suspect. Especially as I imagine he wouldn't exactly be the type to have a string of girlfriends, either. He'd be very much a one-woman man.'

'Unlike his brother! From what we've heard, Max just had to have a woman – any woman, in tow. And even when he had one he couldn't keep his hands off the others, by all accounts! If you ask me it's not surprising someone decided to clock him one and chuck him in the swimming pool! Oh all right, all right, sir, no need to look at me like that. I know murder can't be justified. But you must agree that occasionally it is at least under-standable and from what we've heard about Max Jeopard . . . He sounds as selfish as they come, doesn't he? Never mind anyone else's feelings as long as his own were gratified. Imagine groping other women at your own engagement party! What must Tess have felt about that!'

'Quite. Or her father, for that matter.'

'You think it's true, what the old lady said about him being dead against the marriage?'

'It wouldn't surprise me. Sylvester and Max would have been chalk and cheese, I imagine. And I should think it's true that Sylvester would much prefer to have Tess settled locally, where they could see her regularly and be able to watch their grandchildren grow up. Of course, for all we know, Max and Tess were planning to settle in this area anyway, or at least to have a house here as a base. We must find out.'

They were both silent for a while, thinking. Then Thanet said, 'The fact of the matter is we're only just beginning to scratch the surface of this case, Mike. Let's find out a bit more about these people before we start trying to draw conclusions. Which reminds me, we mustn't forget that Max Jeopard actually spent most of his time – when he was in this country, that is – in London. There's too much to do today, but I think we'd

76

better try and get up there to take a look at his flat. Tomorrow morning, perhaps.' They were approaching a pub and he glanced at his watch. Twelve-forty-five. 'Might as well pull in here for a bite to eat. Once we get to the Sylvesters' we'll be there for hours.'

The pub was quiet, the service swift, and three-quarters of an hour later they were turning once again into the Sylvesters' drive, just behind another car, a blue Nissan, which took the right fork, towards the bungalow.

'Perhaps we'll have a word with the gardener first,' said Thanet. 'What was his name? Fielding? He might have seen something last night.'

They parked in front of the main house alongside a sleek K-registration BMW convertible at which Lineham cast admiring glances. 'Wonder whose it is,' he said wistfully, running a hand along its bonnet.

'Sylvester's, I imagine. Or his wife's.'

'Or even Tess's. Must be nice to be able to afford to buy your daughter a car like that! They cost around £28,000 new, you know. Probably thirty, on the road. And this latest 325i model is holding its value well.'

Thanet laughed. 'I think you must spend all your spare time reading Auto magazines!'

Lineham grinned. 'Pretty well.'

They walked back down the drive. By daylight last night's impression of prosperity was underlined. The whole establishment was in excellent order and groomed to perfection, a place where weeds would think twice before daring to raise their heads above the soil and shrubs and trees obediently grew to exactly the right dimensions. The lawn edges were knife sharp, the block paving of the drive free of moss and algae.

'Wish my garden looked like this,' said Lineham.

Thanet laughed. 'Too much hard work.'

His smile faded as he saw why the people who had got out of the Nissan were taking so long to get into the bungalow. There were three of them, an elderly couple supporting a much younger woman who was so weak she was apparently incapable of walking alone. With their arms around her waist they were making pitifully slow progress towards the front door, which stood open.

By mutual accord Thanet and Lineham slowed down to allow them time to get themselves organised indoors.

'Think we ought to come back later?' said Lineham.

Thanet shook his head. 'Not much point in putting it off. It doesn't look as though the situation is likely to change much, does it?'

'Their daughter, you think?'

'Must be. Sylvester said they had one.'

'Wonder what's the matter with her.'

'Something pretty serious, by the look of it, poor girl. It didn't look as though she could stand unaided.'

'It must be terrible to see your son or daughter in that condition.'

Cancer, Thanet thought. Or some incurable wasting disease. He pushed away the thought of Bridget in that state. It didn't bear thinking about.

Fielding had obviously seen them heading in his direction and now he came back out of the bungalow, shutting the door behind him.

Thanet studied the man as he introduced himself. The gardener was in his mid-sixties, he guessed, short and whipcord-thin with sparse brown hair and a narrow face on which lines of anxiety were deeply etched. He was wearing a tweed jacket, shirt and tie. Sombre hazel eyes peered out at Thanet from deep sockets.

'You wanted to see me?'

'Just a few questions about last night.'

78

Fielding said nothing, just waited.

'I imagine you were helping in some way?'

'I was overseeing the parking. You can get so many more cars in if they're parked properly.'

'So what time did you come back down?'

'It must have been about a quarter past nine. My wife was watching the nine o'clock news when I got in.'

'We understand you helped look for the Sylvesters' son when he went missing. Did his nurse, Mr Roper, come down and fetch you?'

'Yes, he did.'

'What time would that have been?'

'Somewhere around five to ten, ten o'clock, I should think.'

'And were you indoors all the time during the intervening period?'

'No. Mr Sylvester had asked me to keep an eye open for gatecrashers. You never know these days . . .'

'So you went out, patrolled around?'

'Not exactly. I just came out and walked down to the gate a couple of times, made sure everything was quiet.'

'Did you, on any of those occasions, notice that the pool house was lit up?' A vain hope, but he had to ask.

Fielding shook his head. 'Afraid not.'

'And you didn't actually go into the main house, you say?'

'No.'

'So you saw nothing, heard nothing suspicious, the entire evening?'

Another shake of the head. 'I'm sorry.'

As they walked back to the house Lineham said, 'Pity.'

'If he only walked down to the gate he'd have been too far away to see anything useful anyway. And in any case, we're only assuming the pool house was lit up. If Max's assignation was with a woman . . .'

'True. Light would have been the last thing he would have wanted.'

Suddenly there was the sound of furious barking and a large brown dog came rushing out from the gap between the garages and the house and raced towards them. Thanet and Lineham froze. It was, Thanet saw to his alarm, a Dobermann. It approached at terrifying speed, its eyes narrowed to yellow slits, fangs bared as it continued its frantic barking. Pointless to think of turning to run. He could only hope that it would find their immobility unthreatening.

When it was only ten yards or so away a girl emerged from the same gap. When she saw what was happening she began to run. 'Jason!' she shouted. 'Stay!'

The dog skidded to a halt in front of them but continued barking ferociously.

'Tess Sylvester, presumably,' said Lineham with a nervous laugh.

EIGHT

Thanet had never seen a Dobermann at close quarters before and hoped he never would again. He was prepared to believe everything he had ever heard about their ferocity. He realised that the palms of his hands were damp.

'Jason!' she shouted again. 'Enough!'

The dog stopped barking immediately but did not change its aggressive stance, just stood looking at them, ready to spring, the whites of its eyes showing.

The girl came up alongside it and laid her hand on its head. 'Sit!' she said. Reluctantly, the Dobermann lowered its rear quarters to the ground and was rewarded by a pat and a murmured, 'Good boy!'

Thanet could see why Tess's father apparently doted on her and more than one man had wanted to marry her. Despite her red-rimmed eyes and the dark shadows beneath them she really was a lovely girl, with a clear, almost luminous complexion, lustrous dark eyes and a tumble of luxuriant hair the colour of ripe chestnuts. She was wearing the ubiquitous country uniform of Barbour and green wellington boots.

He discovered that he had been holding his breath. 'Good watchdog!' he said, when they had introduced themselves, relief infusing his comment with apparent enthusiasm.

'He certainly is,' said Tess, fondling the animal's ears. It turned its head, clearly relishing the caress. 'He's an old softie, really.'

'You could have fooled me!' said Lineham.

'Oh, but he is. Really. And once he knows you're supposed to be here, he'll be fine. In fact, just to be on the safe side, I'd better introduce you properly, then there won't be any problem. Give me your hand,' she said to Thanet.

Thanet held it out and she took it between both of hers and rubbed it before offering it to the dog. With difficulty Thanet refrained from flinching. The dog sniffed at it warily.

'You see?' she said. 'I've put my smell on it. Now, next time you meet, he'll associate your smell with mine and know you're a friend.'

Thanet hoped she was right.

'Now yours,' she said to Lineham, and the sergeant reluctantly went through the same process.

Watching, Thanet realised that they had reason to be grateful to the animal for breaking the ice. The diversion had distracted them all from the business in hand.

The aggressive light had magically faded from the dog's eyes and now it trotted around beside Thanet and thrust its nose into his palm.

'See?' said Tess. 'He wants you to stroke him.'

'Amazing,' murmured Thanet, complying.

An awkward silence fell. Somehow he had to bridge the gap between banality and tragedy. 'Miss Sylvester, allow me to offer you my condolences. This is a terrible time for you and I hesitate to say that I need to talk to you, but . . .'

'That's all right. I understand. Go ahead.' But she had

turned her head away sharply and when she looked at him again he saw that her eyes had filled with tears. She bit her lip. 'Naturally I want to do all I can to . . .' She shook her head, unable to continue.

To give her time to overcome her distress, in unspoken agreement Thanet and Lineham turned and began to stroll towards the house, leaving her to trail behind. After a few moments she blew her nose and came up alongside them. Thanet gave her a sympathetic smile and said, 'There's nothing that can't wait, if you prefer.'

She shook her head. 'I'd rather get it over with.'

'Very well.' Quickly, Thanet took her through the events of the evening. Her account agreed with everything they had been told so far. He deliberately avoided questioning her about the incident with Anthea Greenway. There had been plenty of other witnesses and it was pointless to cause her unnecessary distress. The note was a different matter, but she apparently knew nothing about it. She had taken her duties as hostess seriously and during the early part of the evening, before supper, had done her best to circulate among the guests.

Now for the difficult part. 'Miss Sylvester . . .'

'Tess, please.'

'Very well. Tess. I'm sorry, but I really have to ask you this.'

They had reached the house. She had taken them around to the back door, pausing to chain the dog up on the way, and was now removing her boots. Aware of the alteration in his tone she glanced up at Thanet sharply before straightening up. Then, without a word, she opened the door, led the way into the kitchen, stopped and turned to face him, folding her arms and hunching her shoulders as if to protect herself from whatever was coming. 'What?' she said.

'You'll have talked to your parents this morning and be aware that we are treating this as a case of suspicious death. So I have to ask you if there is anyone, to your knowledge, who would be glad to see your fiancé dead?'

The fear faded from her eyes leaving behind a strange blankness, as if she had pulled a shutter down to hide her feelings and then suddenly it was back again, redoubled. 'No!' she cried. 'Of course not!' She put her hands up to the sides of her face, pressing so hard against her cheeks that her features became distorted. Then, without warning, she turned and dashed from the room.

Thanet pulled a face. 'Well handled.'

'No point in blaming yourself, sir. It's not surprising she's a bit fragile today.'

'Looks as though she does have her suspicions, doesn't it? Who, do you think?'

Lineham shrugged. 'Father, brother, Gerald whatsisname, her former fiancé? Take your pick.'

Thanet glanced around. The kitchen was much as he would have expected, the type by now familiar to everyone through the glossy magazines: elaborate wooden units, wall-tiles whose unevenness proclaimed the fact that they were hand-made, terracotta tiles on the floor and every sophisticated gadget known to man. But there was one interesting individual touch, a cork noticeboard set into a specially constructed niche, covered with photographs of varying shapes and sizes. He crossed to take a closer look at it but before he could do so footsteps came clacking along the corridor from the hall and a woman called out, 'Who's there?'

Marion Sylvester came into the room. 'Oh, it's you, Inspector. I thought I heard voices.' She was obviously the type for whom an attempt at glamour is a way of life. Her plump thighs were encased in tight black leggings,

84

her heels were a good three inches high and her black and white sweater sported a striking design of geometrics and swirls. But this morning her eye shadow and lipstick had been unevenly applied by an unsteady hand and the pouches beneath her eyes were testimony of a sleepless night.

'We were talking to your daughter.'

Marion Sylvester groped for a chair and collapsed upon it as if her legs had suddenly become incapable of holding her upright a moment longer. She raked a hand through her hair. 'Oh God, I just don't know how I'm going to cope with all this. Poor Tess. She's absolutely distraught. She's trying to put a brave face on it but she keeps on rushing off to her room and locking herself in. Then there's Carey. All this upset is so bad for him.'

'How is he this morning?'

She lifted her shoulders. 'Who can tell?'

'I'd like a word with him later.'

She looked alarmed. 'I don't know if that would be a good idea.'

'I'll try not to upset him, I promise. And his nurse can be present at the interview.'

She shook her head wearily, as if she had no strength left to argue. 'Oh, I suppose so, then. If you must.'

Thanet turned back to the noticeboard. The photographs had been crammed on to it, many of them overlapping. 'Interesting collection.'

She shrugged. 'It's a thing of mine. I always think it's pointless sticking them into albums, no one ever looks at them. The trouble is, I can never bring myself to throw them out. Some of those have been there for years.'

'So I see.' Thanet's eye had alighted on a group photograph and he leaned forward to look at it more closely. A number of young people were relaxing over tea on the lawn after a game of tennis. There were seven of them, three girls and four boys, some seated on deckchairs and some sprawled on the grass. He realised with a jolt that although they were much younger a number of the faces were already familiar to him. Surely that was Tess, and Hartley Jeopard, and Anthea Greenway and Max, of course, sitting at Tess's feet and looking tanned and debonair. So the others must be . . .

'What are you looking at?' Marion Sylvester's voice, beside him.

He had been so engrossed that he hadn't even noticed her move.

Obviously intrigued, Lineham joined them.

'I am right, aren't I?' Thanet pointed out the faces he thought he recognised.

'Oh yes. I took that myself. They seemed to spend most of the summer holidays playing tennis in those days. You know how it is with kids, they go through these phases. That must have been taken, oh, a good ten years ago now. Some of them have moved away, of course, Hartley and Anthea live in London and so does . . . did, Max. In the normal way of things Carey would be gone too by now, no doubt, if he'd finished his course at university and found himself a job. He was such a clever boy.'

'Which is he?'

Marion laid a scarlet fingernail on a profile beneath a shock of dark hair.

'And who is this?'

'Oh, that's Linda Fielding, our gardener's daughter.'

Thanet looked at the somewhat plain features and sturdy figure of Linda Fielding and with a shiver remembered the frail creature they had seen earlier, who could not now even walk unaided.

'She and Tess and Anthea are the same age,' said Marion. 'They were all in the same class at school, so Linda often used to make up the numbers at tennis. When this photo was taken Tess had a sprained ankle, I remember.'

Now that it had been pointed out to him Thanet could see that unlike the others Tess was not wearing tennis whites. He had been misled by the fact that her summer dress was in a pale colour.

Marion was still talking about Linda. 'Poor girl, she's very ill now, I'm afraid, which is why she wasn't at the party last night.'

'We saw her earlier, when we arrived. What's the matter with her?'

'Cancer, I imagine,' said Marion. 'I haven't enquired too closely, it's obvious it's serious. She's not been well for some time but lately she seems to have gone downhill at an alarming rate. I feel so sorry for the Fieldings. She's their only child and they've always doted on her. They were getting on a bit when she was born and I think they'd given up hope. Though I always feel sorry for kids with older parents, especially if they're only children, like Linda. They never seem to mix well. Linda was never really a part of the group in the same way as the others. I suppose it was partly because, to put it bluntly, she came from a different class, her father was only a gardener, after all, but it wasn't just that. She was always quiet, mousy, never had boyfriends or went to discos. And of course she was a real bookworm, not like the other two girls. Tess has never been what you might call academic and Anthea was always the arty type.'

Thanet wondered why Marion was telling him all this. He was much more interested in hearing about Gerald,

Tess's former fiancé, who was no doubt the other as yet unnamed male in the photograph. Unless, of course, Marion was deliberately trying *not* to talk about Gerald. Which, if true, was interesting. He decided not to interrupt the flow of reminiscence. You never knew when you might learn something useful and in his experience it was good policy, once a witness started to talk freely, to allow him or her to do so.

'I remember the Fieldings were so thrilled and proud when Linda got into Bristol. Unfortunately for her, of course, when she left university in, let me see, it must have been '91, it was right in the middle of the recession and she couldn't find a job. It was awful, really. Mrs Fielding used to be almost in tears telling me about all the job applications Linda kept on sending off, dozens and dozens of them. Most of the time people didn't even bother to acknowledge them, let alone tell her the post had been filled. I think that's terrible, don't you? I mean, they could at least have the courtesy to do that, couldn't they? And after all that education, spending all those years getting a degree, it's so soul-destroying . . . And then, when Linda finally did get a job, the year before last, she'd only been in it a few months when she started getting health problems. She really has had a rotten time.'

She seemed to have run down and Thanet was just going to ask about Gerald when, still gazing at the photograph she said, 'The three girls were all so different – still are, I suppose.'

'In what way?'

'Well, Linda and Anthea were like chalk and cheese. Linda so quiet and shy, and Anthea, well, have you met Anthea yet?'

'Not yet. We did see her briefly, last night.'

'Then you'll see what I mean. The way she was dressed – typical. Anthea always has to be different, always has to be noticed.'

'Who always has to be noticed?' Ralph Sylvester had come into the room. Like Marion he looked as though he hadn't slept much last night. 'I thought I heard voices,' he said, echoing his wife.

'Anthea, dear.'

'Ah, Anthea,' said Sylvester, sitting down heavily at the table. 'Any chance of a cup of coffee, darl?'

'Of course. Would you like a cup?' she said to Thanet and Lineham.

'Yes, please.' They joined Sylvester at the table.

'What did you mean, "Ah, Anthea"?' said Thanet.

'She just doesn't know how to behave, that girl,' said Marion indignantly, clattering kettle and mugs. 'Haven't you heard about the scene she made at the party last night? Disgusting, I call it, making a public spectacle of herself like that. If she wanted to make a fuss why couldn't she have done it in private, that's what I'd like to know, instead of ruining Tess's engagement party?'

'Oh come on, darl, aren't you exaggerating a bit? She didn't exactly ruin it, did she? It was what happened later that ruined it.'

'Well you know what I mean. And you said yourself, last night, that if anyone had a grudge against Max, it was Anthea.'

'Marion!' Sylvester cast an anxious glance at the two policemen. 'Think what you're saying!'

'I'm only repeating what you said yourself!'

'Maybe. But that was in *private*, don't you see?'

'I don't care whether it was in private or not, it's true, isn't it?'

'Perhaps. I don't know. But we ought to let the police

make up their own minds, don't you think? It's hardly fair to Anthea . . .'

'Fair? *Fair*, to *Anthea*?' Marion swung around, hands on hips, eyes blazing. 'What about Tess? Is it fair to Tess that her life has been ruined? Don't talk to me about being fair to Anthea. If she did decide to have another go at him later and shoved him into the swimming pool, then all I can say is that she deserves what's coming to her!'

'All right, darl, calm down. All I'm saying is that you can't go around hurling wild accusations about people.'

'I am *not* hurling wild accusations! I'm simply saying . . .'

Thanet decided to intervene. Rows were often instructive, revealing. People said things they hadn't intended to say. But this one seemed now to be going around in circles. 'Mrs Sylvester,' he said. 'I don't think this is getting us anywhere. We had heard about the scene last night at the party, between Miss Greenway and Mr Jeopard, but so far we haven't managed to find out what it was all about.'

'Who have you asked?'

Thanet wasn't prepared to be specific. 'One or two people.'

'The Jeopards, I bet! And they wouldn't tell you, oh no. Not on your life, they wouldn't!'

'What do you mean?'

'Marion . . .' said Sylvester, a note of warning in his voice.

But she was not to be stopped. She shook her head at him impatiently. 'Why should I keep quiet? What do we owe them, you tell me that? Do you think I didn't know they never thought our Tess was good enough for their precious Max? And although Hartley never had a look-in in the favouritism stakes while Max was still alive, now there's only him they're closing ranks, don't you see? Hartley is still carrying a torch for Anthea and they don't want to upset him by saying anything that would compromise her!'

So he'd been right about Hartley and Anthea, thought Thanet. But he would like to know more, much more. 'Mrs Sylvester. Would you please explain exactly what you are talking about?

She spooned coffee into the mugs. 'Sugar?'

They shook their heads.

She plonked the mugs on to the table and sat down. 'Only too glad to oblige,' she said.

NINE

'I always did think Anthea was keen on Max, didn't I, Ralphie?'

Sylvester merely grunted and took a gulp of his coffee, so Thanet assumed he wasn't disagreeing.

'But of course Max never had eyes for anyone but Tess. Or Tess for him. Proper little pair of teenage love-birds they were, weren't they, Ralph? Oh, I know you didn't approve. You thought Tess was too young to have a steady boyfriend, but I could see there was no point in trying to discourage them. And you have to admit, they really were rather sweet together, weren't they?'

Another grunt, another slurp. Sylvester obviously had no intention of contributing to the conversation at present.

Lineham leaned forward and opened his mouth, no doubt to ask how it had come about, if Max and Tess had only ever had eyes for each other, that they had both apparently had a serious relationship with someone else. Thanet gave an almost imperceptible shake of the head. *Let her tell it her own way.* It was enough. Thanet and Lineham had worked together for so long and had built up such a rapport that the merest hint or flicker of an eyelid was enough to communicate the desired message. Lineham shut his mouth and sat back again.

Marion Sylvester hadn't noticed this little exchange but her husband had and Thanet was pretty certain that he had interpreted it correctly. The man was no fool.

'The trouble was,' Marion went on, 'Tess could never really understand this itch Max had to travel. Well, it was more than an itch, wasn't it, Ralph, it was more like a . . . a . . .' Marion groped for the word.

'A compulsion?' suggested Thanet.

'Yes, that's it. That's it, exactly. A compulsion. It took me a long time to realise that's what it was – years, in fact. For ages I just used to think he was plain selfish, going off whenever he could and never considering Tess's feelings. It upset me, to see how hurt she used to get. But in the end I accepted that that was the way he was, and there was nothing to be done about it. I mean, he was always the same, wasn't he, Ralph? The minute he was old enough he was off backpacking in the summer holidays.'

'Too much money,' Sylvester intervened unexpectedly. 'And too used to having things his own way. Spoilt rotten, that boy was. He could always twist his mother around his little finger. Pity his father died when he did.'

'Max was about thirteen then, I believe?'

'Something like that.'

'What work did his father do?'

Sylvester shrugged. 'He was some sort of high-powered civil servant, I believe.'

'Anyway,' said Marion, 'Max got a place at Oxford and decided to spend the whole of his gap year travelling. You can imagine how upset Tess was, when he told her. But you had to admire her. Once she saw he wasn't going to change his mind she decided to do a Cordon Bleu course while he was away and then do her secretarial course in Oxford, to be near him when he went up the following October.'

'I had the feeling he wasn't too pleased about that,' said Sylvester. 'We were there when she told him. I think he liked the idea of being footloose and fancy-free while he was at university.'

Marion gave her husband a reproachful glance. 'I think you imagined all that. I think he was thrilled to bits.'

Sylvester gave a cynical snort. 'Thrilled! Huh!'

Marion frowned. 'Anyway, that was what she did. And when she'd finished the course she stayed on, got a job in Oxford for the rest of the time he was there. I think she took it pretty much for granted that they'd be married when he'd taken his degree. So you can imagine how she felt when at the end of his final term he told her out of the blue that he wasn't ready to settle down yet. His year in the Far East had made him realise that he wanted to be a travel writer and if they were to have any future together she must understand that he had to be free to travel, whenever and for as long as he wished. So in a few days' time he would be leaving on a trip to China and planned to be away at least a year, perhaps longer. Imagine, all the arrangements were already made and he hadn't said a word about it till then! Well, that was the last straw! That was when she first broke off with him.'

'So that would have been in – let me see – June '89.'

'Right,' said Sylvester.

'Yes,' said his wife. 'Mind, I think she was sorry later that she'd acted quite so hastily. Particularly, I remember, when she realised she was going to miss the College Ball. It's such a very special occasion and I think she thought he wouldn't go at all if he couldn't take her. Also, I suspect she thought he wouldn't manage to find another partner. Girls are always in short supply in Oxford and most were already fixed up with partners by then. But no. She discovered later that Max had immediately got in touch with Linda, of all people, and invited her instead! Linda was in her first year at Bristol by then. He'd never looked twice at her before and never did again, to my knowledge, but I suppose beggars can't be choosers and he just wanted to show Tess she wasn't the only girl in the world.'

'Did it to spite her, more likely,' said Sylvester.

Marion sighed. 'Perhaps. I don't know. Anyway, as I say, Tess was especially upset about that. I think she thought he'd beg her to go with him, this one last time.'

'Max wasn't exactly the begging type.'

'That's not true! He certainly begged her in the end, didn't he, when she was –'

Sylvester cut in swiftly. 'I told Tess at the time, "You've only got yourself to blame. You told him you didn't want anything more to do with him, and he obviously took you at your word."'

Thanet suspected that Marion had been going to say, 'When she was engaged to Gerald'. Interesting that her husband had stopped her from doing so. Did Sylvester seriously think that the police wouldn't find out about that?

'Anyway,' Marion went on, 'off he went to China and he was gone for over a year, didn't come back until, when? The end of November, wasn't it, Ralph? He just turned up on the doorstep as if he'd never been away and nothing had ever gone wrong between them! I couldn't believe it! What a nerve!'

'I told her then, she ought to have nothing more to do with him,' said Sylvester. 'But would she listen? Oh no, not Tess.'

'But you know how miserable she was all the time he was away, Ralph. She nearly drove me mad, moping about the house. And I was worried, too. She was off her food for so long I was afraid she was getting anorexic. So although I was cross with Max, when he just turned up like that, I was so relieved to see her happy again I could have forgiven him anything.'

'Until the next time,' said Sylvester. 'It was all very well while he was living at home writing his book, but the minute it was finished he was off again!'

Lineham's frown of concentration told Thanet that the sergeant, like him, was having problems keeping up with all these comings and goings. 'That would have been when, exactly?'

'The following June,' said Marion. 'June '91. And that I do remember because it was just after Tess's twenty-first. We planned a big party for her and I know she was convinced that Max was going to propose that night. She knew his book would be finished by then and she thought it would be a sort of double celebration. But he didn't. The very next day, in fact, he told her he was planning another trip. She was, well, devastated, wasn't she, Ralph? That was when I realised that the situation was never going to change, that that was the way Max was, and if she wanted him, sooner or later she was just going to have to accept it. And that was what I told her. But she just couldn't. Accept it, I mean. Not then, anyway. Well, I suppose at that age you've got all these romantic notions. You think you've got to come first with the one you love, don't you? So this time Tess said that was it. Absolutely and finally it. She told Max that if he did go off again it was goodbye Tess. And he went. *Finito*.'

'That,' said Sylvester, 'was when I stepped in. Rather than face the prospect of having Tess drooping around the house like a wet fortnight for God knows how long, I thought it would do her good to do a bit of travelling herself, might help her to get Max out of her system. We've got various relatives dotted around the globe, so to start with I put together a package with a few frills like first-class air travel thrown in, and off she went, to Australia and New Zealand, to begin with.'

Thanet could see that Lineham was thinking, *And very nice, too! It's all right for some!* 'And did it work?'

The Sylvesters consulted each other with a glance. Then Marion shrugged. 'To some extent yes, I think so. It took Tess's mind off Max and certainly gave her a taste for travel herself. The trouble is, travel to Tess means staying in comfortable hotels, eating gorgeous food, going shopping and sightseeing, whereas so far as I can gather Max prefers to rough it, go native, if you like. So there's never been any suggestion she should go with him.'

'I imagine he feels that that kind of travel is more likely to give him interesting experiences to write about,' said Thanet.

'Perhaps. I can't see the appeal myself. Give me a bit of comfort, any day! Anyway, for the past few years both Tess and Max have been away quite a bit and when they did come home they seemed to miss each other. Tess came home for Christmas that first year, '91, but Max was still away in South America. Then he came home the following May, for the publication of his book.'

Thanet's antennae twitched. There had been a subtle alteration in Marion's tone there. Why?

'I'm getting confused,' said Lineham. 'I thought Mr Jeopard came back from South America last Christmas.'

'Yes, he did.'

'And he'd been away two years?'

'That's right.'

'So why did he go back there for such a long period of time when he'd already done one lengthy trip out there?'

'Oh, I see what you mean,' said Sylvester. 'Because he hadn't quite gathered all the material he needed. But he was away much longer than he'd intended the second time. In fact, at one point his mother hadn't heard from him for so long that she was afraid something dire had happened to him. And it had. We heard later that he might well have died. He'd fallen seriously ill while in the Amazonian jungle and been taken in by natives who looked after him for months until he was strong enough to be transported to the nearest hospital, which was some distance away. Even then it was some time before he was fit to travel.'

All good copy for the book which would now never be written, thought Thanet.

'Anyway, to get back to what I was saying, when he came back in '92 for the publication of his book, Tess had gone off to the States. But would you believe, the first thing he did was to come around here looking for her?'

By now this didn't surprise Thanet in the least. However many ups and downs there had been in the relationship between Max and Tess, clearly there had existed between them some magnetism which they were powerless to resist.

'Just turned up on the doorstep again, didn't he, darl?'

Marion nodded. She stood up abruptly and began to clear away the coffee mugs. 'Anyone fancy another cup?'

'Yeah, I wouldn't mind,' said Sylvester.

Thanet and Lineham shook their heads. Thanet was watching Marion closely. Her husband didn't seem to have noticed anything, but for the last few minutes she had been very quiet. Thanet was convinced that some-

98

thing had occurred to her which had had the effect of disrupting the earlier steady flow of reminiscence. What could it be?

'If I'd been here I'd have sent him packing,' said Sylvester. 'Anyway, it was soon after that he took up with Anthea. Now that was a new one. He'd never shown any interest in her before. Though like my wife says, she'd always thought that Anthea fancied him. Trouble was, by then Anthea was living with Hartley.'

'Ah.' So it had been that serious between Hartley and Anthea, thought Thanet. How must Hartley have felt, when Max waltzed home from wherever he'd been and in default of Tess being around, stole Hartley's girl from right under his nose? 'How did that happen?'

'It was at the party Mrs Jeopard gave to celebrate the publication of Max's book, I believe,' said Sylvester. 'Thanks, darl.' He took the fresh cup of coffee Marion had produced for him. 'We were invited but we didn't go, did we? I thought he had a bloody cheek asking us, after the way he'd treated Tess. Not that it should have surprised me. He had the nerve for anything, if he wanted it. I suppose that as Tess's parents he was hoping to get us on his side again. Anyway, if that was what he wanted he was disappointed. And the next thing we heard, Anthea and Max were being seen everywhere together.'

'It didn't last that long,' said Marion, rejoining them at the table. 'Max took off again in the autumn for that second trip to South America – would have gone earlier, in my opinion, if it hadn't been for the fact that his mother was ill and even he couldn't bring himself to be that callous.'

'So what happened with Anthea? Did she go back to Hartley?'

Marion shook her head. 'No. And to my knowledge

Hartley's never had another girlfriend, before or since. I felt really sorry for him, I can tell you. Though I must say it did surprise me when he first took up with Anthea. I wouldn't have thought she was his type, I'd have said she was too, well, flamboyant. But there's no accounting for taste, is there?'

'And what about Anthea?'

Sylvester gave a cynical little laugh. 'From what happened last night, I gather she'd counted on Max coming back to her.'

'What did happen, exactly?'

Sylvester and his wife glanced at each other. She gave a little nod. *You tell it.*

He took a sip of coffee and narrowed his eyes in thought, remembering. 'Well, Anthea arrived late.'

'Wanted to make an entrance, probably,' said Marion, unable to resist joining in, 'make sure her little exhibition had the maximum effect.'

'What time exactly, do you know?'

Sylvester frowned, thought. 'Sorry, no.'

'Could you say if it was before or after nine o'clock?' Thanet was still anxious to find out if this little episode had taken place before or after the note was handed to Max.

'No, I'm afraid not. All I know is that most of the guests had arrived by then and there was quite a crowd. I was in the same room as Max and I saw Anthea appear at the door. I happened to be facing that way but in any case you couldn't really miss her, of course, in that red Chinese outfit she was wearing. She stopped in the doorway for a minute, glancing around as if she was looking for someone – Max, I realised, because as soon as she spotted him she marched straight across to him, elbowed her way into the little group of people he was talking to, and put her hands on her hips. It was obvious she was out to make trouble and almost before she'd said a word everything went quiet.

'"Hullo, Max *darling*," she said. Then she stepped forward and quite deliberately slapped his face, really hard. It sounded like a pistol shot, and if there was anybody in the room who hadn't been aware of what was going on, they knew about it now. You could have heard a pin drop. "You bastard!" she said. "I wish Tess joy of you." Then she swung around and stalked out. You should have seen Max's face! The shock! He couldn't believe she'd actually done it!' Retrospectively, Sylvester was clearly enjoying Max's discomfiture.

'What did he do?' Thanet was genuinely interested. What did people do, in embarrassing situations like that?

Sylvester shrugged. 'Pretended to laugh it off. Rolled his eyes, grinned around at everyone and said, "Wow!" They laughed, of course, as he'd intended them to, and gradually conversations started up again. No prizes for guessing what they were talking about, of course. I was livid, I can tell you. I didn't know which of them I was more angry with, Anthea for making such a scene at Tess's engagement party, or Max for messing around with one of Tess's friends in the first place.'

'But why did she wait until last night?' said Lineham. 'I assume there would have been plenty of other opportunities for her to tackle him before then?'

'Of course there would!' said Marion. 'Max has been home since Christmas, that's three whole months. That's why we were so furious with her. She's just an exhibitionist, that's all.'

'And I suppose she wanted to cause him maximum humiliation,' said Sylvester. 'It wouldn't have been enough to do it in private.'

'Well she might have thought of Tess!' said his wife. 'She is supposed be Tess's friend, isn't she?'

'I know, I know. Don't get cross with me, darl, I agree with you, for God's sake!'

'And do you know,' Marion said to Thanet, 'she even had the nerve to stay on at the party, afterwards!'

'We didn't want to cause more unpleasantness by asking her to leave,' said Sylvester.

Thanet said, 'I'm surprised, in the circumstances, that you asked her to sit with your daughter while I talked to you, last night.' Though Marion had been against it, he remembered.

'Well,' said Sylvester, wearily, 'last night we were all so shell-shocked we weren't thinking straight. I just suggested the first person who came into my mind and it happened to be Anthea. She's been around so long she's practically part of the family.'

'Which is what makes her behaviour all the worse,' said Marion. 'I'm only thankful Tess wasn't actually there to see it. It would have been so humiliating for her.'

'Maybe if she had been, Anthea wouldn't have done it. Maybe she checked first, and picked her moment,' suggested Sylvester.

But Marion was obviously not inclined to give Anthea the benefit of the doubt. 'You're too good-natured by half, Ralph.'

Thanet thought there had been enough discussion of Anthea. 'There's one person in that group photograph we haven't mentioned yet,' he said. 'I believe it must be Gerald Argent. I understand your daughter was engaged to him before Max?'

They exchanged dismayed glances. 'Yes, she was,' said Sylvester. 'But what's that got to do with it?'

'Oh come, Mr Sylvester, don't pretend to be so naïve!

102

Your daughter is engaged to one man. She breaks it off and becomes engaged to another, who is then found dead in a swimming pool on the night of their engagement party.'

'You're not suggesting Gerald had anything to do with Max's death, are you?' said Marion.

'That's utterly preposterous!' said Sylvester.

'Is it? Is it, Mr Sylvester? Just think about it.'

'It is if you know anything about Gerald!' said Sylvester.

'Gerald wouldn't hurt a fly!' said Marion.

If the general public knew how often this was said about those who had committed the most atrocious acts, they would ban the phrase for ever, thought Thanet. 'How long was your daughter engaged to him?'

They exchanged glances. *I suppose we'll have to tell him.* 'Six months,' said Sylvester reluctantly.

'But they'd been going out together for ages before that,' said Marion, apparently anxious not to make Tess seem too fickle. She turned to her husband. 'When did they start?'

He frowned, and they worked it out between them. Since Tess finally broke it off with Max the day after her twenty-first birthday, they had not seen each other until three months ago, when Max came home at Christmas. Tess had spent a year in America before finally returning home in the spring of '93. Not long afterwards she had begun to go out with Gerald and her parents had heaved a sigh of relief, believing what they wanted to believe, that their policy had worked and Tess had finally got Max out of her system. The previous autumn, when Gerald had been promoted to managerial status at the bank in Sturrenden where he worked, they had become engaged.

A June wedding had been planned and everything had gone smoothly until Max's return at Christmas, when yet again he had tried to take up with Tess. But this time, to the Sylvesters' relief, Tess had said she didn't want anything to do with him. Unfortunately he had refused to take no for an answer. He had at once launched into a single-minded campaign to win her back. Letters, flowers and presents arrived daily, and on one occasion he had even hired a light aircraft to float a banner, with 'Tess, I love you' written on it, across the sky. But still she had resisted.

Then, for the first time, he proposed.

'When was that?' said Thanet.

'About ten days ago,' said Sylvester grimly. 'Marriage had never been mentioned before.'

'I think it had dawned on him that this was his last chance,' said Marion, 'that if he didn't get Tess now he would lose her for good. I tried to tell her that this didn't mean he had changed, but I could see she was weakening. "He must have," she said, "or he wouldn't have asked me to marry him." I told her I meant he would still go off on his travels when he wanted to, that I really didn't believe she would be able to stop him. And d'you know what she said? She said, "It's no good, Mum. I've come to realise that a bit of Max is better than no Max at all, and if that's what I have to settle for, then I shall." "What about Gerald?" I said. And she just shook her head. "Oh, Gerald," she said. "He'll be hurt, of course, and I'm sorry. But between the two there just isn't any choice. I've never loved anyone but Max, and I don't think I ever shall."'

Marion's face suddenly crumpled. 'I don't know what she's going to do!' she cried. 'I don't know how she's going to bear it!'

Sylvester got up and put an arm around his wife's shoulders. 'We'll see her through, somehow,' he said.

She turned her face into his shoulder. 'Oh I hope so, Ralph. I do hope so.'

Thanet caught Lineham's eye. *I think we've done all we can here, for the moment.*

It was time to interview Carey Sylvester.

TEN

On the way up to Carey's room, however, they ran into Barbara Mallis. She was carrying a pile of sheets and towels and she smiled at them over the top of them. 'Oh, good morning, Inspector, Sergeant.'

Thanet was never one to pass up an opportunity. 'Ah, Mrs Mallis. I wanted a word with you. Would now be a convenient moment?'

'Yes, of course.' There was a table opposite the top of the staircase and she laid down her burden of household linen and turned to face them. 'How can I help?'

Despite the emotional turmoil which surrounded her she appeared calm and self-controlled, and was the first member of the household Thanet had encountered this morning to look as though she'd had a good night's sleep. The care she took over her appearance was clearly habitual: her make-up was immaculate and her hair drawn back this morning into an elegant chignon which Thanet did not think suited her. It emphasised her pointed nose and did nothing to conceal the deeply etched frown lines. She was wearing tight jeans and an expensive-looking sweater appliquéd in an abstract design of whorls and zig-zags dotted with seed pearls and clusters of beading.

'Is there somewhere a little less public where we could talk? You have a flat in the house, I believe.'

'Yes. This way.' She turned and led them up a further, narrower flight of stairs to the attic floor, but Thanet had not missed the hesitation. She hadn't wanted to take them into her private domain. Why? Because of a natural reluctance to have her privacy invaded, or for some other reason?

The flat surprised him, and Lineham, too, judging by the look the sergeant gave him after a quick glance around. Stretching across the whole length and width of the house, with dormer windows at the front and velux roof lights at the back, it consisted chiefly of one huge open space with a door at one end leading presumably to bedroom and *en suite* bathroom. In one corner a compact little kitchen was divided off by a unit of open-sided shelves from a dining area with sophisticated glass-topped table and tulip-shaped chairs. The living space was comfortably, even luxuriously furnished, with thick fitted carpet, festoon blinds at the recessed dormer windows and dralon-covered three-piece suite. Perhaps efficient housekeepers were in such demand these days that lavish accommodation would be regarded as a natural perquisite of the job?

'Nice flat,' he said, and was interested to note that an expression which he was unable to interpret flickered in Barbara Mallis's eyes, and was gone. What had it signified? he wondered. Why should such an innocuous comment produce any reaction at all, other than mild gratification?

'Yes, isn't it. Would you like to sit down?' Her tone implied that she would like the answer to be no, they wouldn't, as their visit was to be brief.

She had been forthcoming enough last night and so partly out of perversity but also because he was interested to find out why she wanted to get rid of them quickly, Thanet accepted the invitation. 'Thank you.'

She chose to perch on the very edge of one of the armchairs. *I'm a busy woman. I hope this won't take long.*

'How long have you been with the Sylvesters, Mrs Mallis?' said Thanet when they were settled.

The question obviously surprised her and Thanet was interested to see that she looked wary.

'Since '91,' she said. 'Why?'

'Just interested to fill in a little background. What happened to the previous housekeeper?'

'There wasn't one. I was the first.' Thanet's cocked eyebrow forced her to continue. 'When Carey came to live permanently at home after being in and out of hospital, they found Mrs Sylvester couldn't cope. So they decided to get someone in to run the house. At that point she was still trying to look after him herself. It was hopeless, of course. Absolutely hopeless. He was so unpredictable. To be honest, if she hadn't given up, if they hadn't got Mike Roper in to look after him, I don't think I would have stayed. You can't imagine what it was like when Carey was free to roam around at will. The trouble was, he hated taking his medication – they all do, I believe, all these schizos, it's the one thing they loathe and it's the one thing which keeps them reasonably normal. That was what was wrong with that Ben Silcock or Ben Silcox, whatever his name was, who climbed into the lion's den at London Zoo. Remember?'

Thanet remembered only too well. Anyone who had seen the television footage of the unfortunate man being mauled by a full-grown lion wasn't likely to forget it. He nodded.

'You know what I mean, then. Without proper medication they go haywire. So in those days, when you ran into Carey you never knew what to expect. It was pretty unnerving, I can tell you.' She looked around and got up to fetch her cigarettes, waited until she had lit up before going on. 'Sometimes he'd carry on as though he was terrified of you and other times . . . the things he used to say! Talk about bizarre! And sometimes he'd just ignore you and talk to his voices. Most schizos hear voices, apparently, hear them and talk to them. Well, I don't know if you've ever been at close quarters with someone who's hearing voices, but believe me it can be pretty scary. I was very relieved when Mike arrived, I can tell you.'

'Was Carey ever violent?' said Thanet.

'Sometimes. Not that he ever actually attacked anyone, to my knowledge. But I do remember once he smashed in his TV with a chair. Said it was trying to get inside his head, control him. And before Mike came he tried to commit suicide more than once. Mike told me there's a terrifically high suicide rate among schizos – one in ten, I think he said. It was after the second attempt that they decided to get a live-in nurse.' She lifted a shoulder and blew out a lungful of smoke. 'It was the obvious thing to do, really. They could afford it.'

Her attitude was cold, almost callous. The suffering of everyone involved in such a desperate situation had obviously left her unmoved. There was, it seemed, only one person who mattered to Barbara Mallis and that was Barbara Mallis.

'So what about now? Is Mr Roper efficient?'

'Seems to be. Carey never goes out alone and I know Mike makes sure he really does take his medication.'

'So last night was unusual, in that Carey did get out?'

'Yes, very. Some idiot unlocked the door and didn't

relock it, I believe. Mike blames himself for not actually removing the key when he went downstairs, and let's face it, it was pretty careless of him, when the house was full of people.'

'Habit, I suppose, if that's what he always does.'

'Perhaps. Anyway, I can't imagine why they didn't think of looking in the dog kennel earlier. Carey's always been very fond of Jason and of course Jason's an outdoor dog, he's never allowed in the house.'

Thanet couldn't visualise himself ever wanting to squeeze into a kennel with a Dobermann, but then Tess had said that the dog was 'an old softie' so perhaps it wasn't that surprising. Perhaps Carey had found comfort in proximity to the animal he loved.

'To return to the party, then,' he said. 'We've been told that Mr Jeopard was handed a note during the evening, somewhere around nine o'clock. Did you by any chance witness this incident?'

She shook her head.

'And have you recalled anything else you feel we ought to know?'

Another negative.

'Right, well, I think that's about all for the moment.' He was interested to note the relief in her eyes and the alacrity with which she jumped up. What was he missing? On the way to the door he paused. 'Oh, by the way, I forgot to ask Mr and Mrs Sylvester. Where were Tess and Mr Jeopard going to live after they were married?'

'In London.' The gleam of malice in her eyes was unmistakable. It was clear that she had taken pleasure from the thought of her employers' disappointment if Tess had moved away from the area. Was this because she had a specific grudge against them, or was her nature such that she always enjoyed the spectacle of other people's misery? Could this be why she had stayed so long in this particular household?

'And if she had married Mr Argent?'

'I believe they were house-hunting locally.'

On the way downstairs Lineham said, 'Pretty keen to get rid of us, wasn't she?'

'Yes. I wonder why?'

'And it was Mike this, Mike that, did you notice?'

'Think there might be something going on there?' Another possible reason why Barbara Mallis had stayed? Thanet wondered. And if so, had her interest been reciprocated? Personally he would as soon have curled up in bed with an anaconda, but there was no accounting for taste and both she and Roper must be starved of a social life. Certainly they must have seen a lot of each other over the last few years.

'Rather him than me,' said Lineham.

'Well, let's not jump to conclusions.'

They were back on the first-floor landing and they followed Marion Sylvester's directions to Carey's quarters. He and Roper shared a self-contained suite of rooms at one end of the first floor. The single entrance door to the premises was at one end of the landing corridor and Thanet understood why someone last night might have thought it led to a bathroom. Though surely the fact that the key was on the outside, not the inside, should have given them pause for thought? He said so to Lineham, while they waited for an answer to their knock.

'Might have had too much to drink, sir.'

'True.' Thanet sniffed. 'What's that smell?' As so often happens with smells out of context it was familiar but he could not place it.

Lineham wrinkled his nose. 'Turps.'

There was the rattle of a key in the lock, the door

opened and a more powerful waft of turpentine gushed out to meet them. Thanet had not met Roper last night and in view of what he had just been thinking about Barbara Mallis he was interested to see that the nurse was indeed a very personable man, with good physique and an air of alert competence. He was in his early forties, Thanet guessed, and was casually dressed in jeans and sweatshirt.

Introductions made, Thanet asked how Roper's charge was this morning.

'Not too bad. I've seen him better.' The voice was low pitched, slightly nasal, with a hint of cockney accent.

'He's recovered from last night's escapade, then?'

Roper shrugged. 'Don't suppose he's given it another thought.'

'Does he know about Max Jeopard's death?'

'I told him. I had to, with policemen all over the place.'

'How did he react?'

'There wasn't much reaction at all. He just looked at me for a moment, then went back to what he was doing.'

'Which was?'

'Watching television.'

'We'd like a word with him, if possible.'

Roper hesitated, then stood back. 'Try not to upset him.'

This was going to be tricky, thought Thanet. He'd never interviewed anyone with this particular mental condition before, and found that he was feeling slightly apprehensive. Don't be stupid, he told himself. Fear of mental illness, he knew, was universal, but Carey was stabilised, his nurse would be present . . . Treat him like any other witness, he told himself. Just be particularly aware of his responses, that's all, on the alert for the first sign of trouble.

Roper led them through a minute hallway into a room on the right. It was, Thanet realised with a jolt of surprise, set up as a studio. Hence the smell of turpentine. Nobody had told him Carey painted. Perhaps painting was regarded as therapeutic, part of his treatment programme? In any case it was, he thought, an excellent idea. Carey was a virtual prisoner in his own home. Something had to be done to fill in the long hours of incarceration.

Carey was of medium height and had his father's stocky build. He was standing in front of an easel with his back to them, head on one side as if considering the work in progress. To Thanet this looked a meaningless daub of shrieking colour – brilliant blue, green and purple slashed with black. Glancing about, Thanet saw that similar canvases were stacked around the walls, each one transmitting powerful waves of chaos and turbulence.

'Someone to see you, Carey,' said Roper. 'Two policemen.'

Only a twitch of the shoulder betrayed the fact that Carey had heard.

Thanet waited a moment and then walked slowly forward until he was able to see the young man's face. Carey was frowning at the painting and as Thanet watched he jabbed the brush he was holding at his palette and added another jagged black streak to the picture.

Thanet said nothing. Would Carey have any curiosity, or was his self-absorption total?

Carey shot a glance at him, so lightning-swift that Thanet almost wondered if he had imagined it.

'You've come about Max,' he said.

Thanet was startled. He didn't know what he had expected, but it wasn't this calm, rational tone. Which made what Carey said and did next all the more shocking.

He put up his arms as if winding them around some-one's neck, closed his eyes in pretended ecstasy and moved his hips sinuously, as if crotch to crotch. 'Oh Max, darling,' he said, in a high-pitched voice, 'promise me you won't go away again. Promise?'

Tess, Thanet realised. At some point Carey had seen Max and Tess together.

Carey opened his eyes and said, once more in a per-fectly normal, reasonable tone, 'Good riddance, if you ask me.'

'You didn't like Max?'

'He was shit. Shit. Shit, shit, shit . . .'

He was becoming increasingly agitated and Roper stepped forward to lay a soothing hand on his arm. 'OK, Carey, calm down.'

Carey jerked his arm to shake him off. 'Leave me alone. I'm fine.' He dabbed at his palette again, scarlet paint this time, and then twitched the brush at the painting. Brilliant red droplets flew from the bristles and spattered on to the canvas, like drops of blood. Some of them trickled down, others hung there, globules of viscous crimson.

'You've known Max for a long time, haven't you,' said Thanet, grimly determined to press on despite increasing doubts that there was any point in doing so.

This time Carey startled him by bursting into song, beating time to the music with his paintbrush. '"Boys and girls come out to play, the moon doth shine as bright as day,"' he sang.

'Yes, you used to play tennis with him,' said Thanet. 'I saw a photograph, downstairs. You and Tess and Anthea and Linda and –'

114

'Linda's ill, you know,' said Carey, interrupting him. 'I don't know what's the matter with her, but she's ill.'

'We can see the Fieldings' bungalow from our sitting-room window,' said Roper by way of explanation.

'They say I'm ill too,' Carey went on. 'Do you think I look ill?' He suddenly left the easel and walked across to a mirror on the wall. He leaned forward and peered into it. 'I look perfectly healthy to me. And all the witches agree. What do you think?'

Nonplussed by the comment about witches, which had been uttered in a perfectly matter-of-fact manner, Thanet decided to ask his questions and terminate what increasingly seemed to be a pointless exercise. 'I just wanted to ask you if you saw him last night? Max, I mean.'

Carey returned to his stance in front of the easel but did not respond.

'Or if, when you were outside – er – keeping Jason company, you saw anything at all unusual?'

'Good dog,' muttered Carey. 'What a good boy!'

Thanet gave up.

'Waste of time,' commented Lineham, when they were outside.

'We had to try.'

'What d'you think, sir? D'you think he had anything to do with it?'

'Impossible to tell. If he did, he seems to have been invisible. There were enough people looking for him. Presumably most of the guests would know him, being friends of the family. If any of them had seen him in the house they'd surely have said so.'

'Some of them must have seen him, even if it didn't register. He must have come downstairs, to get outside.'

'True.'

'He probably slipped out through the kitchen.'

'In which case . . .'

Both of them were remembering that at the other end of the corridor which led to the kitchen was the door to the pool house.

'So if he'd turned left rather than right . . .' said Lineham.

'Exactly.'

'He obviously didn't like Jeopard.'

'Not surprising. Doesn't sound as though many people did.'

They had almost reached the top of the stairs now and as they did so purposeful footsteps clacked across the parquet floor in the hall below.

Thanet put out his hand. *Wait*. They drew back a little. You could learn a lot about witnesses when they thought they were unobserved.

Barbara Mallis appeared, heading for the front door, dressed to go out in suede jacket and high heels.

Just as she was opening it another door clicked open somewhere beneath them and Marion Sylvester called out, 'Are you going anywhere near a shop that might be open?' She sounded slightly hesitant, diffident almost, about asking.

As if he thought his wife had been calling him, Ralph Sylvester appeared in the sitting-room doorway and simultaneously Barbara turned and said, 'I might be. Why?'

Her tone surprised Thanet. Surely a housekeeper would not normally address her employer in that peremptory manner? He realised that she was not aware of Sylvester's presence; the front door, which she was holding ajar, was preventing him from being in her line of vision.

'My husband would like some cigarettes, please.' There

was a slight emphasis on the first two words, and a hint of defiance, as if the fact that it was Sylvester's request made it legitimate for Marion to make it.

Without a word of acknowledgement Barbara Mallis turned on her heel and left. Below them a door softly closed. Sylvester turned and went back into the sitting room, but not before Thanet had glimpsed his face. It was grim.

'Well, well, well!' said Lineham. 'Interesting.'

'Quite. What did you make of it, Mike?'

'I'm not sure. It sounded as if Mrs Sylvester was almost afraid to ask.'

They started to descend the stairs, keeping their voices down.

'And, more to the point, as though Mrs Mallis had the power to refuse,' said Thanet.

'As if she was the one with the upper hand. In fact,' said Lineham slowly, 'almost as if she's got some sort of hold over her.'

'My thought exactly.'

'But what?' Lineham grabbed Thanet's elbow. 'Sir, look at that!' They were halfway down the stairs by now and through one of the glass panels which flanked the front door they had a clear view of Barbara Mallis driving off in the BMW convertible which Lineham had admired earlier. 'It can't be hers, surely!'

'Not exactly the sort of car you'd expect a housekeeper to drive,' said Thanet. 'Let's go and find out.'

Ralph Sylvester was still in the sitting room, standing at one of the front windows, gazing out.

Thanet joined him and was just in time to see the BMW turn out of the drive on to the road, giving him a convenient opening. 'Nice car.'

A brief conversation elicited the information he needed.

According to Sylvester Mrs Mallis had bought the car the previous year with money inherited on her father's death.

'Think that's true, sir?' said Lineham, when they were outside.

'We'll look into it. If it's not, of course, we have to ask ourselves where she did get the money from. It's not just the car, is it? That flat is over the top for a housekeeper and she must spend a pretty penny on clothes. In fact, Mike . . .'

They looked at each other.

'Blackmail?' said Lineham.

ELEVEN

'I wouldn't put it past her, would you?' said Lineham as
he started the car. 'And by the look of it, it's Mrs
Sylvester she's blackmailing. I wonder what she's got on
her. Er . . . where now, sir?'

'Gerald Argent next, I think.'

Lineham glanced at his clipboard of names and addresses. 'He lives on the Ravenswood estate.'

This was one of the new estates which had mush-
roomed around the edges of Sturrenden despite the Green
Belt policy supposedly followed by successive govern-
ments.

'I was wondering earlier,' said Thanet as Lineham put
the car into gear and moved smoothly off down the drive,
'why Mrs Mallis had stayed so long in this job. I shouldn't
have thought it was quite her cup of tea, being stuck out
here in the country. I thought perhaps it was Roper who
was the attraction, as we suggested earlier.'

'Well, he is a good-looking guy, and Mrs Mallis does
seem to have an eye for the opposite sex, as we saw last
night!'

Thanet studiously ignored the reference. 'But now I'm
wondering . . . If she's got something on Mrs Sylvester
and is getting her to pay up for keeping quiet about it,

well, she's on to a good thing, isn't she? She wouldn't leave without good reason.'

A couple of hundred yards down the lane they saw the Sylvesters' gardener, Fielding, strolling towards them. Equipped with binoculars and briar stick he was obviously out for a Sunday afternoon walk. Thanet raised a hand in greeting and briefly envied him the freedom to enjoy it. But not for long. It was a lovely day, true, a typical March spring day with blustery winds, fluffy clouds and fat buds about to burst on every tree and hedgerow, but at the moment there was nothing he would rather be doing than pursuing this investigation. The process of delicately feeling his way into a whole new mesh of relationships was the part of his work which interested him most of all. People fascinated him and despite the long years of police work he still on the whole liked them, enjoyed meeting them and trying to understand what made them tick. And this particular case promised a rich harvest.

'Perhaps,' said Lineham suddenly, 'it's Mrs Sylvester who's having an affair with Roper! She's a pretty sexy type, isn't she, and they must see a lot of each other, living under the same roof day in, day out. And Mrs Mallis found out about it, threatened to tell Mr Sylvester.'

'Could be. Did you see Sylvester's face, in the hall, after that incident between his wife and Mrs Mallis? He knows something's going on, that's for sure. And Mrs Sylvester is definitely trying to hide something, wouldn't you agree? So perhaps that's what it is, an affair with Roper. As a matter of fact I was wondering why Roper has stayed so long, too. It must be a pretty soul-destroying job.'

'You're telling me! Those paintings!' Lineham shuddered. 'If that's what the inside of Carey's head feels like I wouldn't wish his state of mind on my worst enemy. And Roper is shut up with him month after month. I don't know how he stands it! I wonder if he ever gets a break.'

'Oh, I should think so. He'd be entitled to holidays like anyone else, I imagine. But on a day-to-day basis . . . He hasn't even got the company of colleagues to make it bearable. So he must also have a pretty powerful reason to have stuck it as long as he has, and it could be one of the women who's the attraction. Yes, I think we need to take a closer look at both Roper and Mrs Mallis. We'll put DC Martin on to it. He enjoys digging into people's backgrounds.'

They were silent for a while, mulling over what they'd heard so far today. At the beginning of a case there was so much to take in it was difficult to assimilate it all.

'Bit of a tangle, isn't it, sir,' said Lineham eventually. 'A real game of musical chairs. I've been trying to work it out. Let's see if I've got it straight. First it was Tess and Max, on and off, then it was Hartley and Anthea, then Max and Anthea, then Tess and Gerald, then Max and Tess again. Is that right?'

Thanet laughed. 'I think so. You're right, it is a tangle.'

'Mind,' said Lineham, 'I think I can understand why Max kept on backing off like that. Sounds to me as if when they were younger Tess was a bit too clinging. I suspect he felt stifled and it made him want to escape.'

'And he finally succumbed when he realised he was in danger of losing her for good.'

'And when he felt she'd got the message that he wasn't going to be tied down too much. That's the way I see it, yes.'

'I'll tell you what all this reminds me of. The Alicia Parnell case, remember?'*

'Yes I do. As I recall, that also involved a group of young people who'd been inseparable in their teens. Yes, you're right.'

'It seems to happen sometimes, doesn't it. You get a group of teenagers with a certain, what shall I call it, chemistry? between them and it seems that whatever happens in later life they never quite break away from each other, not entirely anyway. And there's often one person around whom the others seem to pivot. In that case it was the lad who committed suicide, if you remember. What was his name? Paul something? And in this, it seems to be Max Jeopard.'

'Yes. People like him seem to expect the world to revolve around them and blow me, it does!'

Thanet grinned. 'Sickening, isn't it!'

'Too right it is! No, but seriously, I'd say Mr Sylvester wasn't far off the mark when he said Max was spoilt rotten. You could tell by the way his mother talked about him that she thought the sun shone out of him. And people like that, well they seem to go through life behaving as though they've got a divine right to have their own way. And what gets me is the fact that they usually do! I mean, look at the way he waltzed in and pinched his brother's girlfriend from under his nose! And it wasn't even as though he was serious about her, he was just amusing himself because Tess wasn't around. Imagine how Hartley must have felt! It would have been bad enough hearing his mother sing Max's praises all his life without that happening! And then, a couple of years later, he does exactly the same thing to Gerald! If you ask

* Last Seen Alive

me it's not surprising he ended up in someone's swimming pool!'

'You are getting hot under the collar, Mike.'

'Yes, well, people like that get up my nose.'

They had reached the outskirts of Sturrenden now and Thanet fell silent to allow Lineham to negotiate the big roundabout and edge his way into the one-way system. When they were moving smoothly again he said, 'We mustn't forget Anthea, either. It's obvious she expected to take up with Max where they left off before he went away on his last trip. And you know what they say about a woman scorned.'

'Yes. "Hell hath no fury" as la Mallis says. I'm quite looking forward to meeting her, aren't you, sir? She sounds a real little spitfire. I have the feeling she really enjoyed making that scene at the party. I bet she'd rehearsed it over and over until she'd got it just right.'

'She certainly has a powerful dramatic instinct. I imagine it had all the more impact because she said so little. It's interesting that that brief incident brings her into such sharp focus. I don't know about you, but I already have a very clear picture of her. Whereas Gerald is a much more shadowy figure.'

'Though according to Mrs Mallis he still had enough gumption to cut Max dead in public, at the party.'

'True. And I'm sure she was right when she called him Mr and Mrs Sylvester's blue-eyed boy. I'm certain they would much have preferred him as a son-in-law. They'd have kept Tess close to them then, seen their grandchildren grow up . . .'

'And he's got a nice steady job as bank manager. I don't blame them. I know which I'd have chosen as a son-in-law myself.'

'Whereas if she'd married Max he'd have whisked her

off to London and given her a good deal of heartache into the bargain.'

'So what are you saying, sir? That you think it might have been Sylvester who shoved him into the pool?'

'Well, we only have Mrs Mallis's word for it so far but she did say she saw Max making a pass at more than one girl at the party. Sylvester might not have been too pleased about that.'

'I bet Jeopard thought himself irresistible!' Lineham was peering out of the window and now he swung left, entering the Ravenswood estate. Serried ranks of newly-built houses marched off in all directions. The developer had attempted to introduce variety by using half a dozen different designs and setting them back at varying distances from the road, but the effect was still depressingly uniform. Perhaps, thought Thanet, they would look better when the trees and shrubs reached maturity. At the moment there was little to soften the expanses of raw new brick.

'Maybe he was. It sounds as though he had an eye for the women. I even got the impression that Mrs Mallis was hinting he'd made a pass at her. The point is, Mike, if Sylvester saw Max flirting with other girls, saw that Tess was hurt by it, maybe he decided to tackle him about it. Say he took him into the pool house to talk because he knew they wouldn't be disturbed in there. Then they argued, it came to blows and, well, he may not have intended to push him into the pool but when it happened he certainly wasn't going to fish him out.'

'Oakleaf Crescent,' muttered Lineham. 'I'm sure it's along here somewhere. Ah yes, there it is.' He signalled and turned right, then glanced at Thanet. 'You're not suggesting the note was from Sylvester, sir? A bit unlikely, don't you think? Wouldn't he have been much more likely to have a word in his ear?'

'Not necessarily. He may have thought Max would refuse. So he might have resorted to subterfuge, sent a note which pretended to be from a woman, suggesting an assignation, on the assumption that Max would probably turn up through sheer curiosity.'

'Yes! Now that is a possibility. Though for that matter, anyone else could have done the same.'

'True. Let's hope Wakeham manages to track the note down.'

'Here we are. Number twenty-one.' Lineham pulled in neatly alongside the kerb.

Tess's erstwhile fiancé lived in a tiny mid-terrace box which looked as though it wasn't much more than one room wide and one deep.

'Bachelor pad?' said Lineham as they took the two strides which covered the concrete path to the front door. He rang the bell, which immediately burst into a truncated version of 'Home Sweet Home'.

Thanet winced. He hated doorchimes. 'Looks like it. Mrs Mallis did say he and Tess were house-hunting before Max arrived back on the scene.'

'I expect Daddy was putting up the cash,' said Lineham 'After all, he wouldn't want his little girl to have to live in a style to which she was not accustomed.'

'Oh come on, Mike. Argent must be earning a decent living. Bank managers aren't exactly paupers and I believe bank employees get preferential rates on mortgages.'

Lineham rang the bell again. 'Looks as though he's out.'

'What a pain! We'll have to come back later.' They returned to the car and Thanet glanced at his watch. Four-fifteen. 'Where does Anthea live?'

Lineham consulted his clipboard. 'Donnington.'

So they'd have to retrace their steps. Thanet groaned. 'Stupid of me. If I'd had any sense I'd have checked before we left the Sylvesters' and we could have gone there first.'

'My fault too. I did think of suggesting it.'

'Ah well, back we go then.'

But Thanet wasn't really too put out. They could have rung Argent first, to make an appointment, which would have avoided the risk of wasting time, but early on in a case Thanet often preferred to keep people guessing. Besides, the time was never entirely wasted; it was often quite useful to have a short breathing space. It gave you the opportunity to step back a little and reflect and it was always useful to get some impression of a witness's life-style. Argent's chosen career had indicated that in all probability he was a steady, careful type and to Thanet's mind his house had confirmed that predictably he was both unostentatious and prudent, the sort of man who would never run before he could walk and who would bide his time until he could achieve what he truly desired. How would such a man react when his patience apparently paid off and then his prize was snatched away from him? Was it possible that as Lineham would no doubt put it, the worm had turned? According to Barbara Mallis, Argent had originally refused the invitation to the engagement party – scarcely surprising in the circumstances. But then he had changed his mind and turned up. Why? Was it a purely masochistic impulse which had driven him to attend, or had he had something more sinister in mind than a mere snub?

Fortunately, as it was Sunday, the traffic was light. Ten minutes later they were back in Donnington. The village was small, consisting chiefly of one main street and a few clusters of cottages on little side-turnings to left and right. The motor car was gradually turning far too many villages into little more than dormitories, thought Thanet; there was no village shop and even the pub looked as though it had seen more prosperous days.

Wistaria Cottage also looked as though it had come down in the world. The owner – Anthea? Her parents? A landlord? – was obviously either hard up, lazy, incapacitated or indifferent to the deterioration of his property. It was a typical Kentish cottage, mellow red brick to the first floor and tile-hung above, separated from the pavement by a rickety picket fence which badly needed a coat of paint. The two tiny patches of earth on either side of the uneven path sported a fine crop of weeds. Grimy window panes, peeling paint and rusting door knocker all added to the general air of neglect.

The woman who answered the door was wearing black leggings and a loose multicoloured tunic top in panels of different materials sewn together with blanket-stitch. The effect was as off-beat as the cheongsam last night and for a fleeting moment Thanet thought that it was Anthea. Then he registered the lines on the woman's face, the texture of skin from which the bloom of youth had faded and he realised that it must be her mother. The likeness was remarkable but this woman was in her forties.

When he told her who they were her eyes flashed. 'I don't know why you're bothering. We should be hanging out the flags, that the world has one bastard fewer in it today.'

'We have to make enquiries, Mrs Greenway. May we come in?'

She cast a defiant glance up and down the road as if to

127

say to the neighbours, *Yes, it's the police. So what?* Then she turned. 'Suit yourself.'

They stepped straight into a small square sitting room. It struck chill and dank, as if it were rarely used and was, Thanet thought, quite the most cluttered room he had ever seen. Every available square inch of surface on mantelpiece, windowsills and table-tops was jammed with an extraordinary collection of objects ranging from ornaments of every possible description, some broken and some intact, to shells, stones, pebbles and bits of driftwood. There were so many pictures and prints crowded together on the walls that there was virtually no wall-surface to be seen, and even the ceiling was partially concealed by bunches of dried flowers of all colours, shapes and sizes, some in woven baskets, suspended from hooks screwed into the beams. There was an all-enveloping smell of cats and Thanet counted at least three, curled up on the chairs. Lineham wrinkled his nose in distaste at Thanet as one of them jumped down and followed its mistress into an equally cluttered kitchen and finally into a glass structure built right along the back of the house, too ramshackle to be called a conservatory. Here too the windowsills were crammed with objects, this time interspersed with potted plants. A steamy warmth gushed forth to meet them, emanating from an oil convector heater. The windows were running with condensation and in here the smell of cats was overpowering. Thanet found that he was breathing through his mouth and seeking the source of the stench he traced it to several litter trays, some of which he noted to his distaste had been used more than once. Mrs Greenway was evidently of the school which considered the great outdoors to be anathema to her pets.

Restraining an impulse to rush to the door and fling it

open, he forced himself to look around, realising at once that for the second time today he was in a studio. Unlike Carey Sylvester Mrs Greenway worked in watercolour; a large table loaded with pots of brushes, boxes and tubes of paint and all the other accoutrements of a watercolourist stood in front of the window. Nearby was a smaller table with a still life set up on it, a carefully arranged group of kitchen objects on a harlequin-patterned cloth – a stainless steel kettle and saucepan, some dessert spoons and three silver eggcups.

Thanet gestured at the painting upon which she was obviously working. 'May I?'

She shrugged and nodded, her expression still hostile.

Leaning over to look at it he saw at once what he had not appreciated before, that all the objects in the still life were shiny. It dawned on him that what interested her was the reflections. Each object reflected the others, the shapes distorted by the curved surfaces, as were the diamonds of hazy colour cast up by the cloth. The degree of detail was astonishing. If part of an artist's task is to enable the viewer to look at the world with new eyes, she was certainly succeeding. He glanced up at her with respect. 'This must be incredibly difficult to paint.'

Sensing his genuine interest she thawed a little. 'It is a bit complicated, yes.'

He studied it a moment longer before straightening up. 'I believe a famous writer once said, "If it wasn't difficult everybody would be doing it."'

That amused her and she even managed a slight smile. 'I never thought of it like that but yes, I suppose that's true.'

'It must take you ages to complete a painting. This is so detailed.'

'It does, unfortunately. I'm afraid I work at a snail's pace.'

'And the fewer you finish, the fewer you have to sell.'

'If you can sell them at all!'

'Yes. I imagine it's not the easiest field in which to make a living.'

'You can say that again!'

She was now almost ready to be cooperative, thought Thanet. 'I suppose you collect all this sort of thing for your work.' He waved a hand at the crowded windowsills.

'I'm a real magpie. You just never know when something is going to come in useful.' She sat down in front of the table, swivelling the chair around to face them as if conceding that she was now ready to talk. 'There's only one spare chair, but it's warmer in here than in the sitting room. Tip the cat off, if you like.'

Thanet glanced at the basket chair to which she had referred. The cat which had followed her in was now firmly ensconced upon it, engaged in its ablutions, one leg stuck up in the air. The cushion, he noted, was plastered with cats' hairs. 'It's all right, we'll stand.'

'Or there are a couple of stools in the kitchen.'

Thanet glanced at Lineham and the sergeant went off to fetch them.

'Actually, it was your daughter we wanted to talk to.'

Her expression hardened. 'I assumed as much. But I'm afraid you're out of luck. She's terribly upset. She's still in bed, been there all day.'

The stools, Thanet was relieved to see, were made of wood and reasonably clean.

'I'm afraid we really have to talk to her.'

'Won't I do, instead? She can't tell you anything I don't know.'

'Were you at the party last night?' Thanet was pretty sure she hadn't been. He hadn't seen two Greenways on the guest list.

She shook her head.

'In that case, we really must see her.'

'She won't get up. I know she won't.'

'Would you try to convince her it would be a good idea? She'll have to talk to us sooner or later and it would be far better for her to get it over with.'

Mrs Greenway stared at him for a few moments, considering what he had said, trying to make up her mind. Then her mouth tugged down at the corners. 'I suppose you're right.' She stood up. 'All right, I'll try. But I can't promise anything.'

TWELVE

When she had gone Lineham said, 'D'you think we could open the door for a few minutes, sir, let some fresh air in?'

'Better not. She might not be too pleased and we don't want to upset her now she's come around.' Thanet sat down on one of the stools Lineham had brought.

The sergeant reluctantly followed suit. 'How can anyone live in an atmosphere like this?'

'They're used to it, presumably, don't notice it any more.'

'Don't notice it? How can anyone fail to notice it? I've spent so long holding my breath I thought I would suffocate!'

'Breathe through your mouth, Mike. And stop being such an old woman. I don't like it any more than you do but we have to do this interview and that's all there is to it.'

Lineham looked mutinous and muttered, 'We ought to get extra pay for this sort of thing.'

'Danger money you mean?' said Thanet with a grin.

Lineham gave him a sheepish look and then, his normal good humour reasserting itself, grinned back.

'What'll we do if Anthea won't come down, sir?'

'Make an appointment for her to come in to Headquarters, I suppose. Anyway, let's hope that doesn't happen. I'd much prefer to talk to her now.'

They were in luck. A few moments later Mrs Greenway returned and said, 'She's getting dressed. She'll be down shortly.'

'Good. Thank you.' Thanet waited until she had sat down and then added, 'I gather you weren't too keen on Max Jeopard.'

She grimaced. 'How did you guess!'

'Would you mind telling us why?'

'Where do I begin?'

'Oh, it's not as bad as that, surely,' said Lineham.

'You didn't know him.'

'No,' said Thanet. 'But we're learning.'

'Well, you've come to the right person. I've known Max since he was in his teens. He and Anthea used to run around in the same crowd of young people. They were always in and out of each other's houses, so one way and the other I saw quite a lot of them.'

'You're talking about Max, his brother Hartley, Tess and Carey Sylvester, your daughter Anthea, Gerald Argent and Linda Fielding?' said Thanet.

'You haven't wasted much time, have you! Yes, that's right.'

'So tell us about him,' said Thanet.

Mrs Greenway frowned. 'I always find it difficult to describe people I know well. I suppose,' she said reluctantly, 'the most striking thing about him was his, well, I suppose you'd call it charisma. He could charm the birds out of the trees, could Max. To begin with you thought, what a delightful young man! Then after a while it began to dawn on you that this façade – his politeness, good manners and so on – was all just a means to an end, that of getting his own way. Sooner or later, everybody always ended up doing what Max wanted. It took ages for me to realise this but when I did I wondered why on earth I hadn't seen it before. There's no doubt about it, he was the sort of person who thought he could get away with anything and usually did.'

Until now, thought Thanet grimly. This time he went too far.

'The girls were all dazzled by him, of course,' Mrs Greenway was saying.

'All?'

'Yes. Even Linda, and she was very different from the other two, much quieter and more retiring, and she didn't actually spend as much time with the group as Anthea and Tess. But now and then I'd catch her looking at Max and there's no doubt about it, she fancied him all right. Poor girl, she's desperately ill now, I believe. I feel so sorry for her parents, they absolutely doted on that child. What was I saying?'

'You were talking about Max's fascination for women.'

'Ah, yes. Well, Tess absolutely adored him, of course, and poor Anthea never got a look in. The curious thing about Max was that although he couldn't resist making a pass at any eligible female within arm's reach, there was really only ever one girl he was seriously interested in.'

'Tess.'

'Tess. The trouble was that, being Max, he was determined to have her on his own terms.'

'Which were?'

'That he should have complete freedom to do as he wanted. Max was a great one for having his cake and eating it. So Tess was expected to wait patiently at home while he bummed off around the world for as long or as short a time as took his fancy. I'm not surprised she got fed up with it. It was always Tess who broke off with him, you know, not the other way around. Until, eventually, he went a little too far and discovered that she'd finally given up on him and was about to marry someone else.'

'Gerald Argent.'

'Exactly. When I heard Tess and Gerald were engaged I thought, good for Gerald! I knew he'd always had his eye on Tess but while Max was around he never had a hope. And I must admit to a sneaky feeling of satisfaction that just for once Max wasn't going to get what he wanted. I should have known better! When Max came home at Christmas I think he realised this was his very last chance with Tess and he went all out to get her back. Poor Gerald never stood a chance. He was very cut up about it, I believe, or so Anthea says, anyway.'

'It wasn't the first time Max had pinched someone's girl, was it. I believe he did the same thing to his brother, with your daughter.'

'Typical!' Mrs Greenway clamped her lips together as if to prevent her angry feelings from spilling out against her will and it was immediately obvious that she had no intention of talking as freely about Anthea as she had about the others.

So, how to get her to open up? Thanet tried an oblique approach. 'Tess was away when this happened, I believe?'

'In America, yes.'

'How long had your daughter been going out with Hartley, at that time?'

'I'm not sure. I wasn't counting.'

'Weeks? Months? Years?'

'Oh, months, I'd say.'

'How many?'

'I told you, I wasn't counting!'

'At a rough guess, then?'

'Five, six, I suppose.'

'So it was quite a well-established relationship.'

'Look, if you want to find out about this, you'll just have to talk to Anthea. I'm not prepared to discuss it.'

'Discuss what?' A new voice, from the doorway. Anthea, at last. Her long dark hair was caught up into a pony-tail on the top of her head with an elastic band and she was wearing jeans and a baggy sweater with sleeves so long that only the very tips of her fingers protruded. But although her clothes were much more conventional than last night she still retained a slightly exotic quality, her slightly slanting eyes lending her a touch of the Orient absent in her mother.

'Your love life,' said Mrs Greenway, clearly attempting to shock Anthea into indignation.

Anthea yawned. 'How boring!' she said. She sauntered to the basket chair, picked up the cat and sat down, settling it on to her knee. Almost at once it began to purr.

'I think perhaps your mother is exaggerating a little,' said Thanet, introducing himself. 'I'm simply trying to find out more about Max Jeopard and naturally I have to talk to all the people who knew him.'

'No need to pussyfoot around,' said Anthea. 'No doubt you heard about the little act I put on last night. Ouch! Stop it, Tibbles!' The cat was kneading Anthea's thighs with half-extended claws.

'Act? What act?' said her mother sharply.

'Oh don't fuss, Mum.'

'I want to know what you're talking about!' Mrs Greenway glared at her daughter, willing her to give in, but Anthea wasn't budging. Her mother switched her gaze to Thanet. 'Inspector?'

But Thanet had no intention of alienating Anthea. 'Mrs Greenway, I'm sorry, but I think it would be best if you left us to talk to Anthea alone.'

'No! It wouldn't be right.'

'Oh Mum, really! I am a grown woman, not a twelve-year-old! I agree with the Inspector. It would be easier all round if you went.'

'What is it you don't want me to hear? I insist on staying!' And then, as no one responded, 'You can't turn me out of a room in my own house! I refuse to leave!'

'Very well,' said Thanet, rising. 'Miss Greenway can accompany us to Headquarters, instead.'

'Oh, for God's sake!' said Anthea in disgust. 'What a fuss about nothing! Sit down, Inspector, do. I don't want to go trailing into Sturrenden when we can get it over with more quickly here. Please, Mum, just go, will you? I promise you there's no need to worry. It's no big deal.'

'Well . . . If you're sure . . .'

'I'm sure!'

Mrs Greenway's reluctance showed in every line of her body, in her dragging footsteps and the backward glance she cast over her shoulder.

'I'm her only chick,' said Anthea with a grin when she had gone. 'She can't help it.'

'Perfectly understandable,' said Thanet. 'But now . . .'

'OK, OK, I'll tell you all about it, right? Then if there's anything more you want to ask you can fire away afterwards. I've got nothing to hide.'

'Fine.'

'It's all quite simple really,' said Anthea, with a toss of her pony-tail. 'I don't know how much you've found out about Max yet but you may or may not know that until Christmas he'd been away on a really long trip, in South America. He's a travel writer so naturally he has to travel. The point is that before he went we had a bit of a thing going and I had the distinct impression that when he came back we'd take up where we left off. But we didn't. Instead, he made a beeline for Tess again and just didn't want to know, as far as I was concerned. Well, naturally, I was, to put it mildly, rather pissed off with him.' She shrugged. 'Hence the little scene last night. End of story.'

'If he's been back since Christmas why wait until last night to tell him so?'

'Oh I didn't! Oh no! I told him what I thought of him, believe me, in no uncertain terms.'

'So why tell him again, in public?'

Anthea abandoned her world-weary pose and sat up with a jerk, leaning forward in her eagerness to get them to understand, and the cat, affronted, jumped down and stalked off into the kitchen. 'But that was just the point, don't you see? *In public*. Before, I'd just spoken to him in private but this time I wanted to humiliate him in front of everyone he knew.'

'Including Tess?'

Anthea's expression changed. 'I must admit that was the one thing I felt badly about. I didn't want to hurt her and I made sure she wasn't actually in the room before I staged my protest, but I'm afraid I was so mad with him that every other consideration just went out of the window.'

'*Every* other consideration?' said Thanet quietly. 'Precisely how angry with him were you?'

She stared at him, the animation fading. Then she frowned and narrowed her eyes. 'What are you getting at? You surely aren't suggesting that I . . .? Oh no. You can't be.'

'That you pushed him into the pool?' said Thanet. 'Did you?'

'Don't be ridiculous! As far as I was concerned I'd made my point and that was it, finish!' And she made a chopping movement as if to indicate how final her severance with Max had been.

Apart from a slight puffiness beneath her eyes Anthea had so far revealed no sign of grief or regret at Max's death, thought Thanet. Yet her mother said that she was so upset she had stayed in bed all day and certainly last night she looked as though she had been crying. He distinctly remembered thinking, when he noticed her, that there went someone who had mourned Max Jeopard's passing. So, had the grief been for him, or had there been some other reason for her distress? He had to find out how she truly felt about Max in order to gauge the likelihood of her having had something to do with his death. How could he get behind this show of bravado? 'It looks as though someone did,' he said. 'By all accounts Max was a strong swimmer. No one has suggested that he'd had too much to drink, and it's unlikely that he would have slipped if he'd been in the pool house alone. We think he went there to meet someone.' Thanet glanced at Lineham, who understood at once what Thanet was trying to do, and chimed in.

'We think there was a struggle.'

'That Max slipped . . .'

'Or was pushed . . .'

'And fell into the pool . . .'

'Knocking his head on the side as he fell.'

'So he was unconscious as he went into the water.'

'And whoever it was just let him drown.'

They stopped and Lineham's last words hung in the air, with all their overtones of callousness and deliberate intent on the part of Max's assailant.

Anthea stared at the two policemen, eyes glazed, obviously visualising the scene they had conjured up. Then her lower lip began to tremble and she sucked it in, bit on it and closed her eyes as if to shut out the images in her brain. Two tears squeezed out from beneath her closed eyelids. 'Oh, God,' she said, and covered her face with her hands.

Thanet and Lineham glanced at each other, reading their own emotions mirrored in the other's face. They had achieved their aim but couldn't help feeling ashamed of themselves. Many policemen over the years build up a carapace of insensitivity which enables them to employ such tactics without the slightest qualms of conscience, but Thanet had never been able to do so – nor would he have wanted to. Somewhat pompously he told himself that he was not prepared to relinquish his humanity. At times like this, however, he wondered if somewhere along the line he had done so without even realising it. After all, Anthea had not for a moment denied her anger with Max. Should that not have been sufficient?

'Miss Greenway,' he said gently, leaning forward. 'I'm sorry. Our account was too graphic and I apologise.'

She took her hands away from her face and gave him a searching look, blinking away the tears which were still welling up.

Without a word Lineham handed her a handkerchief and she wiped her eyes before blowing her nose.

'I'll be frank with you,' said Thanet. 'The trouble is that even the most innocent of witnesses feels threatened at being questioned by the police, and resorts to defensive behaviour. It's understandable, of course, but it does get in the way, hold things up.'

'I think I see what you're getting at. I was putting it on a bit. Playing it cool.'

'Yes, but that was your way of coping,' said Thanet. 'I see that now.'

Suddenly and unexpectedly she smiled, for the first time, and Thanet saw how vital and attractive she might be in normal circumstances. 'You're much too nice to be a policeman.'

Lineham rolled his eyes. 'You wouldn't say that if you worked with him!'

'That's enough from you, Sergeant!'

They all laughed and the atmosphere lightened still further.

'OK,' said Anthea. 'Let's try again. Tell me how I can help.'

'I know it might be painful for you, but if you could tell us a bit about Max? It really is helpful to find out how different people viewed him.'

She frowned, picking at some nail varnish which had worked loose. 'It's so difficult when you know someone well,' she said, unconsciously echoing her mother. 'And I've known Max for years, ever since we were in our teens.' She shook her head. 'And I still can't believe he's . . .' She swallowed hard and dabbed at her eyes with Lineham's handkerchief. 'He was so alive, so much, well, larger than life. I know he was self-centred and big-headed but somehow, with Max, you could forgive him because, let's face it, it was justified. He had everything, you see. He was good-looking, intelligent, gifted . . . The fact that he traded on all this just seemed to fade into insignificance when you were with him. He made life so much more exciting, just by being there. That's why he was always the centre of a crowd. He was like a magnet. That was the secret of his success as a travel writer, I think. People would have opened up to him in a way that was pure gold as far as his work was concerned.' She stopped, gave a little grimace and a wry grin. 'That was his good side.'

'And his bad?'

'He was pretty ruthless really. If he wanted something he went for it, no matter who got hurt on the way.'

'And I should think,' said Lineham as they returned to the car, 'that that just about sums him up. What amazes me is that she could see all that so clearly and yet she was still crazy about him.'

'It really shouldn't surprise you, Mike. There are men like that, and women too, and no matter what they do the unfortunate souls who fall in love with them just keep coming back for more.'

'Back to Sturrenden to see Argent?' said Lineham, starting the engine. He waited for Thanet's nod before moving off. 'So what do you think, sir? Think it was her?'

'No, I don't. I may be wrong, of course. She was certainly away from the others long enough.'

Anthea had confirmed that around 9.40, while they were queueing for supper, she had left Gerald and Hartley; to go to the loo, she claimed. There had been a number of women with the same idea and she had had to wait to use the bathroom, passing the time with social chit-chat. Lineham would check the names she had given them but even so, the fact that she had been away a good fifteen or twenty minutes meant that in the general confusion of people milling around at suppertime it would be virtually impossible to pin down timings precisely.

'Now if her mother had been there . . .' said Lineham.

'I know. But she wasn't.'

'I think what made Mrs Greenway so furious with Max was that she could see all along he was only amusing himself with Anthea because Tess wasn't available. She knew Anthea was going to get hurt and there was nothing she could do about it.'

'And being proved right has given her no satisfaction. You're right, Mike.' Thanet was thinking of Bridget and her ex-boyfriend Alexander. 'It's not easy to stand by and see your children get hurt. It's bad enough when it's not intentional, when it's a love affair that just goes wrong, but when you suspect from the beginning that someone is just using your son or daughter for his own amusement and you feel helpless to prevent it ... Oh yes, I can understand how she feels, all right. But if we all went around bumping off people who had jilted our offspring there'd be mayhem.' Why, oh why hadn't they heard from Bridget? Would she ring tonight?

'Anyway, as you say, she wasn't even there.'

This time they were not disappointed. Although dusk was only just beginning to fall there were lights on in Argent's house and a couple of cars parked outside.

'That's Hartley Jeopard's Golf,' said Lineham.

'So it is. Never mind.' Thanet was already out of the car. He wasn't going to be put off now. Gerald Argent was the only member of the group they had not so far met and he was eager to do so. 'Let's see what Argent has to say for himself.'

THIRTEEN

Gerald Argent was the type you'd pass in the street without a second glance, thought Thanet as they followed him through a hall so tiny that there was barely room for more than two people to stand in it. Argent was neither short nor tall, fat nor thin, dark nor fair, and had, on first impressions, no peculiarities of physiognomy to make him stand out from the crowd. It was all the more intriguing, therefore, to enter his living room and be confronted by two shelves of cups and trophies and a number of framed photographs which clearly commemorated the occasions upon which they had been won. Apart from this touch of individuality it was a room which would, Thanet thought, be indistinguishable from hundreds of thousands of others in modern houses up and down the country, simply but adequately furnished with a sofa, two matching armchairs, some adjustable bookshelves, a television set and a CD player. At one end there was a small round modern dining table and four chairs.

Hartley Jeopard unfolded his long frame from an armchair as they came in. 'Good evening, Inspector, Sergeant. I'll be off, then, Gerald.'

'Don't be ridiculous, Hart. I don't mind you staying,

not in the least.' Argent cocked an interrogatory eyebrow at Thanet.

'It's entirely up to you,' said Thanet.

Hartley shuffled his feet. 'No, I think it would be best if I went. Tell you what, I'll go and pick up something to eat. D'you fancy Chinese?'

'Fine by me.'

'OK. Anything special?'

'Up to you.'

The display of photographs was drawing Thanet like a magnet and during this exchange he edged closer to them. The images took on definition, became recognisable. The distinctive silhouettes of ballroom dancers have become universally familiar via the medium of television. Perhaps Argent wasn't quite your Mr Average after all, he thought. Distinction in any field can only be achieved by patience, dedication, perseverance and sheer hard work. He turned to find Argent watching him, and waved a hand at the trophies. 'You must be very good at it.'

Argent shrugged. 'A lot depends on finding the right partner.'

'You obviously have.'

'We've been dancing together for a number of years now.'

'I imagine it's a pretty time-consuming hobby.'

'It does take a fair amount of time, yes. Do sit down.'

'How do boyfriends and girlfriends, husbands and wives feel about that?'

'Much as they would about any other hobby, I suppose.'

'And Miss Sylvester?'

Argent was immediately wary. 'What do you mean?'

'I was wondering how she felt about your spending so

much time with another woman, when you were engaged.'

'June isn't "another woman", as you put it, Inspector. She's my dancing partner and nothing more. As a matter of fact she's engaged herself and getting married in the autumn. Anyway, the question is irrelevant. My engagement was recently broken off as you're obviously aware. And in any case, I frankly don't see that it's any of your business.'

'Oh but it is, Mr Argent, as I'm sure you'll realise if you put your mind to it. In fact, you must think I'm pretty naïve if you imagine I don't appreciate the possible consequences of Max Jeopard's death as far as you are concerned.'

Argent's lips tightened but he did not respond.

'Yes, I see you understand me. Miss Sylvester is free again now, isn't she?'

'I refuse to discuss the matter. I think it's in very bad taste, so soon after Max's death.'

'In my view, bad taste doesn't enter into it, where murder is concerned.'

'It is definitely murder, then?'

'We're treating it as such at the moment, yes. It's difficult to see how it could be anything else. And the plain fact is that yesterday Miss Sylvester was lost to you. Now, she is attainable again, because of Max Jeopard's death.'

'So that makes me a murderer, does it!'

'Not necessarily, no. But you must see that suspicion is bound to fall upon you and it's up to you to convince us that you had nothing to do with his death.'

'Great! I thought that in this country you were innocent until proved guilty, not the other way around!'

'I didn't say that it was up to you to convince the

146

Court that you were innocent, just to convince us. A very different matter. I'm putting this to you quite plainly because you are obviously an intelligent man and I want you to understand that there is no point in trying to be anything less than frank with us.'

'Why should I be less than frank with you? I've nothing to hide.'

'Good!' said Thanet. 'In that case . . .' He glanced at Lineham.

The sergeant took over smoothly and while he put his questions Thanet observed Argent carefully, on the alert for the slightest sign of unease, wariness, dissemblance. When you were doing the questioning you had to concentrate so hard on what you were saying that it was not always possible to pick up these nuances. But try as he would he could detect no sign that the man was lying. Argent's account accorded with that of Anthea and Hartley: he had remained behind in the queue while the other two went off to their respective loos. He had, he claimed, collected his food and then gone to sit down while he waited for them to return.

'We understand that in the first instance you refused the invitation to the party,' said Lineham.

'I don't know why that should surprise you. I would have thought it understandable in the circumstances.'

'Quite. No, we're much more interested in why you later changed your mind.'

Argent shrugged. 'I thought about it a lot before deciding to go after all. As I saw it, the fact of the matter was that although Tess and Max would be living in London we would be bound to see each other from time to time and unless I was prepared to go through life avoiding any possibility of running into them, I might as well start as I meant to go on.'

'Your change of heart did not extend to being civil to Mr Jeopard, though.'

'My God, you have been listening to gossip, haven't you?'

'Naturally we've been talking to everyone who was present last night, yes. What else would you expect, in a murder case?'

'Snubbing someone doesn't mean to say you intend to nip off and kill them later on in the evening, does it? In fact, I'd say the opposite was true. If I'd intended to bash Max over the head and shove him into the swimming pool I'd scarcely have made it quite so obvious I wasn't on speaking terms with him, would I?'

Argent had a point, there, thought Thanet.

Lineham had picked him up quickly. 'Who said anything about bashing him on the head?'

'Nobody! But it's obvious to anyone who knew Max and has even a grain of intelligence that he must have been unconscious when he went into the water or he would have got himself out again. Hasn't anyone told you what a strong swimmer he was?'

Definitely round one to Argent, thought Thanet as they left. Despite his nondescript appearance he was clearly not a man to be underestimated. He said so, to Lineham.

'You're right there!' The sergeant was clearly smarting at having allowed Argent to gain the upper hand.

'He's either a good liar or he has nothing to hide.'

'I agree.'

'But the fact remains, he had a pretty powerful motive.'

'Too true. Tess Sylvester would be a good catch for any man. I mean, she's got everything, including an old man who's rolling in it.'

'I sometimes think you're completely lacking in romance, Mike.'

'That's what Louise says.'

'You'd better watch it! Once your wife starts saying that sort of thing you could be in big trouble.'

Lineham appeared unconcerned. 'She's been saying it since before we were married and it didn't put her off then, so why should it make any difference now? Still, maybe you're right.' He grinned and glanced at Thanet. 'You'll be asking me when I last told her I love her, next!'

Thanet laughed. 'When did you?'

On the drive back to the office they were silent, thinking. Just before they got there Lineham said, 'There is one possibility we haven't considered.'

'What?'

'That Hartley Jeopard and Argent could have been in it together. They seem pretty close.'

'Oh come on, Mike. Haven't we got enough suspects, without you scratching around for further possibilities? Besides, I think we'd both agree that this is unlikely to have been a premeditated murder and I can't really envisage a scenario in which more than Jeopard and one other person were involved.'

Back at the office there were endless reports to read and to write and it was late before Thanet managed to get away. He was tired, his back was aching as usual and all he could think of was getting into bed and sinking into oblivion. He thought that both Joan and Ben would have been in bed long since and on arriving home, therefore, he was surprised to see lights on downstairs. Bad news about Bridget? His mind clicked into higher gear as the adrenalin began to flow.

As he closed the front door Ben appeared in the living-room doorway. He'd obviously been waiting for his father to get home. But there was no sign of Joan, so this was probably nothing to do with Bridget. Thanet breathed a sigh of relief.

'Hi, Dad. I know it's late, but any chance of a word?'

'Yes, of course. The spurt of anxiety had in any case woken Thanet up. He could guess what Ben wanted to talk about and felt guilty that he had scarcely given a thought to his son's future all day. 'Fancy a cup of tea?'

'Thanks. I wouldn't mind a snack as well. You want one?'

'No, I'm not hungry. Had something in the canteen earlier. You go ahead, though.'

Thanet put the kettle on while Ben assembled the makings of one of his famous snacks: bread, margarine, cheese, tomatoes, lettuce, spring onions, cucumber. 'How's the case going, Dad?' he said.

'All right, I suppose. The first day's always a bit hectic. I can never seem to get through as much as I'd like to.'

'Sounds an interesting one, by what I heard on the news. Is it true that it happened at the victim's engagement party?'

'Yes, I'm afraid so.'

'Tough on the fiancée.'

'Quite.'

'They said he was a travel writer.'

'That's right. He'd only written one book so far, but he did pretty well out of it. As a matter of fact I've got a copy.' Thanet had shoved the book Mrs Jeopard had given him into his raincoat pocket before leaving the office and now he went to fetch it, handed it to Ben.

'*Peephole into China*. Mmm. Interesting cover,' said Ben, studying it. He turned the book over. 'This him?'

Thanet nodded. The kettle had boiled and he made the tea, then poured it.

'Looks pretty full of himself.'

Thanet made no comment and Ben, sensing that his father had said all he was prepared to say on the subject, handed the book back and picked up his sandwich and mug. 'Ready?'

They retired to the living room where the embers of a fire still glowed. Both Thanet and Joan loved an open fire and always used it in the evenings in preference to central heating.

Thanet threw a couple of logs on to it then sank back into his armchair with a sigh of relief. 'That's better. So . . . I imagine you want to talk about this new suggestion of yours.'

Ben nodded. 'We didn't have much chance to discuss it last night.' He sank his teeth enthusiastically into his sandwich.

'I know. I'm sorry.'

'It wasn't your fault. And I'm sorry, too, to spring this on you at the end of such a long day. But I don't have any choice. I really do have to make up my mind in the next day or two.'

Thanet grinned. 'I know. But I think we'd better stop apologising to each other, don't you? Now, tell me what you really feel about this and I'll try to do the same.'

Ben took another huge mouthful before replying. 'Well, I know that last night I came over a bit strong. But to be honest, Dad, I still haven't really made up my mind. I suppose I was afraid you'd be so dead set against the idea that I felt I had to present you with a cut-and-dried decision to counter what you were going to say.' He gave a shamefaced grin. 'Knowing you and Mum I should have had more sense.'

'What do you mean?'

'Well, you're not exactly heavy-handed types, are you?'

Thanet smiled. 'We try not to be. Is that a complaint?' He was endeavouring to hide his relief. There was still a chance, then, that Ben might opt for university after all.

This time there was mischief in Ben's smile. 'Well, it doesn't leave much room for adolescent revolt!'

'Is that what this is?'

'No! Well, not exactly. I suppose I feel I've just drifted into the idea of going on to university without really questioning whether or not it's what I really want.'

'And when did you decide that what you really wanted was to go into the police?'

Ben shrugged, finished demolishing his sandwich. 'Oh, I don't know. Years ago, really, if I look back. I've always been very interested in your work, as you know. But I suppose I didn't actually come out with it because in a way I didn't want to seem to be following in my father's footsteps. If you see what I mean. And then I thought, well hang on, this is ridiculous. If it's what I want, that shouldn't stop me doing it. Should it?'

'No, of course not.'

'So, what do you think?'

Thanet paused before replying. He desperately wanted not to say the wrong thing. He chose to prevaricate. 'Would you tell me first how thoroughly you've looked into this?'

Very thoroughly, he discovered. Ben knew precisely what the selection procedure involved, how long the training would be. He was also aware of the graduate entry scheme and its advantages and disadvantages. And of course he had had first-hand experience of the kind of demands police work could make on a man's domestic life, through his father. No, he certainly wasn't going into this with his eyes shut.

'So come on now, Dad. Tell me what you think.'

'All right. I'll try to be frank.' Thanet paused for a moment before continuing. 'As you know, your mother and I have always hoped that if you proved bright enough, you'd go to university. There's no point in pretending otherwise. Nor is there any point in pretending that if you don't we won't be disappointed. At the same time we both feel that it's your life and your career that's at stake and it would be wrong for us to try and impose our wishes on you. So, you have to make up your own mind and the best I can do in the way of advice is to say to you what I would say to any other bright young potential recruit who came along: that you shouldn't rush into this, that you should get some experience of life first. Maturity is a great help in the force, both in terms of relationships with the public, who don't like policemen who look wet behind the ears, and in terms of helping you personally to deal with difficult situations. So I would say go to university and take some time out for travel, either before or afterwards. Then when you've got your degree see if you still feel the same. If you do, then go ahead, and good luck to you.'

'And that really is what you'd say to anyone in my situation?'

'Definitely, yes. The other point is of course that at the moment entry is difficult. Most forces are swamped with applications. But I don't see that as a particular problem in your case. I think you'd have a pretty good chance of getting in, provided you can find a force which is recruiting and you're then prepared to wait several months before starting training.' Thanet felt that he couldn't be fairer than that.

Ben was silent, thinking over what his father had said.

'If you like,' Thanet offered, 'I could arrange for you

to talk, in confidence, with someone else. I'm sure the Super would be only too happy to advise you.'

Ben grinned. 'It's OK, Dad. I trust you. He'd probably only say the same as you. In fact, you're only confirming what I already suspected.' Ben heaved himself out of his chair. 'Thanks.'

Thanet was longing to ask if this meant Ben had reached a decision, but he restrained himself. *Don't push it.* As it was, the outcome looked far more promising than he had hoped.

He had just switched the light off in the sitting room and started up the stairs when the telephone rang. At this hour of the night it could only be an emergency at work or Bridget. Praying that it was the latter he hurried back down and snatched up the receiver.

Relief flooded through him at the sound of his daughter's voice.

'Dad? Oh thank goodness! I'm sorry I haven't managed to get through to you before!'

Apparently Bridget's host family in Adelaide had met her at the airport, scooped her up and borne her straight off into the outback where they were spending a few days at a holiday home lent them by a friend. This had no telephone and Bridget hadn't realised that she would therefore be incommunicado for some time. On their first trip to a town she had seized the opportunity to ring.

'I realise it must be the middle of the night there, Dad, and I'm sorry if I've woken you up, but I felt I must grab the chance.'

'Don't worry. I wasn't in bed anyway. It's a relief to hear from you. It sounds as though you're having a great time.'

'Oh, I am! Love to Mum.'

Thanet would have loved to talk to her longer but they

had agreed before Bridget left that these calls would be brief, because of the expense. Anyway, it was enough just to know that she was safe.

Thanet went to bed a much happier man and expected to go out like a light. But peace of mind, it seemed, was not enough to keep at bay the crowded impressions of the day. Always, at the beginning of a case, there was so much to think of, to remember, to plan, that he tended to find it difficult to go to sleep and tonight was no exception. They shouldn't forget, as he had said to Lineham, that Kent had been only part of Jeopard's life. He had actually lived and worked in London, when he wasn't away on his travels, and presumably had contacts there of which they as yet knew nothing. His publishers, for instance, or his literary agent, if he had one. All his papers and correspondence would be there too. Yes, they really ought to make a visit to his flat a priority. Tomorrow morning they would skim through the reports and if there was nothing urgent they would get clearance from the Met and be off. As Monday was a weekday and parking in the capital such a problem it might be best to go by train – so long as he was back in time for his visit to the chiropractor. Joan would be furious if he missed it after having had to wait for a month before getting an appointment. He wasn't looking forward to it. He didn't know exactly what chiropractors did but whatever it was he was sure it would be painful. And he really didn't think it would do any good anyway. He'd tried physiotherapists and osteopaths but none of them had really made any lasting difference. Experimentally he eased his back, wincing as pain stabbed. Well, it could be worth a try, he supposed. If there was even a thousand to one chance it might help, it would be worth taking it.

He felt as wide awake as ever. Perhaps he should read

for a while? He had brought Jeopard's book up with him. He didn't want to disturb Joan but her deep, even breathing indicated that she was sound asleep. He switched on the bedside light.

Joan stirred and sighed but did not awake and he reached for the book and studied again the inspired jacket design. Was Chinese landscape really as spectacular as that? It looked so mysterious, so exotic, kindling a longing he had never known before, to see other cultures, other climes. He'd never had the opportunity to travel, himself. He and Joan had never been able to afford really expensive holidays and when he was young it hadn't been such an accepted part of a young person's preparation for life. Nowadays it had become almost routine for youngsters to take off either before or after college or university. They even had a name for it. The gap year, they called it. And some of them, like Max Jeopard, got a taste for travel, were never again content to settle for less than constant movement, new experiences. Though very few managed to capitalise on that restlessness as Jeopard had.

Thanet turned the book over and studied Max's photograph again in the light of what he had heard about him today. Yes, there was no denying the charisma of which Anthea's mother had spoken with such bitterness, and although for some that charm evidently wore thin, for others it seemed never to have lost its power. However hard Tess had fought to struggle free of it she had always succumbed in the end, and it had been strong enough to bind Anthea to him through an absence of over two years in the hope that he would one day come back to her.

What made you tick? Thanet silently asked the smiling, confident image. And just how did you overstep the mark? What was it that cost you your life?

Perhaps this book could provide an answer, or part of one.

He opened it and began to read.

FOURTEEN

It was usually Thanet who rose first and took Joan a cup of tea in bed but next morning it was the other way around.

'What time is it?' he said, sitting up with a jerk and squinting anxiously at the clock.

'Don't worry. It's only ten to seven.' Joan sat down companionably on the edge of the bed with her tea.

'I must have slept through the alarm.'

'I'm not surprised, with such a long day yesterday. You fell asleep with the light on. Reading this, I presume.' She reached for Jeopard's book, which had fallen on to the floor.

'Yes. It's fascinating. It was written by the victim. His one and only, as it turned out. His mother gave it to me. She was so proud of him.'

'Poor woman. Imagine how she must feel.'

'Which reminds me!' said Thanet. 'Bridget rang last night.'

'Did she? Oh, good! What a relief! Is she all right?'

'Fine.' Thanet explained what had happened.

'Did Ben wait up for you, by the way? Nothing was said, but I got the impression he was going to.'

'Yes. We had quite a long talk. Did he discuss this new idea of his with you?'

Joan shook her head. 'And I wasn't going to broach the subject. I think he wanted to have a heart to heart with you first. Did you reach any conclusion?'

Thanet related the conversation. 'So it looks as though there might still be a chance he'll opt for university.'

'Oh well, we'll just have to keep our fingers crossed.' Joan was still holding the book and now she tapped it and said, 'Perhaps you ought to give him this to read. It would do him good to travel. Lovely cover, isn't it.' She turned the book over, studied Max's smiling face. 'What an attractive young man!'

'He was only twenty-nine,' said Thanet, suppressing an involuntary little spurt of jealousy. He felt ashamed of himself. Jealous of a man who was almost young enough to be his son, and a dead man, at that! Whatever next?

'What a waste! He looks as though he had a pretty good opinion of himself, though.'

'He did, by all accounts.'

Joan put down her cup, flicked through to the beginning of the first chapter and began to read aloud.

I flew into Beijing – Peking, as it is known in the Western world – three weeks to the day after the massacre in Tiananmen Square, my mind full of the sounds and images we had witnessed on our television screens: the advancing tanks, the terrified faces of the students, the shots, the screams, the blood.

Until then, we had been told, the spirit of optimism had been running high in the young people of the Chinese Republic. They had been convinced that the future was in their hands, that a new era was about to dawn, and they were confident that nothing could stem the tide of revolt against the stultifying tyranny their country had suffered for so long. Had all this hope been crushed out on that hot summer night, extinguished by the ruthless action of the elders of the old regime?

I was about to find out.

'Stirring stuff,' she commented. 'Certainly makes you want to read on.'

'Oh he was talented, no doubt about that. But now I really must get up. I've got to go to London this morning.'

'You haven't forgotten your appointment with the chiropractor?'

'How could I?' said Thanet with a grin. 'You've reminded me often enough!'

After attending the morning meeting and dealing with various administrative matters Thanet and Lineham caught the 9.45 to Victoria. The decision to travel by rail had been clinched by the news that there had been a serious accident on the M20 near Maidstone. Fortunately the train was virtually empty and they were able to talk.

A certain amount of information had come in since yesterday, though nothing particularly constructive. A little research into Sylvester's background had confirmed that he was a successful businessman, dealing in road construction and heavy plant hire. His daughter would have been a catch for any man, as Lineham had pointed out.

Wakeham had found and interviewed the waitress who had handed the note to Jeopard, but had learned nothing useful about the person who gave it to her. She had, she said, been very busy at the time. Someone had simply left it on her tray when she had gone to fetch fresh supplies of drinks. It hadn't been in an envelope, had simply been a small sheet of white paper, folded once and with Max Jeopard's name on it in capital letters. She knew who Max was because he had been pointed out to her as the prospective bridegroom. She had not waited to watch him read it and had been indignant at the suggestion that she might have taken a peek at its contents.

'Pity,' said Thanet. Ethics could sometimes be a hindrance.

Now Lineham said, 'That note. The fact that it wasn't in an envelope suggests that it was written on the spur of the moment. So I wonder where he – or she – got the paper? I mean, you don't go along to a party with a notepad in your pocket, do you?'

'Was there a pad beside the telephone in the hall?' said Thanet.

'I didn't notice, but I imagine there was.'

'Pity we didn't think of this before. We slipped up there, didn't we. I bet it's had a dozen messages scribbled on it since then.'

A further search of Jeopard's clothes had failed to produce the note and so far no trace of it had been found in the swimming pool. If its arrival had not been witnessed by several people Thanet would have begun to doubt its existence.

'There's only one explanation why it can't be found, isn't there?' said Lineham. 'The murderer must have taken it away with him.'

'But how on earth would he have got it back, if it was in Jeopard's pocket? If there was a struggle there would have been no time. Unless he jumped into the pool after Jeopard went in, of course, and took it out of his pocket while he was in the water. In which case he would have been dripping wet. And,' said Thanet, his voice rising slightly in excitement, 'someone was!'

They stared at each other. 'Sylvester!' said Lineham. 'He had to change his clothes, he told us, after going in to pull Jeopard out. But no, that won't work. That was later, much later. Jeopard had been missing for, what, half an hour by then.'

'Missing, but not necessarily dead,' said Thanet.

Lineham stared at him. 'You mean Jeopard might still have been alive when Sylvester found him?'

'It's possible, surely?'

'But that means ... Let's work it out. Say it happened as we suggested before, and it was Sylvester who sent the note to Jeopard, pretending that it was from some girl. Sylvester didn't go to look for him until ten o'clock. Would Jeopard have hung around for twenty minutes waiting for her to show up?'

'He might have, if he was sufficiently intrigued. But there's another possibility.'

'What?'

Thanet leaned forward. 'Say the note was genuine. Say it *was* from a girl. Say it *did* suggest an assignation in the pool house, and Jeopard decided to keep the appointment.'

'And Sylvester saw her leaving, perhaps! Yes. It could have been like that! He would have been furious, to think Jeopard was messing around with another woman at his own engagement party. So there was an argument which got out of control and bingo! The rest, as they say, was history.'

'I don't know,' said Thanet, shaking his head. 'Would Jeopard really have slipped off to meet another woman on an occasion like that? Pretty unlikely, surely.'

'Depends. He strikes me as being the sort of chap who

was easily flattered and also the type who would enjoy an element of risk, of clandestine excitement, if you like. Or he might simply have turned up out of sheer curiosity.'

'But in any case, that scenario wouldn't explain the disappearance of the note, would it?'

'True. But your first suggestion would. That Sylvester engineered the whole thing.'

'Maybe. We'll just have to wait and see. It's pointless to speculate about this, really, when we haven't a shred of evidence to go on.'

Unlike the previous day it was a dull, grey morning and by the time the train pulled into Victoria station it was pouring with rain. Jeopard had lived in the maze of streets behind Victoria and in normal circumstances they would have walked there but today Thanet took one look at the weather and decided on a taxi. There was no point in getting soaked to the skin within minutes of their arrival.

A few minutes later they were deposited in front of a newish block of flats which had no pretension to style and nothing to recommend it, so far as Thanet could tell, but proximity to the main-line station.

'I'd hate to live in a place like this,' said Lineham as he worked his way through the various keys on Jeopard's key-ring to discover which one opened the street door.

'If you want to live in London it's convenient, I suppose.'

'Ah, got it,' said Lineham triumphantly as the door clicked open. 'I wouldn't,' he said as they consulted the list of flat-owners and waited for the lift. 'Want to live in London, I mean. Not if you paid me.'

'Just as well we don't all feel the same.'

Jeopard's flat was one of three on the fourth floor and

as Lineham went through his routine with the keys again the door of the flat across the landing opened a crack and an eye peered out. In the background a radio was playing.

'Who are you?' The voice was female and Thanet tried to sound his most reassuring as he turned and advanced a few steps. 'Police, madam.'

'I wondered when your lot was going to turn up. Thought you'd have been around yesterday. Give us a look at your identification.' A hand emerged through the slit.

The door was still on the chain, Thanet realised as he obligingly laid his warrant card on the outstretched palm. The hand disappeared and the door closed. He grinned at Lineham, who had by now found the key to Jeopard's flat and was waiting impatiently to go in.

Another rattle and the door opened, wide this time. 'Fancy a cuppa?' she said.

Her name was Ellie Ransome and she was tiny, less than five feet tall, with a frizz of improbably red hair and make-up so exaggerated that it wouldn't have been out of place in a circus. She was wearing a ginger-coloured Crimplene suit with a fawn blouse and misshapen down-at-heel slippers which were clearly too comfortable to throw away. Thanet judged that she was well into her sixties. He and Lineham raised eyebrows at each other as she led them into her living room. He had thought, yesterday, that Mrs Greenway's sitting room was the most crowded he had ever seen but in comparison with this it was positively uncluttered. Cardboard cartons of all shapes and sizes were stacked all around the walls from floor to ceiling, sometimes three or four deep, so that there was barely room for the little furniture the room contained. His eyes skimmed over the boxes, registering that they contained – or had contained – chiefly electrical goods of all sizes and descriptions, ranging from microwaves, television sets and CD systems to kettles, toasters and shavers. He and Lineham looked at each other again.

?

Various bizarre explanations flashed through Thanet's mind. This diminutive old woman was a receiver of stolen goods, a fence? In which case she would scarcely invite the police into the flat, surely? A pawnbroker, then? Or perhaps she simply collected empty cardboard boxes?

As if she had read his mind she cast a mischievous glance at him over her shoulder. 'They're full all right. Sit yourselves down and I'll tell you all about them in a minute.' She switched off the radio and cleared a couple of boxes from the settee. 'Shan't be a tick,' she said, heading off along the cardboard corridor to what was presumably the kitchen. 'The kettle's not long boiled, I'd just made me elevenses when I heard the lift.' She nodded at a mug on the only table, which was covered with a mess of newspapers, magazines, and scraps of paper, along with a jampot containing a number of ballpoint pens and a couple of pairs of scissors. A chair in front of it had been pushed back askew as if she had been interrupted in her task. It was obviously the hub of the room's activity. What on earth was she up to?

Thanet was longing to go and take a good look but he and Lineham obediently sat down on the space she had cleared and a few moments later she returned.

'There you are.' She handed them mugs of tea and offered them sugar, which they both refused.

She picked up her own mug and sat down at the table, swivelling to face them. 'Competitions,' she said. 'All

165

this,' she explained, waving a hand at the boxes, the papers. 'I win them.' She looked smug. 'Got the knack, you see.'

'Competitions,' said Lineham. 'You mean when you have to tick the right answers and then write a sentence summing up why such and such is the best product in the world?'

'Got it in one!' she said.

'All this?' said Lineham. He looked slightly dazed.

'All this.'

'But how? I mean, the questions are usually easy enough to answer, but it's always the sentence that's the deciding factor, I imagine.'

'I told you. I got the knack. I just put myself into their position and tell them what they want to hear. And I'm a dab hand at jingles, I can tell you.'

'I'm amazed!' said Lineham. 'I don't know a single person who's ever actually won anything in that way.'

'That's because they don't take it serious enough. I really work at it, I can tell you. Spend hours at it, every day. It might take a week to come up with a really good sentence or slogan or whatever.'

'I've even wondered if these competitions are genuine.'

She smiled and her eyes lit up. 'Oh, they're genuine, all right. I've had some really lovely holidays, cruises and that. You name it, I've won it.' Her face fell. 'No, I tell a lie. I still haven't won a car. Or the big one.'

'The big one?' said Thanet. He knew this conversation was a waste of time but he was enjoying it immensely. Such interludes were one of the unexpected joys of his work.

'A house,' she said. 'You know, cottage in the country, with roses round the door.'

'But,' said Lineham, 'why bother to duplicate like this?

166

I mean, who wants more than one microwave, for example.'

'Oh I don't *keep* them,' she said scornfully. 'They're me income. Me old-age pension, if you like, me hedge against inflation. I win 'em, then when I need money I sell 'em.'

'You don't get much for second-hand goods, surely?' said Lineham.

'You'd be surprised. If people know they're brand new, still in the box and have never been opened ... And I always tell them, if you're not satisfied, bring it back within fourteen days and I'll give yer yer money back. They hardly ever do. I run one or two ads in the local paper every week. Never fails.'

She was really enjoying this, Thanet realised. If she lived alone, opportunities to talk about her somewhat unique talent must be rare. And Lineham was the perfect audience.

Once again she tuned in to his thoughts. 'Nice to have a bit of company for a change,' she said. 'I sometimes feel I'm the only person left alive in this dump, during the day. They all go off to work and the place is like a morgue.' She pulled a face. 'If you'll pardon the expression, in the circs. I heard about the poor lad across the way on the wireless.'

'Did you know him well?' said Thanet.

'Nah ... Scarcely passed the time of day with him. He was always polite enough, mind, not like some, these days. But he was away so much and when he was here he just shut himself up in there for hours on end. Never seemed to go out to work.'

'He worked at home, I expect,' said Lineham. 'He was a writer.'

'Really? What did he write about?'

167

'He'd only written one book so far,' said Thanet. 'A travel book, about China.'

'Ah . . .' Comprehension dawned. 'So that was why he was away such a lot.'

It didn't look as though she could tell them anything useful. 'So you don't know anything that might help us?'

'Ah well now, I didn't say that, did I!'

Thanet waited. Clearly she was enjoying her moment of suspense. She put down her mug and leaned forward, lowering her voice as if someone might be able to hear if she spoke too loudly. 'There was a girl, come around asking for him.'

'When was this?' said Lineham.

'Night before last. About seven.'

Saturday, then, the night Jeopard died. 'You hadn't seen her before?'

She shook her head. 'She was a foreigner. You know. Darkish.'

'Black, you mean?'

'More like sort of olive. I should think she was Italian or Spanish, something like that. Her English was hopeless, I could hardly make out what she was saying.'

'What was the gist of it?'

'She was looking for Mr Jeopard.' Ellie Ransome shrugged. 'I couldn't help her. I didn't have the foggiest where he was. So I suggested she came back next morning, yesterday.'

'And did she?'

'Yes. I was late getting up, I always have a lie-in on Sundays, so I hadn't heard then that he was dead, or I might have told her. I dunno. I might not've. It's not very nice breaking news like that, is it? Anyway, she obviously didn't know. Her English was so bad I shouldn't think she'd bother to turn the radio or telly on. I just told her I

168

thought he must be away for the weekend and she ought to leave coming back until today. I said she ought not to come too early, so as to give him a chance to get home if he'd stayed over until this morning.'

'And has she?'

'Not yet, no.'

Thanet left his card in case the girl turned up later.

'Someone he met in South America?' said Lineham as they crossed the landing.

'Sounds likely.'

'Must be pretty keen, if she's followed him over here.'

Jeopard's flat was smaller than Ellie Ransome's and a far cry from the sophisticated bachelor apartment with which Thanet's imagination had endowed him, consisting of a cramped sitting room, a shoebox of a bedroom, a galley kitchen and a bathroom so tiny that there was barely room for the door to close when one was standing inside.

'This shouldn't take long,' said Lineham, after they had taken a quick look around. The place was minimally furnished, could almost have been any impersonal hotel room had it not been for the outsize desk, which was set at a right angle to the window and took pride of place. On it were ranged computer, printer, telephone, fax machine, neatly stacked sheaves of papers and all the other accoutrements of a writer's life.

'Looks as though he used this place chiefly for work,' said Thanet, picking up a pile of typescript and flicking through it. A cursory glance was sufficient to tell him that this was Jeopard's current oeuvre, on his experiences in South America. He had completed about 120 pages. 'I suppose he wouldn't have wanted anywhere too big, with the sort of life he led, not while he was still a bachelor, anyway. It would just have been an encumbrance.'

The wastepaper basket was overflowing and there were crumpled sheets of paper all over the floor around it. Thanet up-ended it. Most of the rubbish was discarded sheets of typescript and perforated strips torn off the edges of computer paper, but there was one interesting item, an airmail letter with a Brazilian stamp.

'Look at this, Mike,' he said, holding it up. It had been torn through, unopened. The sender's name was on the back and Thanet held the two pieces of envelope together to decipher it. 'It's from a Rosinha Gomes, with an address in somewhere called Manaus. The girl who called yesterday, no doubt. And he didn't even bother to read it.' He extracted one of the torn sheets of writing paper and peered at it. 'Don't suppose you speak Portuguese, by any chance?'

Lineham shook his head. He was working his way through the drawers of the desk.

Thanet put the letter in his pocket. He could get it translated later. 'Found anything interesting?'

'Only this.' Lineham held up an address/telephone book.

'Is his agent's number in it?' said Thanet.

Earlier attempts to ring Jeopard's publishers in order to get hold of this had been unproductive and they had decided that the offices probably didn't open until ten. It was Jeopard's agent rather than his publishers that Thanet was anxious to talk to. He suspected that he – or she, for he'd heard somewhere that the majority of literary agents were women – would have had rather more contact with Jeopard than his editor.

Lineham found several possible names with 071 telephone numbers, but it was impossible to tell which, if any, was the one they wanted. A brief session at the telephone quickly yielded results, however, and they were able to arrange an appointment for half an hour's time.

'She's called Carol Marsh,' said Lineham as they went down in the lift. 'Of Marsh and Walters Literary Agency. It's in Golden Square, just off Piccadilly.'

Thanet had never met a literary agent before and wasn't quite sure what he expected. Someone rather brash, perhaps, certainly sophisticated and probably somewhat intimidating, wearing the kind of clothes normally dubbed 'power dressing' – short skirt, silk shirt, tailored jacket. Carol Marsh was therefore a surprise, a plump woman in her forties wearing a rather drab ankle-length dress. She was carefully made-up, however, and her very short blonde hair had been expertly styled. She welcomed them with a smile appropriately tinged with sadness. 'I've never been interviewed by detectives before. It'll be a new experience. Though I could wish that it had been under pleasanter circumstances. It was such a shock, to hear of Max's death on the news yesterday.'

Her assistant was despatched for coffee and they all sat down. It was a pleasant place in which to work, thought Thanet. The sash windows overlooked the square and there were two whole walls of books.

He waved a hand at them. 'Are these all by your clients?'

She smiled and nodded. 'For my sins.'

'It must be very satisfying, to see the fruit of your labours set out before you like this.'

'Oh it is. Not a satisfaction granted to your profession, I imagine. I love my work. Most literary agents do.'

'I can imagine. To discover a new talent, foster it, see it succeed . . .'

She grimaced. 'Like poor Max, you mean. Yes. It's such a tragedy.'

Her assistant arrived with the coffee and she waited until the cups had been handed out before saying, 'He had a brilliant future before him, everyone said so.'

'He was certainly talented. I was glancing through his book last night. His mother lent it to me.'

'It did very well. I was looking forward to his next. It was on South America. He had some amazing experiences out there.'

'So I understand.'

'They would have made fascinating reading.' She sighed. 'Now it will never be finished. Such a shame. He was well on with the writing of it, I believe.'

'Yes, he was. We've just come from his flat.'

A calculating gleam came into her eyes. 'You've seen the typescript?' she said eagerly. 'How much of it was there?'

'About 120 pages.'

'I wonder if there was any more on disc.'

'I've no idea.' Thanet's tone was dismissive. A certain amount of conversation was allowable, to break the ice, but he hadn't come here to discuss Jeopard's work in progress.

She picked up his disapproval at once and echoed his thought in words. 'But you haven't come here to talk about Max's work.'

'It was obviously an important part of his life and we can't just ignore it. Had he made any enemies in his professional life, do you know?'

'Someone who hated him enough to kill him, you mean? Good grief, no! In any case, in literary circles any back-stabbing is likely to be verbal rather than physical.'

'You really cannot think of any reason why anyone should wish to harm him, or any issue over which some-one would have been likely to quarrel with him?'

She shook her head. 'No. Definitely not. Max could be irritating, true. He was rather big-headed, and the fact that he had good reason to be wasn't enough to stop him getting on your nerves, sometimes. Though . . .'

'What?'

She was hesitating. 'It's just that he did rather have an eye for the opposite sex.'

'You have someone specific in mind?'

'Well, to put it bluntly, he found women irresistible. And as he was a very attractive man, on the whole it worked both ways. Put Max in a room with a woman and he couldn't help making a pass at her. To be frank, I felt rather sorry for that fiancée of his. So far as I could see, she'd have had nothing but heartache ahead. And she's such a beautiful girl, too, she could have had anyone she chose.'

'So what are you suggesting? That there's a jealous husband somewhere in the background?'

'I'm not thinking of anyone in particular. It's just that with Max it's something that's bound to spring to mind.'

And that was really all she could tell them. To her knowledge Max had no close friendships in connection with his work and had bought his flat because he found it easier to work there than at home in Kent. He had, she said, intended keeping it on after his marriage, for this purpose.

'Complete waste of time,' said Lineham gloomily, on their way back to Victoria.

But Thanet didn't agree. Little by little he was building up a picture of Max Jeopard and the life he had led. Somewhere in that tangled web of relationships lay the solution to the mystery of his death.

Thanet was determined to leave no stone unturned until he found it.

173

FIFTEEN

As soon as Thanet and Lineham walked through the door at Headquarters the constable on desk duty pounced.

'Inspector! The Super wants to see you the minute you get back.'

'Oh? What about? Do you know?'

'I'm not sure. It could be something to do with the phone calls from Mrs Jeopard. She's been ringing all morning, wanting to speak to you, and in the end she asked to be put through to him. Anyway, whatever it is he's pretty worked up about it.'

'Better go straight in, then. Mike, send someone off to collect that notepad, will you? And see if you can find someone to translate this.' Thanet handed over the letter from Brazil found in Jeopard's wastepaper basket.

He hesitated for a moment before knocking on Draco's door, bracing himself. Draco in one of his moods could be pretty overwhelming.

'Come!'

Thanet had heard that tone of voice before. No doubt about it, Draco was definitely on the warpath about something. What could Mrs Jeopard have been saying to him?

'Ah, Thanet. About time too. Where the hell have you been?' Draco's dark eyes were snapping and he raked his fingers through his short curly hair – not for the first time, by the look of it; it was standing on end like a bottle brush.

'To London, sir. I did tell you I was going, at the morning meeting –'

'Yes, yes.' Draco waved an impatient hand. 'But what the devil took you so long?'

'Well it does in fact take quite some time to –'

'Oh never mind, never mind. The point is, how often have I given instructions that the families of victims are to be kept informed about what is going on?'

So that was what this was all about. Mrs Jeopard must have been complaining that she wasn't being kept up to date. This was one of Draco's current hobby-horses and on the whole Thanet was inclined to agree with him. In this instance, however, he felt somewhat aggrieved. It was only twenty-four hours since he had seen Jeopard's mother and there had been nothing as yet to report. He opened his mouth to say so, but wasn't given the chance.

Draco had jumped up and begun to pace about in front of the window: three steps to the right, pause for speech, three paces to the left. 'You know how I feel about this. It's an absolute scandal that sometimes victims' families are left completely in the dark, that cases even reach court without their being informed!'

'I agree, sir. And we never allow –'

'Mrs Jeopard has been trying to get hold of you all morning, without success. Just think what she must be going through!'

'But we –'

'How would you like it, if you were in that situation, tell me that?'

'Well naturally I'd –'

'Exactly! So the very least you could have done is get someone to ring her in your absence.'

This time Thanet made no attempt to respond. What was the point? But it seemed the Superintendent had had his say. He glared at Thanet. 'Well?'

Draco would never listen to excuses. Thanet took a deep, unobtrusive breath. 'What would I have told her, sir?' His tone was as calm, as reasonable as he could make it.

Draco stared at him, lips pursed. Then he clasped his hands behind his back. 'Don't ask me! That's your job! Something, anything, to make her feel that we're not sitting around twiddling our thumbs.'

Prudence battled with a sense of injustice and lost. 'But there really wasn't anything to tell her!'

'Then tell her that!' Draco put his hands on his desk and leaned forward, thrusting his chin out. 'Just so long as you remember that she had a right to know.' He straightened up and waggled his fingers. 'Within reason, of course. No need to dot the i's and cross the t's.'

Pointless to argue. 'I'll detail someone to give her a ring each morning, sir,' Thanet said stiffly.

The concession won, Draco sat down with a thump, pulled a file towards him and opened it. 'Good.' His tone was already absent-minded. Clearly, the interview was over.

Feeling like a schoolboy who has been unjustly accused by his headmaster Thanet left the room and walked upstairs fuming.

Lineham took one look at his face and said, 'Like that, sir, was it?'

Thanet related the conversation.

'Sounds par for the course to me,' said Lineham.

176

'You weren't on the receiving end! I mean, I agree with him, Mike! Victims' families should be kept up to date with what is going on. But what's the point of ringing just to say there's nothing to report?'

'You don't need to convince me, sir.'

'It's just a waste of time and manpower!'

'Well, if it'll keep him happy, it's a simple enough thing to organise. Honestly, sir, it's not worth getting so worked up about.'

'I just object to being ticked off unfairly!'

'You don't object if it's justified, then?' said Lineham with a grin.

Thanet glowered at him, then reluctantly grinned back. '*Touché*, Mike. And you're right. It's not worth getting steamed up about.' If he was honest with himself, Thanet realised, it was hurt pride that was making him react like this. He sat down at his desk. 'Anything new come in?'

'Ellie Ransome rang at about 12.30, apparently – the competition lady. So I rang back. She said the girl came back again soon after we left. She still hadn't heard that Jeopard was dead so Miss Ransome felt she had to tell her. She had hysterics on the spot. Miss Ransome took her into her flat to try and calm her down and tried to find out more about her, where she was staying and so on, but the girl was so upset and her English so poor that she was more or less incoherent. Miss Ransome gave her your card and tried to get her to understand that she really must contact us.'

'But she hasn't yet, I gather?'

Lineham shook his head.

'And this was, what?' Thanet glanced at his watch. 'Three hours ago. Hmm. Well, we'll just have to hope she does. It may not be that important, of course.'

They were soon to find out. Half an hour later the

177

constable on desk duty rang through to say that a Miss Gomes was asking for Thanet.

'I'll be right down.'

Thanet had pictured a tall Spanish-style beauty with an abundance of tumbling dark curls but for the second time today he was wrong. The girl who rose in response to his greeting was small, tiny in fact, and looked very young, little more than a child. She reminded Thanet of someone and almost at once he realised who it was: Tess Sylvester. She could have been Tess's younger sister. Was this what had first attracted Jeopard to her?

She looked very nervous, fearful even, and Thanet put himself out to set her at her ease, taking her into the least depressing of the interview rooms and despatching someone for a tray of coffee and biscuits.

She was wearing a short, loose raincoat and she slipped it off as she sat down. It was as she twisted to drape it over the back of her chair that Thanet saw that she was pregnant. The bulge was slight but unmistakable. He wondered if Lineham had spotted this and glanced at him, but the sergeant was fiddling with the recording equipment.

Remembering the airmail letter, so callously torn across unopened and discarded as rubbish, Thanet's opinion of the man dropped several notches further. Max must surely have been told about the pregnancy months ago.

'Now, how can we help you, Miss Gomes?'

'The woman, she tell me . . . Is true?' she said. 'Max is . . . 'e is dead?'

'I'm afraid so.'

Her forehead wrinkled. 'Afraid?'

This was going to be difficult. And there was no way he could get hold of an interpreter who could speak Portuguese on the spur of the moment. He would just have to do his best and try to make sure there were no misunderstandings. 'Sorry. Yes. Max is dead.'

She stared at him, her eyes huge, the tears welling up again and spilling over to trickle unheeded down her cheeks. 'I see him,' she said.

'I do not understand,' said Thanet, speaking slowly and clearly.

'I want see 'im.' Impatiently she flicked the tears away. 'Per'aps there is mistake.'

So that was it. She had come to view the body. She wasn't convinced that Jeopard was dead, Thanet realised, and wouldn't be until she had seen for herself. He shook his head. 'No mistake.'

'I see 'im,' she repeated. Her jaw set stubbornly. 'I mus'.'

'Very well,' said Thanet. If the girl was carrying Jeopard's child she surely had the right to view its father's body. He could tell she hadn't understood that he had agreed, though. He nodded emphatically. 'Yes. We will take you to see him.'

She relaxed a little, sat back and now, for the first time, picked up her cup of coffee and drank, cupping her hands around it as if to draw comfort from its warmth.

'Did you know Max long?'

She looked puzzled. 'Max long?'

Thanet tried again. 'How long did you know Max? Weeks? Months?' This was going to take some time but might be his only opportunity of talking to her and he was determined to learn as much as he could. Slowly, patiently, he extracted her story.

She lived in the city of Manaus, which was in central Brazil, on the Amazon. Max Jeopard had been brought in by some tribesmen to the hospital where she was a nurse – she was, astonishingly, twenty-two, several years older than Thanet had first thought. Her English wasn't good enough for her to explain exactly what had been wrong with Jeopard but he had been very debilitated. The next part was predictable – according to Rosinha they had fallen in love and he had flown back to England in December, promising to return as soon as possible. She had been convinced that when he did so, they would marry. But she had never heard from him again.

'He gave you his address?'

She shook her head. 'I find a . . . how you say? A letter go in it . . .'

'An envelope?'

'Yes. An envelope. Empty. In a book he leave. So I write. I write many, many time, but he no reply. And then . . .' Her hands rested gently on her stomach.

'The baby.'

Lineham's startled face told Thanet that the sergeant hadn't guessed.

'Baby. Yes.'

She had been frantic when, about a month after he left, she realised she was pregnant. Her religion barred her from having an abortion and further letters to Max telling him the news had still elicited no response. When she finally plucked up the courage to tell her parents they had thrown her out, told her they didn't want to have anything more to do with her. She knew the time would come when she wouldn't be able to work any longer and decided that her only option was to come to England and find Max. Now she didn't know what to do. She had only been able to afford a one-way ticket and her limited funds were almost gone.

Her story finished she dissolved once more into tears and Thanet and Lineham exchanged glances. How would he feel, Thanet wondered, if it were Bridget in this situation? But she wouldn't be, of course. Under no circumstances would he and Joan cast her out, as this girl's parents had done. Even allowing for a different society, a different culture, he simply couldn't understand the mentality of such people in this day and age. What was to be done?

Thanet left a policewoman sitting with the girl while he and Lineham withdrew to confer.

The sergeant was equally concerned about her. 'What are we going to do, sir? We can't just take her to the morgue, show her his body then pack her back off to London on the train. What will become of her? With no money, no work permit, nothing?'

'I agree. We must think of something.'

'Social services?'

'We could try, but I doubt that they'd regard it as their responsibility.'

'They might come up with some suggestions, though.'

'True. Better get on to them then, Mike. No, just a minute . . . I wonder . . .'

'What?'

'It might be worth a try. Tell me, how d'you think Mrs Jeopard would react to the idea of a grandchild?'

Lineham stared at him. 'You think she might take the girl in! That's a brilliant idea, sir! Max was the apple of her eye! You're right, it would be worth a try! Let's go and suggest to Miss Gomes that she meet her.'

Impulsive as ever, Lineham was already moving towards the door but Thanet caught his sleeve. 'Just a minute, Mike. Not so fast. Let's think about this. Say Mrs Jeopard does take her in. What sort of a life would she have? Would *you* like to live with the old lady?'

'No way. But I'm not young, homeless, penniless and pregnant.'

'And in the long term there'd be legal problems too, bound to be. She's only over on a short visit, remember. What happens when her visa runs out?'

'But as you say, sir, all that is in the long term. Surely the main thing at the moment is to make sure she has a roof over her head in the immediate future? And it would buy her time, to take stock of the situation and to adjust to the shock of Jeopard's death.'

'If she stays, she's bound to find out he had just got engaged to someone else.'

'True. And, OK, that'll be hard. But not as hard as finding herself on the streets.'

'All right, Mike. You win. We'll suggest it to her. But not until we've got the visit to the morgue over, first. I don't believe she can think beyond that, at the moment anyway.'

'We'll take her ourselves, sir?'

'Oh, I think so, don't you? She's got enough to cope with without being made to feel like a parcel that's being handed on from one policeman to another.'

'You think we ought to tell her about Tess?'

'I'm not sure. Probably not. We don't know yet whether Mrs Jeopard will take her in and even if she does, the girl's English is so poor it could be ages before she found out, so she'd have time to adjust to the situation gradually. No, better not to say anything about it at the moment.'

'It's odd that she hasn't yet asked any questions about how he died, don't you think?'

'I really don't believe she's accepted that he has, yet. When she's done so, and when she's got over the initial shock, that's when she'll start asking questions. But that might well not be today.'

And Thanet was right. Rosinha's reaction to the sight

182

of her lover's lifeless face was predictable: she fainted. When she came to she was clearly in a state of shock and inclined to go along with whatever Thanet suggested. A tiny spark of interest briefly kindled in her eyes when Max's mother was mentioned but on the brief drive out to the Jeopard house she remained silent and sunk in misery, wiping away the tears which rolled down her cheeks in a never-ending stream. It wasn't until they turned off the road under the stone archway at the entrance to the Jeopard's drive that she paid any interest at all to her surroundings.

'This is Max's 'ome?' she said, peering out of the window at the lovely old timbered house.

'Yes, Miss Gomes,' said Lineham.

Hartley's Golf was again in the garage barn, alongside the Astra.

'Hartley's here, I see,' said Thanet. He wondered how Max's brother was going to react to the arrival of Rosinha Gomes. 'He's Max's brother,' he explained to her.

She nodded. 'I know. Max tell me about 'him. 'E is, 'ow you say, with money?'

'Yes, an accountant,' said Thanet. 'Now, I think it would be best if you stay here while I go and . . .' No, no good, he could tell by the look of anxious concentration already spreading across Rosinha's face. Try again. 'You stay here, I go talk to Max's mother.'

She nodded her comprehension. 'I wait.'

Once again it was Hartley Jeopard who opened the front door. Did he look relieved when Thanet said that it was Mrs Jeopard he had come to see? Thanet couldn't make up his mind. Hartley showed him into the galleried hall, where his mother and aunt were taking afternoon tea.

'About time!' said Mrs Jeopard.

Thanet couldn't think what she meant for a moment,

then realised that she assumed he had come to make the report Draco had promised her. As if he had the time to do so in person! Some people really didn't have a clue!

'Well?' she demanded. 'Have you any news for us?'

'Not as far as the investigation is concerned.'

She opened her mouth, presumably to make some scathing comment, but Thanet jumped in first. 'But I am arranging for one of my men to be in touch with you each day, to keep you up to date. And as soon as there is anything of importance to report, I will contact you myself.'

The wind taken out of her sails, she contented herself with saying, 'Good.' She did not, however, offer him a seat.'

'But this afternoon I have come about another matter. If I could have a word with you in private, perhaps?'

'I have no secrets from my son or my sister, Inspector,' she said stiffly. 'You may speak freely.'

Thanet was surprised. He would have expected a woman in Mrs Jeopard's position, dependent upon others for her slightest need, to relish the prospect of having the small measure of power involved in knowing something they did not. 'It's up to you.' But still he hesitated. Ought he to try to persuade her to see him alone?

'Well?' she said impatiently. 'What is it?'

Mentally, Thanet shrugged. He had tried, after all. If she regretted it later, then that was her affair. He didn't feel, however, that he could remain standing while he told them about Rosinha. 'May I sit down?'

She gave a grudging nod and he chose a small upright chair, moving its position slightly so that he could see their faces. Then he gave them a brief account of how he had learned of Rosinha's existence and of her subsequent visit to Headquarters. He was hesitating over how best to break the news of her pregnancy when Mrs Jeopard interrupted his narrative.

Leaning forward, she said, 'May I assume that all this rigmarole has a point, Inspector? I really cannot see that one of my son's former girlfriends has anything to do with me!'

She had given him his opening. 'Oh but she has, Mrs Jeopard, I assure you. You see, she is carrying your grandchild.' He couldn't help a spurt of satisfaction as he saw how the news affected her: her eyes flew open wide with the shock of it and her pale skin was infused with a tide of colour from neck to temple. Her sister looked equally shocked, as did Hartley. Neither of them had said a word until this point but almost at once Hartley burst out, 'Are you sure? I mean, is it true?'

'She is certainly pregnant. That is obvious.'

'When is the baby due?' said Louisa Burke.

'In a few months, I imagine. What I haven't yet told you is that her parents have turned her out, refuse to have anything more to do with her. She used the last of her money to fly over here to see Max, relying on the fact that he would help her. Now she is virtually destitute and of course desperately upset over your son's death – still in a state of shock, in fact, after seeing his body. She insisted on doing so. Until then I don't think she really believed he was dead. I didn't feel we could put her on a train back to London in that state and in her situation. That was when I thought of you.'

'Where is she now?' said Hartley.

'Outside, in the car.'

Three startled faces glanced towards the window as if they could see through bricks and mortar to this stranger who had suddenly entered their lives. Then Mrs Jeopard spoke for the first time since he had broken the news. 'How do we know that the child is Max's?'

'You don't. Not at this stage. Later, of course, when the baby is born, this could easily be confirmed by blood tests. But frankly, I doubt that she would have flown all this way if it weren't.'

'Poor girl,' said Louisa Burke. 'What a terrible situation to be in.'

Her sister shot her an admonitory look. 'Really, Louisa, tell you any sob story and you'll swallow it hook, line and sinker! We've heard enough from Max about the conditions in central Brazil to make any tale like this suspect.'

'But why should she make it up?' said Louisa stubbornly.

'If people are desperate enough they'll try anything on,' said Hartley, ranging himself alongside his mother.

Hartley would, after all, have a lot to lose if his brother's child came on the scene, thought Thanet.

'And if her parents have kicked her out . . .' Hartley went on.

'But to be completely alone, and to come all this way . . .' said his aunt. She turned to Thanet. 'What is she like?'

'What does it matter?' snapped Mrs Jeopard, clearly exasperated by her sister's unwonted opposition. 'I hope you're not suggesting we should actually *do* anything about this.' She shot a venomous glance at Thanet. 'I really can't imagine why you should have brought this . . . girl here at all. I suppose you thought you could just shuffle off the responsibility by dumping her on our doorstep.'

'But Eleanor,' protested Louisa, determined not to give up, 'surely, if she's carrying Max's child, she *is* our responsibility. By no stretch of the imagination could she be called the Inspector's.' She gave Thanet a shy smile. 'I think it was very caring of him to bring her to us.' She ignored Eleanor's snort at the word 'caring'. 'It would have been only too easy for him just to put her on the train back to London and wash his hands of her.'

'If she was as close to Max as she claims, she's bound to know he comes from a fairly well-off family,' said Hartley. 'When she found out he was dead I bet she asked you for our address, didn't she?' he said to Thanet.

Thanet shook his head. 'She didn't ask a single question about Max's family. She was so distraught after such a shock that I think she was incapable of thinking rationally at all.'

'What did you think of her, Inspector?' said Louisa. 'Did she strike you as being the calculating type?'

'Not in the least.'

Eleanor Jeopard gave a derisory snort. 'A pretty girl can pull the wool over most men's eyes,' she said. 'Especially if she has a sob story to tell. She could have slept with dozens of men, for all we know, and the child could have been fathered by any one of them.'

Louisa Burke stood up, in an unconscious need, perhaps, to repudiate her usual subservience to her sister and underline the importance of what she was about to say. 'Have you thought what will happen, Eleanor, if we refuse to help her or have anything to do with her? With no money, what will she do? Where will she go?'

'Back on the streets, perhaps, where she probably belongs.'

How callous can you get? thought Thanet.

Louisa Burke was equally shocked. 'I can't believe you really said that, Eleanor. You'd actually be prepared to let that happen? When she might be carrying Max's child? Your grandchild, as the Inspector so rightly points out?'

Hartley intervened. 'We could pay her air fare back to Brazil.'

'And then what?' said his aunt. 'From what we hear, she has no resources there. And,' she added, turning back to her sister, 'can you really tell me that you are prepared to let her disappear into the blue? That even if her story is genuine and this is Max's baby, you're willing to lose touch with her permanently?'

This had struck home. Eleanor Jeopard's lips tightened and for the first time since Thanet had told her that Rosinha was pregnant a hint of doubt appeared in her eyes.

'Would it not be sensible,' he said, 'to play safe? As I said, when the child is born it will be a simple matter to establish whether or not Max is the father.'

She was weakening, he could tell. She was blinking rapidly and her mouth was working, her hands plucking restlessly at the mohair rug which covered her knees.

He pressed home his advantage. 'Can you risk,' he said gently, 'never knowing for certain?'

SIXTEEN

'That was what clinched it,' said Thanet. 'She knew that if she let Rosinha walk away now without even seeing her, she might lose contact with her completely and she would never know for sure if it was Max's baby. She couldn't bear the prospect of that.'

He and Lineham were driving back to Sturrenden. Mrs Jeopard had reluctantly volunteered to take Rosinha in, for the moment at least, making it clear that this was only a temporary arrangement while the situation was considered and enquiries into Rosinha's background were made, and Hartley was going to drive the girl back to London to collect her suitcase from the hotel.

Lineham grinned. 'I'd love to have seen the old bat's face when you told her.'

'I just hope we've done the right thing.'

'Stop worrying, sir! As I said before, at least the girl will now have a roof over her head.'

'But for how long, Mike? I did make it clear to Mrs Jeopard that I was pretty certain Rosinha wouldn't be allowed to stay here permanently. You'd better ring Croydon to find out what the position is. We don't want to be accused of encouraging illegal immigrants!'

'What time did you say your appointment is, with the chiropractor?'

'Five o'clock.' Thanet glanced at the dashboard clock. It was twenty to five. 'I should just make it.'

But he hadn't allowed for late-afternoon traffic. They should have gone out to the Jeopard house in separate cars, he realised, then he could have gone straight to the clinic. He didn't feel he could ask Lineham to hang about waiting for him while he kept the appointment and by the time they'd got back to Headquarters and Thanet had picked up his car it was already five past. He arrived at reception twenty minutes late.

'I'm so sorry. I do apologise. The traffic . . .'

The receptionist was middle-aged, with a round, pleasant face, wispy brown hair put up in a precarious bun and layers of flowing garments of ethnic design. She gave him a reassuring smile, revealing a set of perfectly even over-large false teeth. 'Don't worry,' she said. 'Miss Carmel has only just finished with her previous patient and you are the last for today.'

Janet Carmel was brisk and businesslike in tracksuit and training shoes. She was in her late thirties, tall and slim with straight fair hair caught back in a pony-tail and very direct blue eyes. Knowing that her profession abounded in unqualified practitioners, Thanet had taken care before making the appointment to check that she was a registered chiropractor. She had, he discovered, taken a full-time four-year course at a College of Chiropractic.

Medical history noted, he found himself stripped to his underpants, gowned and lying on his back on an examining couch which she cranked up to an appropriate height for the treatment. He had rarely felt so vulnerable. What was coming next? What, exactly, did chiropractors *do*?

'I think I've changed my mind about this,' he said with a nervous laugh.

She recognised that he wasn't entirely joking and gave a reassuring smile. 'Don't worry,' she said. 'It'll be all right, I promise.'

Believe her, Thanet told himself. She is qualified, after all.

'Now,' she said. 'I want you to extend your right arm up into the air and clench your fist. I am going to say "Hold", and try to push it down. I want you to resist the pressure if you can. Do you understand?'

'I think so.'

'Right, then.' Miss Carmel grasped his clenched fist in her left hand, inserted her right hand under Thanet's back, and simultaneously pressed her fingers against one of his vertebrae and pushed against his extended arm. 'Hold.'

Thanet successfully resisted the pressure and his arm remained in a vertical position.

'Good,' she said. 'Again.' Pressing her fingers against a different vertebra she repeated the process. He again resisted the pressure against his right arm. What on earth was this telling her? he wondered. Over and over again she went through the same motions. 'Hold . . . Hold . . . Hold.'

Thanet was beginning to think that this was a completely pointless exercise when suddenly, when she said 'Hold', his right arm seemed to lose all power of resistance and she pushed it down with ease.

'Ah,' she said, and repeated the same pressure, the same movement, this time pushing his arm down with only one finger.

'Why did it do that?' He was astounded. His mind was telling his arm to remain vertical, his body was refusing to obey.

191

'Because your brain knows that there is something wrong in that area. This is where your major problem is. It's as I suspected, when you told me about the original injury to your back, heaving that lawnmower into the boot of your car.'

'So what's wrong, exactly?'

'It's your sacroiliac joint, the big joint at the base of your spine. It's been strained and it's unstable. Over the years the instability has increased and because it's a major weight-bearing joint your body has had to compensate, thus putting strain on other joints. This is why your back pain has been so general.'

'So can anything be done to put it right?'

'I can certainly put it back in position. The problem is going to be getting it to stay there in the long term. As this is a long-standing injury the ligaments holding it in position have become stretched and slack so they can't hold the joint together. Your body is now used to the instability; it's been programmed to accept it, so to speak. One of the difficulties is going to be in reprogramming your brain to a different assessment of the situation.'

'That doesn't sound very optimistic.'

'I wouldn't say that. I can't promise anything, but I think there's a good chance it could be treated successfully. It would take time, though. You can't eliminate twenty years of damage in a matter of weeks.'

'So what sort of timescale are we talking about?'

'It's really impossible to tell. What I would propose is that we begin with a course of four weekly treatments, then reassess the situation. By then I should have a good idea of whether or not it's going to work.'

'But you think there's a chance that it might.'

'A good chance, yes.'

'Then I'll try it. After all those years of backache any chance is worth taking!'

'Right, then. Turn on to your right side, please.'

Apprehensively, Thanet allowed his position to be adjusted to her satisfaction, trying not to tense up in anticipation of what was coming. Relax, he told himself. Relax.

'Try to relax,' she said. Then grasping his left shoulder firmly with one hand, his right hip with the other, she performed a rocking, twisting movement which culminated in a final jerk. There was a cracking sensation at the base of his spine and it was over.

'On your back again now, please,' she said calmly.

Gingerly, Thanet turned over. His spine was still intact, it seemed.

Reverting to her diagnostic procedure she went through the same process as before. This time, to his further astonishment, when she pressed the place where his arm had formerly shown no resistance it remained firmly in the air.

'Ah, that's better,' she said, with satisfaction.

The treatment continued. At one point, to his surprise she donned rubber gloves and putting her fingers into his mouth did some uncomfortable pressure movements inside, for cranial adjustment, she told him. Finally she inserted two large wedges under his buttocks, one on each side. These, she told him, were pelvic blocks and they realigned the sacroiliac joint and stabilised it. This process would also inform his brain that this was how things should really be in that region. When he left he was to take a ten-minute walk before getting into his car, to give both brain and body time to adjust to the new situation.

Thanet walked out of the consulting room feeling dazed. He couldn't believe that someone had at last told him

193

what, specifically, was wrong with him. Conscientiously taking his brief walk he was aware of a new ease of movement and absence of pain in his lower back. He had been warned that this might not last; after each of the first few treatments the joint would probably slip out of alignment again quite quickly. But for the first time in twenty years something constructive had actually been done to tackle what he had come to believe was an intractable problem and he felt a cautious optimism. Was it really possible that some permanent improvement could be achieved? He had arrived a sceptic and left a convert. He couldn't wait to tell Joan all about it.

He arrived home before she did and started preparations for supper. She was surprised to see him. 'I didn't expect you yet!'

'I came straight home after my appointment.'

'So how did you get on?' She took another look at his face and her eyebrows went up.

He held up his hands in a gesture of surrender and laughed. 'All right, I admit it. You were right and I was wrong!'

'Really? You mean, she actually managed to do something constructive?'

'It was amazing!'

They sat down at the kitchen table while Thanet described the experience in detail. Joan listened with complete attention, her mobile face as responsive as always. When he had finished, she said, 'Well, I'm delighted, of course, darling. Absolutely delighted. But please, don't get too excited about it. She did say she couldn't *guarantee* any long-term improvement.'

'I know. But what she did, it's made so much difference! The fascinating thing is that I wasn't expecting it to. Just the opposite, in fact, as you know. Which makes it all the more convincing, don't you see?'

'Yes, of course I do.' She got up, came around the table and kissed him. 'All the same, let's not get carried away. Let's just wait and see, shall we? I just don't want you to be disappointed if it doesn't work.'

'Talk about role reversal!' said Thanet. 'Usually I'm the one advising caution!'

His mood of euphoria lasted overnight and next morning he was up earlier than usual, delighted to find that the ever-present discomfort in his back was still considerably diminished. He felt as though he were firing on all four cylinders instead of the usual three and for once was at his desk before Lineham.

The sergeant's eyebrows went up when he saw him. 'You're looking very pleased with yourself today!'

'It's the chiropractor. She was amazing!'

'Really? That's great!' Lineham had seen at first hand how Thanet had suffered over the years and his pleasure was genuine. 'You think she really might be able to help you?'

'She says she's willing to try, and thinks there's a good chance she can. I'll tell you all about it over a pint, later, Mike. I've been trying to catch up on the reports I didn't write last night. Have a look through what's come in, will you?'

For a while both men concentrated on their work. Finally Thanet sat back and said, 'Well I think that's it. So what's new?'

'Well, I'm afraid I haven't found anyone to translate Rosinha's letter yet. Does it matter, now we've seen her?'

'Shouldn't think so. No, leave it.'

Lineham consulted his notes. 'DC Carson says the notepad was still there beside the telephone on the table in the hall at the Sylvesters' house, so he's sent it off to forensic with an urgent request for comment.'

'Good.'

'It would be terrific if they came up with something, wouldn't it?'

'Don't suppose for a minute that they will. It's a long shot, but worth trying. What else?'

'You remember Sylvester told us that Barbara Mallis said she'd inherited money from her father? Well DC Martin says the old man is still alive and kicking and living in a council flat off the Old Kent Road. He's a retired bus driver. Looks as though we were right, doesn't it? No one could afford a BMW on a housekeeper's salary.'

'I agree. We'll go and see her again. Though I doubt that we'll get anywhere. She's not the type to cave in easily. What does Martin say about Roper?'

'Ah, well, he's a different matter. You know we were wondering why he'd stayed so long with the Sylvesters? Apparently he's paid almost double the going rate. I suppose they feel it's worth it, to keep someone who really knows how to handle Carey. Also, and this is the point, he has a young sister who has psoriasis very badly – you know, that really extreme form of skin disease – and he's spending a fortune on trying to find an effective treatment for her. His mother can't speak too highly of him.'

'He could still be involved with Mrs Sylvester, though, couldn't he?'

'Yes. And if he is, Barbara Mallis would be ideally placed to find out. So if she is blackmailing Mrs Sylvester, that's probably why.'

'Maybe.' Thanet was frowning.

'What's the matter, sir?'

'I don't know, Mike. Say we're right. Say that is what's going on, and Sylvester suspects it. What possible relevance could it have to Jeopard's murder?'

'You've said yourself, sir, often enough, that you can never tell what relevance a fact might have, in a murder case.'

'True. All the same . . .'

'Sir! Look at the time!'

Draco was a stickler for punctuality and Thanet had barely one minute to get downstairs to the Superintendent's office for the morning meeting. He didn't want to risk incurring Draco's displeasure again, after yesterday, and he shot out of his chair and down the stairs as fast as he could move. Boon had evidently given up on him and gone in.

Draco's eyes went to the clock as Thanet entered. 'Ah, Thanet. We were just about to begin.'

The Superintendent took Tody and Boon briskly through their reports and listened intently to Thanet's. Then he opened a file on his desk.

Thanet's heart sank. He knew the signs. What now?

Draco sat back, steepling his fingers. 'I've been thinking about your case, Thanet. This lad Carey, the Sylvesters' son. He's a schizophrenic, you say?'

'Yes, sir.'

'You've interviewed him?'

'As best I could, sir. It was . . . rather tricky.'

'In what way?'

'Well, one second he'd be rational, the next he'd be talking nonsense.'

'Is he dangerous?'

'I don't know, sir.'

Draco gave what Thanet privately thought of as his crocodile smile; danger lurked behind it. 'Then may I suggest you find out?' He sat forward, picked up a newspaper cutting from the file in front of him and fixed Thanet with a gimlet-like stare. 'I've been doing some research. This is an article from the *Daily Telegraph*, a reputable newspaper I think you will agree, whatever the colour of your politics. Admittedly it dates from last year, at the time of that television programme about the Zito case, I expect you remember all the fuss, but all the same the facts it gives are very interesting. If you remember, Zito was killed by a diagnosed schizophrenic who had been released into the community. As a result the National Schizophrenia Fellowship collated some figures. Just listen to this. According to them, in the year following Zito's death there were seventeen cases of killings by schizophrenics, five of which were carried out by former mental hospital patients who had shown previous violent behaviour. Longer-term research had shown that over the thirty-three months up to the December before the article was written, there had been thirty-eight fatal attacks. Thirty-eight, Thanet! Over one a month!' Draco tossed the cutting on to his desk. 'I think the facts speak for themselves.'

Thanet felt bound to defend himself. 'As I understand it, sir, they are only dangerous if they don't take their medication. And Carey Sylvester is closely supervised, with a full-time nurse to look after him.'

'But I understand he escaped and was loose on the night of the murder.'

Thanet didn't like the word 'loose' in reference to Carey any more than he had when Mrs Jeopard had used it. It made the lad sound like a wild animal and he was, after all, a human being. 'Yes, sir. But –'

Draco shook his head. 'All I'm saying, Thanet, is that I

think you ought to look into this more closely. Which hospital was he in?'

Thanet realised to his chagrin that he didn't know. 'I'll find out, sir.'

Draco's hairy eyebrows arched, but showing unusual restraint he refrained from comment. He closed the file and brought the meeting abruptly to a close. But as they were on the way out he called Thanet back.

'Get this put up on the noticeboard for me, will you?'

Outside Boon said, 'What is it?'

The three of them stopped to read it. Draco's distinctive handwriting marched across the page.

You are reminded that the families of victims should always be kept up to date with what is going on in the relevant investigations.

G. Draco

'What brought that on?' said Boon.

'Me,' said Thanet. 'Well, actually it was Jeopard's mother. She kept on ringing me up yesterday and I was in London, so she got herself put through to the Super. He hauled me over the coals as soon as I got back.'

'Hard luck,' said Boon.

It would have given Thanet tremendous satisfaction to screw the piece of paper up and toss it into the nearest wastepaper bin, but restraining himself with difficulty he handed it to the desk sergeant. 'Put this up, will you?'

Lineham looked up as Thanet came in. 'The PM is fixed for later on this morning. What's the matter, sir? Not more trouble?'

'I'm not exactly the Super's blue-eyed boy at the moment, Mike. He thinks we've been remiss in not looking into Carey's background more closely.' Thanet sat down with a thump. His back protested and he clutched it. 'Oh, no!' He hoped he hadn't dislodged the joint again.

'What?'

'Oh, nothing.' He couldn't be bothered to explain. It was too complicated. 'The trouble is, he's probably right.'

'But . . .'

'No, Mike. Put Martin on to it right away. Get him to find out all he can about Carey's medical history – which hospital he was in, how long he was there and so on. Tell him to find out which psychiatrist he was under and to make an appointment for us with him as soon as possible – this afternoon, perhaps. And make sure that Carson understands that he has to ring Mrs Jeopard every single morning to keep her happy. Tell him to use his common sense about what to tell her. With any luck, though, with Rosinha's arrival she'll have something else to occupy her mind now. Which reminds me. Did you get through to immigration at Croydon last night?'

'No. They were closed. But I spoke to them just now, while you were in the meeting.'

'And what did they say?'

SEVENTEEN

'It's not too hopeful, I'm afraid,' said Lineham, reaching for the sheet of paper on which he had made notes. 'First of all it doesn't look as though Rosinha would have applied for an entry clearance certificate which is essential as a preliminary to getting permission to stay here. If she had applied for one, giving pregnancy as a reason, she wouldn't have got it without documentation – a letter from the child's father, for instance, and we can be pretty sure from what she says that Jeopard didn't provide her with one. So she would have come into the country in the normal way. No visa is required and provided she could satisfy immigration that she was a genuine visitor and convince them that she intended to return to Brazil, there would have been no problem about entry and she would then be able to stay for six months.'

'Six months. That means she could in fact have the baby over here. Does that mean it will have British nationality?'

Lineham was shaking his head. 'No. Definitely not. Even if the father is British, unless the parents are married the child would be of Brazilian nationality and permission to stay longer than six months would be refused.'

'Ah.' Thanet could see problems looming. 'We'll have

to tell Mrs Jeopard all this. Perhaps we should have looked into the matter more thoroughly before taking Rosinha to meet her. She's going to be pretty upset if she sees her through her pregnancy and then finds the baby is whisked off to Brazil.'

'I still don't see what else we could have done.'

'In any case, it's too late now to worry about it.' Though Thanet knew that he would.

'So, what's on the agenda for this morning, sir?'

'Another visit to Mrs Mallis, I think.' Because although, as he had said to Lineham, it was difficult to see how the fact that the housekeeper might be blackmailing her employer could have any relevance to the case, Thanet's instinct kept tugging him back to the Sylvester household. Something was going on there, and he was determined to get to the bottom of it. And it was, after all, the place where the murder had happened. Why was that? he wondered. Why had Max Jeopard met his death in that particular place and at that particular time? His engagement party should have been an occasion for celebration but instead of a day for rejoicing it had become a day for dying.

As they were about to leave, however, DC Martin knocked on the door.

'About Carey Sylvester, sir . . .'

'That was quick.' Thanet sat down again.

'I got on to someone very helpful at County Hall.'

'So?'

'Well, apparently Carey would have been in the catchment area for St Augustine's, Canterbury, but that was finally closed down at the end of '93 and patients now go to the new, purpose-built wing at Sturrenden General. There are only sixty beds there and patients are admitted only if it's absolutely necessary. Someone like Carey

Sylvester, who has his own nurse, wouldn't have a chance unless something went dramatically wrong.'

'So if St Augustine's is closed, what would have happened to his medical records?'

'They go with the psychiatrist, provided he stays in Kent. If he moved out of the area, the files would go to his successor. But we're in luck, there. Dr Damon, who treated Carey, is actually in charge of this new wing at Sturrenden General. I rang his secretary to request an appointment for you and she said they'd have to discuss the matter with management first. I stressed the urgency and she promised to try and get back to me today – later on this morning, if she could.'

'Well done!' said Thanet. 'Let's hope they agree.' Even if they didn't, there would be sufficient new information to pacify Draco. And he had to admit that the Super was right, as usual. Carey's medical history was a loose end which should be followed up.

The heavy rain which had greeted them in London yesterday had moved south-east at a snail's pace and was only now clearing Sturrenden. Outside the banks of dense cloud were moving away and a brightness in the sky hinted that the sun was doing its best to break through. The country lanes were still awash with water and more than once Lineham had to slow down in order to negotiate huge puddles which had spread halfway across the road. Thanet sat gazing out at the drowned landscape and planning the best way to tackle Barbara Mallis about the suspected blackmail. She wasn't going to give in easily and admit it, that was certain. So would it be best to be polite and devious, or come straight out with the accusation? No, not the latter, he decided. That would simply put her back up and get nowhere. The softly softly approach, then.

Lineham agreed. 'Think we'll get anywhere?'

'Frankly, I doubt it. But we can try. She's the only person we know for certain is lying at the moment.'

'We've only Sylvester's word for it that she claims to have inherited money from her father. He could have got it wrong, misunderstood her, whatever . . .'

'That's true. We'll have to tread carefully, hope we can catch her out.'

As they turned into the drive of the Sylvester house the sun came out at last, illuminating it as if a spotlight had been turned on. It looked so innocent, thought Thanet. Who, passing in the lane, would ever have guessed that behind its walls murder had so recently been done?

Fielding, the gardener, was squatting by a blocked drain in front of the house. He had the cover off and was ramming a flexible metal rod down it.

'Trouble?' said Thanet.

'Too much water coming off the roof too fast,' said Fielding. 'If there's any kind of obstruction, this drain can't take it. It has a sharp bend a short way along, it's always causing problems.'

It was Tess who answered the door. The Dobermann was beside her and advanced to nose at Thanet's hand. With difficulty he prevented himself from flinching and managed to pat the dog's head. 'Good boy.'

Tess smiled. 'You see?' she said. 'I told you he'd remember you.' She looked a little better today, her eyes less bloodshot, the skin beneath less puffy.

Thanet smiled back. 'It's Mrs Mallis we've come to see.'

'She's in the kitchen.' Tess stood back to let them in.

'Thank you. We know the way.'

She nodded and turned back to the open door of the sitting room, where the television set was on. The dog's toenails clicked rhythmically on the parquet floor as he followed her.

Barbara Mallis was preparing the family's evening meal, a casserole by the look of it. She was cutting up stewing steak and dropping it into a large green Le Creuset pot. Bags of various root vegetables lay on the table. She was wearing a neat blue and white checked overall to protect her clothes and her hair was caught up into a French pleat. As usual she was carefully made up and sported a number of pieces of jewellery. In addition to earrings Thanet counted four rings and three gold necklaces of varying thicknesses and designs. He wondered how she managed to maintain her long varnished nails in such good condition.

She didn't look too pleased to see them but she invited them to sit down. 'You don't mind if I go on with this?'

'Not at all. You must spend quite a lot of time in here, with – how many? – six adults to cook for?'

'I do, yes.'

'Do you do all the cleaning too?'

'Oh no. A woman from the village comes in every day. I supervise her, do the food shopping and organise the running of the house in general. And cook, as you say.' She dropped the last batch of meat into the pot and set it on the hotplate of the Aga. It began to sizzle almost immediately and she reached across to switch on the extractor fan.

This was rather noisy and Thanet had to raise his voice. He regretted agreeing that she should continue with her preparations. 'You like the job?'

A shrug. 'It's all right.' She was stirring the meat vigorously with a wooden spoon to prevent it sticking.

How to put this tactfully? 'I imagine the Sylvesters are generous employers.'

She gave him a sharp look over her shoulder. 'I don't see that's any business of yours, Inspector.'

'I'm not sure whether it is or not.'

She removed the casserole from the heat, closed the hotplate lid and turned to face him, giving him her full attention for the first time. 'And just what, exactly, do you mean by that?'

So much for the softly softly approach. It had been naïve of him to imagine that he could approach the subject of money without putting her on the defensive. He would have had to come out into the open sooner or later and it was obviously sooner. 'How much, exactly, do you earn, Mrs Mallis?'

'I told you. I don't see that it's any of your bloody business!'

'Oh, but I'm afraid it is, Mrs Mallis. Whether you like it or not. You are living in a house where murder has been committed and –'

'You're not implying that *I* might have had anything to do with it?'

'We're keeping an open mind at the moment.'

'And what does that mean?'

'Just what I say. You were here, in the house, when Mr Jeopard died –'

'Along with about a hundred other people! Are you hounding them, too?'

'Hounding? Oh come, Mrs Mallis, don't you think that's an exaggeration?'

'No, I do not! You barge in here asking questions about my private affairs . . .'

'About your salary, specifically. Now why should that upset you so much, I wonder?'

She was silent for a moment, glaring at him. Then she said, 'I just don't see that it has anything to do with you.'

'But I disagree, I'm afraid.'

She said nothing, just waited, and he saw the muscles along her jawline ripple as she clenched her teeth.

'You see, he said, 'you present something of a mystery. And I'm afraid that we cannot afford to let mysteries go unsolved in a house where we're investigating a murder.'

Still no response.

'We couldn't help noticing, you see, that you seem to have rather an extravagant life-style for someone who lives on a housekeeper's salary. One has only to look at you to see that you spend considerable sums of money on your appearance . . .'

'I have no one else to spend it on,' she said between clenched teeth. She was containing her anger with difficulty, restraining herself only because she wanted to know exactly what cards were in his hand.

Thanet hoped the trump up his sleeve would catch her unprepared. 'Also, Sergeant Lineham and I were surprised to see how luxurious your flat is.'

'As you suggested, the Sylvesters are very generous employers,' she said. 'And they appreciate the service I give them. Ask them, they'll tell you! They just want to make sure I stay, that's all. So they provide me with a really nice flat. Big deal!'

'Then there's your car,' said Thanet. 'Sergeant Lineham is very interested in cars, aren't you, Sergeant? You noticed it right away.'

'I did,' said Lineham, nodding. 'Very nice, too.'

'But a BMW convertible?' said Thanet. 'How much does a BMW convertible cost, Sergeant, do you know?'

'I checked,' said Lineham. 'Around £26,000, for a K-reg. 325i in good condition, like Mrs Mallis's. Probably more, if it has certain extras.'

'Really? At least £26,000, then! As much as that! I

wonder how many housekeepers could afford to spend so much on a car?'

'There's always hire-purchase, of course,' said Lineham. Barbara Mallis opened her mouth, but before she could speak Lineham added, 'Something we could easily check.'

She shut it again.

'True,' said Thanet.

She really was furious at being driven into a corner like this. Her hands curled into claws at her sides as if she would like to fly at Thanet and scratch his eyes out. With a violent movement she folded her arms across her chest, as if to try and hold her anger in. 'If you must know,' she spat out, 'I bought that car with money I inherited from my father when he died a couple of years ago.'

Got you! thought Thanet. 'Really?' he said. 'How strange. I could have sworn that DC Martin said he'd actually spoken to – what was Mrs Mallis's father's name, Sergeant?'

'Waycom.'

'Yes, that's it. Waycom. An usual name, wouldn't you agree? Yes, I'm certain DC Martin said he was talking to him only yesterday. Er . . . Did you say something, ma'am?'

She had gone white, then red. 'How dare you!' she said. 'How dare you pry into my private life! You had no right!'

'Every right, I'm afraid,' said Thanet. 'And the sooner you understand that the better.' He leaned forward. 'Look, Mrs Mallis, I don't enjoy browbeating anyone . . .'

'You could have fooled me!'

'Well it's true. I don't. But sometimes I am driven to it. You must admit you're not exactly being cooperative. I'm not asking for details, just a general clarification of your financial position. All I want is the truth, pure and simple, then we'll leave you in peace.'

She stared at him, lips pressed together in a thin hard line. Would she give in?

Thanet doubted it. She had nothing to lose, perhaps everything to gain, by remaining silent.

Her eyes narrowed then suddenly she seemed to relax. She unfolded her arms and rested her hands lightly on the metal bar of the Aga behind her. Her lips curled in a malicious little smile. 'Then you'll have to go on wanting, won't you, Inspector. And there's not a thing you can do about it.'

She was wrong, of course, but at the moment Thanet did not feel justified in pursuing the matter further. If it became necessary, he would do so. So he contented himself with lifting his hands in apparent defeat. 'It's up to you.'

Back in the car Lineham said, 'She's got something to hide, no doubt about it.'

'I agree. I'm just surprised she reacted so strongly. I'd have thought she'd realise that would make us even more suspicious.'

'You caught her by suprise, I suppose.'

'Perhaps.'

Back at Headquarters they ran into Doc Mallard hurrying down the stairs. He looked harassed.

'Ah, there you are, Luke. I'm in a bit of a rush, I'm afraid. But I thought I'd just pop in to let you know the PM didn't come up with anything unexpected. Jeopard died of asphyxia, drowning if you like, not from the blow on the temple. I expect the diatom test to confirm that.'

'Remind me what that is.'

'Sorry, I really haven't got time to explain just now. Next time I see you, perhaps.'

209

'Don't worry, we'll look it up. Thanks for letting us know.'

'Not at all. 'Bye.' And he was gone.

'So,' said Lineham, 'it's as we thought. He must have been unconscious when he went into the water.'

'And someone just left him to drown,' said Thanet grimly.

In the office there was a note from DC Martin on his desk. 'Good, we've got an appointment with Dr Damon at 2.30 this afternoon, Mike.'

'Great.' But Lineham had only half heard him. He had gone straight to the bookshelves and was looking something up. 'I can't remember precisely what a diatom test is, either. Ah, here we are. "Diatoms . . . microscopic algae found in water . . . In drowning, they're sucked into the lungs and during the moments of struggling they enter the bloodstream . . . Presence in body tissues proves that victim was alive when entering the water." So, conversely., their absence presumably proves he wasn't.'

'Quite.' This murder may not have been premeditated but it had certainly been intentional. He said so, to Lineham.

'I agree, sir. So which of them d'you think could be sufficiently callous to stand by and watch him drown?'

'I don't know. I don't feel we're getting anywhere at the moment, Mike. We seem to be just casting around in the hope of finding a lead, and allowing ourselves to be sidetracked by Rosinha, when we should have been concentrating on the case.'

'We couldn't just ignore her situation, could we, sir?'

'I know, I know. But what have we done today, you tell me that. What exactly have we achieved?'

'Not a lot, I admit.'

'And where do we go next? Oh come on, Mike. Let's go to the canteen and have a bite to eat.'

'Perhaps we'll strike lucky with Carey's psychiatrist this afternoon,' said Lineham as they picked up their lunchtrays.

'Perhaps,' said Thanet.

But in the mood he was in, he doubted it.

EIGHTEEN

At the hospital Lineham set off along the seemingly endless corridors with confidence. His wife Louise was now once again a Ward Sister here, as she had been before their marriage. She loved her work and had found it very hard to give up during the years when Richard and Mandy were too young to go to school. She had stuck it out, however. She was a strong character, a woman of principle, and she believed that if you chose to have children you should be prepared to look after them during those early, formative years.

'I'd hate to put them with a childminder,' she'd once said to Thanet. 'I want them to learn to behave as Mike and I want them to, not how some stranger thinks they ought to. And I couldn't bear to think that someone else was instilling her values into them instead of mine. Especially these days, when moral standards generally are so low.'

Thanet agreed with her and said so, but wished she didn't always make him feel he was being preached at. 'Why are people like Louise, who invariably believe they're in the right, so wearing?' he'd said to Joan.

Joan had laughed. 'Because they usually are right?'

In any case, Thanet had always been thankful that it was Lineham who was married to Louise, not him.

'Mike! What are you doing here? You didn't tell me you had to come to the hospital.' Louise had emerged from a door as they were passing. She looked trim and efficient in her uniform, her dark hair neatly tucked away beneath her cap.

'Didn't know myself until this morning.'

'Where are you going?'

'The new psychiatric wing.'

Louise rolled her eyes. 'Very swish.'

They chatted for a moment or two before continuing on their way. Thanet was beginning to wonder if they would ever get there when Lineham pushed his way through swing doors and they entered a new and glossier world. Sturrenden General had been built in Victorian times and although it had been modernised over the years it was still rambling, inconvenient, and badly adapted to contemporary requirements. For years there had been talk of abandoning it and building a new hospital on the outskirts of the town but the prohibitive cost of doing so, allied to a vigorous Save Our Hospital campaign, had resulted in the status quo being maintained, with various concessions to changing policy. The building of the psychiatric wing had been one of them; the closure of the older mental hospitals and the release of former mental patients into care in the community had made some new provision for those who needed hospital care essential.

They had stepped into a circular foyer with a hexagonal dome of obscured glass and short corridors leading off it like the spokes of a wheel. Over the entrance to each of these was a name – Stour, Rother, Medway, Beult, Len; Kentish rivers, Thanet realised. Was there some deep psychological significance to the fact? In the centre was a round reception desk with a green and white striped

213

canopy suspended above it. The effect was cheerful without being over-stimulating – a carefully achieved balance, Thanet guessed.

The receptionist was young and pretty with glossy shoulder-length hair the colour of a ripe horse-chestnut. 'Ah, yes. He's expecting you. It's the third door on the left along Medway.'

Thanet's knock was answered at once.

'Come in.' The voice sounded weary.

And its owner looked it, thought Thanet as they entered.

Dr Damon and his room were in complete contrast. He was small, tired, and balding, whereas his surroundings were aggressively new and resplendent. Seated behind a huge mahogany desk in an executive-type black leather swivel chair with high back, he looked somehow diminished, as if the years of functioning in shabby outworn surroundings had left an indelible imprint upon him.

Introductions made, Thanet said, 'As you'll have gathered, this is about Carey Sylvester.'

'Yes.' Damon picked up a black ballpoint pen which lay on the file before him – Carey's file, Thanet presumed – and began to slide it through his fingers, turning it over again and again. 'I've been half-expecting you. But before we begin I must make several points clear. First, I want it understood that this discussion is entirely off the record.'

'Agreed.'

'And I also want your assurance that nothing I tell you today would be used in any future Court proceedings.' Damon laid the pen down on the desk blotter, carefully aligning it with the edge of the file.

'Understood.' Thanet could appreciate the psychiatrist's caution. He had seen enough expert witnesses put through the mill by able Counsel to appreciate why

Damon was being careful to spell out the ground rules for this interview. He himself was always very careful how any material which might subsequently be used in Court was obtained.

The telephone rang and Damon picked it up. 'Excuse me. Damon here. Sorry, no, not at the moment. Yes, as soon as I can.'

He replaced the receiver and folded his arms across his chest. 'Also, and I must make this clear although I'm sure you are already well aware of the fact, my main concern must be to safeguard my patient's privacy.'

'Yes. We appreciate that.'

'Good.' The psychiatrist unfolded his arms and sat back in his chair. 'In that case, I'll naturally do what I can to help. I assume I'm right in thinking this is about the murder on Saturday night at the Sylvesters' house?'

'Yes.'

'And you suspect that Carey is involved?'

'Not necessarily, no. He is only one of a number of suspects.'

'But I don't see how the question could arise. As I understand it, the Sylvesters employ a qualified nurse, full time, to look after Carey. I cannot, in fact, think of another single patient of mine who is so well cared for, out of hospital.'

Thanet explained how Carey had come to be wandering about. 'And unfortunately, it was just at the time of the murder.'

Damon tutted. 'What rotten luck.'

'Naturally, what we would really like is your professional opinion as to whether Carey would be capable of killing someone.' Thanet knew that there wasn't the slightest hope of getting it, but he had to ask.

'I'm sorry. You must see that I can't possibly give you an answer.'

'Would you, then, be prepared to tell us whether or not he has ever shown violent tendencies?' Another vain hope, Thanet knew.

'I'm sorry. Again, I can't help you there. What I can tell you is this: it is very difficult to make categorical statements about schizophrenics. The very nature of their illness renders them so unpredictable that it is virtually impossible to generalise.'

'Is there anything you can tell us, which might be of help?'

The telephone rang again and again Damon spoke into it briefly. Then he passed a hand over his bald head and looked thoughtfully at Thanet. 'Well, I can say this. If this murder you're investigating was premeditated you can rule Carey out. If schizophrenics commit murder it is almost invariably on impulse. That is one generalisation I can make. Usually it's because something, something which to us may seem completely irrational, triggers them off.'

'Have you any idea what that something might be, in Carey's case?' Once more there was little point in putting the question, but Thanet felt he had to.

Damon was shaking his head almost before Thanet had finished speaking. 'I can't answer that, I'm sorry.'

The telephone rang yet again. 'Damon here. Yes, I see. I'll come at once.' He was already rising. 'I'm sorry, Inspector. A minor crisis. I really must go.'

Outside Lineham said, 'Well, a fat lot of use that was.'

'I agree. All we learned really is that we can't rule Carey out and we knew that already. Still, at least the Super will be satisfied.'

But Thanet was wrong. Back at Headquarters they ran into Draco in the entrance hall.

'Ah, Thanet. Martin tells me you've been to see Carey Sylvester's psychiatrist. How did you get on?'

Thanet told him.

'And that's it? You couldn't get any more out of him than that?'

'He was being very careful, sir, covering himself in case it ever came to Court.'

'But doesn't the man realise that meanwhile we have a murderer running around loose, and it could be his precious patient?'

Thanet contented himself with a shrug. When Draco got on to his high horse there was little point in trying to present any other point of view.

'It's an absolute disgrace that in cases like this the police shouldn't have free access to information they consider relevant!' Draco stumped off along the corridor, irritation in every line of his body.

Back in his office Thanet found that somehow his hand had found its way into his pocket and emerged clutching his pipe. He looked at it wistfully. Gradually, over the years, forced by the strength of medical opinion, public disapproval of anyone who emitted clouds of smoke and, closer to home, Lineham's intense dislike of the habit, Thanet had managed to cut down on his smoking and now allowed himself the luxury of only one pipe a day, usually in the evening, after supper. But just occasionally, in times of stress or frustration, he still found himself lapsing.

He suspected that this was going to be one of those times.

Besides, he always thought best with a pipe in his mouth, especially if it was lit.

Lineham had noticed and was grinning. 'Going to give way to temptation, sir?'

'Why do I sometimes wish you didn't know me so well?'

'Oh go on, sir. Light up. Indulge yourself for once. I'll survive.' Lineham was already going through the routine they followed at such times, opening the window and propping the door ajar so as to create a through draught.

'Thanks, Mike.' Thanet fed tobacco into his pipe. 'Well, as I was saying earlier, we don't seem to be getting very far, do we?'

'Perhaps we ought to interview Carey again.'

Thanet shook his head. 'What's the point? You saw what he was like. He lives so much in a world of his own you can't be sure of the truth of anything he says. Even if he confessed I'd have serious doubts about it. No, as I see it, the only possible way in which we could be certain he was guilty would be if we found some material evidence to prove it.'

'Not much chance of that, is there!'

'Precisely. No, we'll just have to put Carey on the back burner for the moment, whether Draco likes it or not, and get on with examining all the other possibilities. Which at the moment means only one thing.' He struck a match and lit up, feeling a blissful sense of relaxation steal through his veins. All right, he told himself defiantly. So I'm addicted. As long as I keep the habit under control, as I usually do, what's the harm?

'Reports?'

Thanet nodded. 'Reports.' When there was much to do and many leads to follow it was only too easy to overlook some detail which at the time may have appeared unimportant but which in the light of subsequent knowledge proved otherwise. Although neither of them enjoyed the process, experience had taught them the value of constant reassessment so they now settled down to read their way steadily through the material which had come in so far. From time to time they would comment, discuss, but for the most part they just read, absorbed, immersing themselves in the case.

It was when Thanet was scanning his own report on the interview with the Sylvesters on Sunday morning that he remembered something which had puzzled him at the time. 'Mike?'

'Mmm?' Lineham was deep in a report.

'I've been meaning to mention it. When Mrs Sylvester was filling us in on the background of Max and Tess and the others, did you notice anything odd when she was talking about the time when Max came back for the publication of his book?'

Lineham was frowning. 'I don't know. I don't think so. Oh, hang on a minute. It's coming back to me now. Yes, now you mention it, I did. She sort of dried up, didn't she?'

'Yes. I wondered why, at the time. I think it must have been something she remembered, something she didn't like remembering. I wonder what. Of course, it might not be relevant to the case.'

'But there again, it might,' said Lineham.

They stared at each other, thinking.

'Which year was that?' said Lineham. 'When Jeopard's book was published?'

'Nineteen ninety-two. In May, I think Mrs Sylvester said.'

'And Mrs Mallis started work there in '91. When did they get Roper in to look after Carey? We know it was some time later because she was talking about what it was like before Roper arrived.' Lineham began shuffling through the reports. 'Ah, here we are.'

'What are you getting at, Mike?'

'Just that I wondered if what Mrs Sylvester was remembering might be connected with the blackmail.'

'You mean, if Mrs Sylvester was having an affair with Roper, it might have been around the time of Max's book being published that Mrs Mallis saw whatever it is that's given her a hold over her?'

'Could be . . .' Lineham was still perusing a report. 'No. That's no good. According to Martin, Roper didn't start work at the Sylvesters' until the autumn of '92.'

'Unless . . .' said Thanet slowly. A new and bizarre idea had suddenly struck him.

'Unless what?'

'It's just occurred to me. Say we're right about the blackmail, wrong about the reason.'

'Well?'

'Just think, Mike. Look at the facts.' Thanet began to tick them off on his fingers. 'Everyone's been telling us that Jeopard is not only attracted by women, but also attractive to women. As his agent said, "Put Max in a room with a woman and he couldn't help making a pass at her." What if –?'

'Mrs Sylvester!' said Lineham, suddenly seeing what Thanet was getting at. 'Yes! Could be! I mean, she's a good-looking woman if you like that type, and she's in pretty good shape for her age. And Tess was away at the time, so when Max came looking for her as Mrs Sylvester said he always did . . . You could be right, sir! And if Mrs Mallis saw them together, now that really would give her a hold over Mrs Sylvester! I mean, just think how Sylvester would feel, if he knew! He can't stand the man and not only his daughter but his wife succumbs to him!'

'Exactly, Mike. And if he found *that* out . . .'

'Some motive!'

But now Thanet was shaking his head. 'No. It's a bit far-fetched, don't you think?'

'Oh come on, sir, think of some of the things we've seen in the past. In comparison with them this is positively run-of-the mill!'

'I suppose so. The trouble is, how do we prove it?' It would be difficult if not impossible to worm such information out of any of the people involved, but Thanet knew he had to try and he was already on his feet.

'Back to the Sylvesters'?' said Lineham.

Thanet nodded. 'Back to the Sylvesters'.'

NINETEEN

This time it was Barbara Mallis who opened the door. 'Oh no, not you again!' she said.

'Relax,' said Thanet. 'It's Mrs Sylvester we've come to see this time. Is she in?'

'Just got back.'

'And Mr Sylvester?' It was only 4.45 and Thanet was hoping Sylvester would still be at work. It would be impossible to interview Mrs Sylvester on such a delicate topic with her husband present.

'He's not home yet.'

Barbara Mallis led them to the sitting-room door, tapped and stuck her head in. 'Police,' she said.

Thanet and Lineham exchanged glances. The house-keeper's lack of respect for her employer verged on insolence. If she really was blackmailing Mrs Sylvester, thought Thanet, nothing would give him greater pleasure than to see she got her just deserts.

In the sitting room the glow of a coal-effect gas fire imparted an atmosphere of cosiness to the scene. Marion Sylvester and Tess were sitting companionably together over afternoon tea – the sort of tea one rarely came across these days, Thanet noted. A splendid fruit cake with one slice cut out of it took pride of place and there were plates of sandwiches, too, and scones, jam, cream. If Tess and her mother indulged themselves in this way every day he was surprised they weren't both grossly overweight. Perhaps, in the present circumstances, it was a classic case of eating for comfort. He averted his eyes from all the goodies as his mouth began to water.

Mrs Sylvester had obviously been shopping, cheering herself up as women often do by going out to buy herself something new. There were several carrier bags lying about and she had been showing Tess her purchases – a brightly coloured skirt and jacket were draped over one end of the sofa and on the floor two pairs of shoes nestled in tissue paper in opened boxes. The faces she and Tess turned towards the two policemen were full of weary resignation.

'Would you like a cup?' said Tess, getting up with a marked lack of enthusiasm. 'I can easily make a fresh pot.'

Thanet shook his head reluctantly. He made it a rule never to accept such an offer grudgingly made. 'We'd like a word with Mrs Sylvester if we may.'

Tess looked at her mother, who nodded. 'Off you go, lovey.'

'You're sure?'

'Quite sure. Really. Take these up for me, will you?' Marion Sylvester put the lids back on the shoeboxes and scooped them up, thrusting them into Tess's arms. Then she draped the skirt and jacket on top. 'Thanks.'

'She's looking a little better today,' Thanet said, when Tess had gone.

Marion grimaced. 'She's putting a brave face on it. But I don't think she'll ever get over it, not properly. I'm afraid poor Gerald was always second best. Do sit down, for heaven's sake. I can't stand people looming over me.'

On the way over Thanet had given some thought as to the best way to broach the subject, but had come to no satisfactory conclusion. It was, whichever way you looked at it, going to be a tricky interview and he had finally decided to play it by ear.

'Mrs Sylvester,' he began, 'you will appreciate that during the course of a murder investigation we come across all sorts of things which may or may not be relevant. Some of them are, shall we say, delicate matters, and we have to look into them because we have to make up our minds whether they are or not. Relevant, that is.'

She was already looking wary. Today she was wearing cornflower blue leggings and matching sweatshirt exactly the colour of her eyes. Her figure was good and if only she didn't wear such heavy make-up she would, as Lineham had said, be an attractive woman. Thanet could understand why a womaniser like Max might have made a play for her. But she was waiting. He must press on. 'I do want to make it clear that if anything . . . private is uncovered, and proves to have nothing to do with the investigation, it will remain absolutely confidential.'

'I don't see what you're getting at, Inspector.'

But her body was betraying her. Her legs were crossed and the foot which was suspended in mid-air had begun to twitch. Thanet knew that extremities are often less controllable than facial muscles.

He persevered. 'There are two things we couldn't help noticing about your housekeeper.'

'Mrs Mallis?' Her voice was shrill and she must have realised it. Her next words were consciously in a lower register. 'What's she got to do with it? Really, Inspector, I haven't a clue what you're going on about.'

'The first,' said Thanet, ignoring the interruption, 'is that she does appear to be remarkably affluent for someone in her situation. Her car, for instance, is a much more expensive model than you'd expect a housekeeper to run.'

'I don't see what it's got to do with me, if my house-keeper chooses to spend all her money on a BMW.'

'It's puzzling to know how she can afford it.'

'If you must know,' said Marion, 'though frankly I can't see that it's any of your business, she bought it with some money she inherited.'

'From . . . ?'

'From her father, dammit! Do you always go about poking and prying into people's private affairs like this?'

'Only if we feel it necessary, Mrs Sylvester. As we do, I'm afraid, in this case. So that's what she told you, is it? That she inherited the money from her father?'

'Yes.' The monosyllable was over-emphatic. There was defiance in it, and a hint of fear, too, as if she could foresee what was coming.

'Well, I'm afraid you have been grossly misled. Mrs Mallis's father is very much alive, and living in the East End – in a council flat off the Old Kent Road, if I remember rightly. That's correct, isn't it, Sergeant?'

Lineham nodded. 'He's a retired bus driver, ma'am.'

'So you see, even if he had died, which he hasn't, it doesn't sound as though he'd be in a position to leave his daughter enough money to buy a BMW.'

Marion Sylvester lifted her shoulders. 'So she got the money somewhere else. I didn't enquire further. Perhaps she won it on the pools.'

'Then why not say so?'

'How should I know?' Her voice was raised, her self-control slipping. 'If she chooses to tell lies about it, that's nothing to do with me!'

'Isn't it?' said Thanet softly.

She opened her mouth to challenge him, but she didn't dare. He guessed she was too afraid of the answer. She stared at him. He could see in her eyes what she was thinking. *He knows*, she was thinking. *He knows.*

The certainty that he was right about all this was growing all the time. But he had to get her to admit it. As he had said to Barbara Mallis earlier, he didn't enjoy browbeating anybody, but this could be crucial to the case.

'You see, the second thing which we couldn't help noticing about your housekeeper was her manner towards you, her employer. It verges on insolence, especially when she thinks she is unobserved.'

Marion jumped up. 'Sorry, but I've had just about enough of this. I don't see why I should have to put up with being interrogated in my own house. Would you please leave. Now.'

Thanet stood up. 'By all means, Mrs Sylvester. But if we do, I'm afraid I shall have to insist that you accompany us to the police station for further questioning.'

She stared at him, her look of desperation heightening the sympathy he already felt for her.

'Look,' he said gently. 'You must accept that one way or another we have to talk about this. Why don't we try to discuss it calmly? Please, sit down again, won't you?'

The flash of defiance had evaporated and her shoulders sagged in defeat as she returned slowly to her chair.

Now was the time to bring matters out into the open. 'She's blackmailing you, isn't she?'

Marion's lips tightened and her hands clenched together.

Please, let her admit it, thought Thanet.

Then, at last, when he had almost decided she was

going to persist in her denials, she took in a deep breath as if inhaling courage and gave a reluctant nod.

'Threatening to tell your husband if you didn't pay up?'

Another nod.

'And this has been going on since the May of '92?'

He saw the flash of astonishment in her eyes, that he should know so much. 'How . . . How did you find out?'

'I assume it happened when Max came looking for Tess, as he always did? She was away, wasn't she?'

'Stupid!' she whispered, shaking her head in dismay and disbelief at her own weakness, foolishness. Her voice grew louder. 'I was so stupid!' She beat one clenched fist against the palm of the other. 'Stupid, stupid, stupid! One stupid mistake, and God, how I've been paying for it ever since! It was only once, you see. He caught me at the wrong moment. I'd . . . Oh, what's the point of making excuses. It happened. And I've never been allowed to forget it, not for a single day.'

'I assume Mrs Mallis has some kind of proof with which to back up her story, should it ever come to that? What is it?'

'Another idiotic mistake,' Marion said bitterly. 'I wrote to Max, telling him it must never happen again. I was so ashamed. My husband . . . I love my husband, Inspector, I really do. He's a good man. I wouldn't hurt him for anything. And Tess . . . Oh God, there was Tess, too. She'd never forgive me. So I wrote. It was just a note, very brief, but it was difficult to write and I had several goes before I was satisfied. If only I'd burned my first attempts! Another unbelievably stupid mistake, a real catalogue of them, isn't it? But I just tore the rough drafts up and threw them in the wastepaper basket. I knew Ralph would never dream of going through my waste paper and piecing together stuff I'd thrown away and it was him I was thinking of, he was the one I didn't want to see them. I never thought of her. How naïve can you get? Oh God, this won't have to come out, will it, Inspector? You did mean what you said, about it being in confidence if it wasn't connected with the case?'

'Yes, I did.' Thanet didn't have the heart even to hint that her confession had just doubled her husband's possible motive for Jeopard's murder. But he had to prepare her in some way. 'But if it's your husband finding out that you're worried about, I think I ought to warn you . . . You remember the other day, when you were in the hall? Mrs Mallis was going out and you called after her, to ask her to pick something up?'

She nodded, afraid of what was coming.

'We were on the landing and saw what happened. You didn't realise but your husband, thinking that you were calling him, perhaps, came to the sitting-room doorway. He heard the way she spoke to you. I could see the look on his face.'

Still she said nothing, but a horrified awareness crept into her expression as she understood the significance of what Thanet was telling her.

'Yes,' he said. 'I think he knows – or at least suspects. Not the details, perhaps, but in principle.'

As he watched, tears welled up in her eyes and spilled over, running down her cheeks unheeded. 'No,' she whispered, shaking her head. 'No. You're wrong.'

'I don't think so.'

'He would have said. He would have told me.'

'Would he?' said Thanet. 'Are you sure that, like you, he didn't simply prefer to pretend it wasn't happening?'

She buried her head in her hands. 'Oh God,' she sobbed. 'What'll I do? What'll I do?'

Suddenly the door opened and Sylvester burst into the room, rushed to his wife, dropped to his knees beside her and gathered her protectively into his arms. 'It's all right, darl,' he murmured. 'It's all right. Ralphie's here now. Hush, it's all right.' He ignored the two policemen completely.

Tess must have left the door ajar, Thanet realised, burdened as she had been with her mother's purchases, and Sylvester must have been listening outside. Engrossed in the interview Thanet hadn't heard him arrive and wondered how long he had been there. Long enough for his chief emotion to be concern for his wife rather than anger that Thanet appeared to have reduced her to tears, anyway.

Lineham raised his eyebrows at Thanet and jerked his head towards the door.

Thanet shook his head. His instinct too was to leave the Sylvesters alone for a while, give them some space and privacy, but he couldn't afford to.

Now, if ever, could be the moment for the truth to come out.

TWENTY

Marion Sylvester's sobs gradually diminished and her husband fished a handkerchief out of his pocket and pushed it into her hand. Without raising her head to look at him she eased herself away a little, wiped her eyes, and blew her nose. Finally, still without meeting his gaze, she whispered, 'You heard?'

Sylvester nodded, his face grim. 'The bastard! I could – ' Awareness of what he had almost said pulled him up short and he looked uneasily at Thanet.

'And did you?' said Thanet. 'Kill him?'

'No!'

'But you knew there was something wrong between your wife and Mrs Mallis. We could tell, the other day.' And Thanet explained what they had seen.

Sylvester stood up and taking his wife gently by the hands tugged her out of her chair to sit beside him on the sofa. There he put his arm around her and she leaned into his shoulder, drawing comfort from his proximity. Her mascara was smudged, her face tear-stained, her eyelids swollen with crying and she looked subdued, but it was obviously an immense relief to her to know that her husband knew the truth and had apparently forgiven her. If Sylvester had heard her admission of what had happened between her and Max, Thanet realised, he had also heard her declaration of love for her husband, and it was obvious which mattered to him most. It was equally obvious that she still hadn't perceived the new danger in which her admission had put him.

'Something wrong, yes,' said Sylvester. 'But I didn't know what, until a few minutes ago.' He squeezed his wife's hand and gave her a loving look. 'You should have told me, darl,' he said. 'Putting yourself through all that for nothing.'

Now, for the first time, she met his gaze squarely and returned his look of affection with a tremulous smile. 'I couldn't,' she said. 'I was afraid you'd . . .'

'What? Beat you or something? Not my style, darl, you know that.'

'No, that you'd leave me,' she said.

'Leave you? You can't get rid of me as easily as that, you ought to know that by now!'

She smiled again, shook her head.

'We've only got your word for it,' said Thanet, 'that you didn't know until a few moments ago.'

'Well, you're never going to prove otherwise, are you? You couldn't, anyway, because it's true.'

'Even if it is, you must see that you are still are a prime suspect.'

'What?' cried Marion. 'Ralph is? You can't be serious!'

'Oh, but I am,' said Thanet. 'Just think about it for a moment. To begin with, you didn't like Jeopard, did you, Mr Sylvester, and you especially didn't like the way he kept messing your daughter about, blowing hot and cold so that she never knew where she was with him. Also, I believe you genuinely thought she would be unhappy with him. You suspected he'd be unfaithful to her, cause her a lot of heartache, and you couldn't bear the prospect of that. No, you much preferred the idea of having Gerald Argent as a prospective son-in-law, didn't you, and so did you, Mrs Sylvester. That was obvious, from the way you both tried to keep him out of our discussion the other day. He's so much more suitable in every way, isn't he – a nice, steady sort of bloke with a good, respectable job, and if Tess had married him she would have continued to live locally, you'd have seen a lot of her and have been able to watch your grandchildren grow up. Jeopard, on the other hand, was going to whisk her off to London where you'd hardly ever see her and, worse, would more than likely sometimes take her off on those long trips of his. She would, in short, to a greater or lesser extent be lost to you and you hated the idea of that, especially as your son, in his own way, tragically already is.

'So it seems to me quite possible that when Tess finally succumbed to his blandishments once more, broke off her engagement to Gerald and agreed to marry Max instead – and seemed so eager to do so that she was even prepared to utilise all the wedding arrangements you had already made instead of delaying matters by having to start all over again – you decided the time had come to act. I'm not saying you actually *planned* to kill him. Perhaps you thought it would be worth trying to buy him off, as so many men have done before you when confronted with unsuitable suitors for their daughters . . .' And yes, that shaft had found its mark, Thanet could tell. Was this, in fact, what had happened? Had Sylvester tried a bribe, and failed, lost his temper and shoved Jeopard in the pool instead? 'I'm right, aren't I?'

'What if you are?' said Sylvester. 'Right about trying to buy him off, that is. But wrong about everything else.'

'You didn't tell me you'd offered him money, Ralph.'

Sylvester patted her hand. 'No need for you to know, darl, was there? And we must make sure Tess never finds out, either. She'd never forgive me.'

'How could she find out? I'm certainly not about to tell her.'

'What do you mean, wrong about everything else?' said Thanet.

'I tried offering him a nice fat bribe over a week ago, the day after Tess told me she was going to marry him instead of Gerald. Met him in town, gave him a slap-up lunch. Offered him a hundred thou.'

Thanet saw Lineham's lips pursed in a soundless whistle.

'But it wasn't enough,' said Sylvester bitterly.

'He refused?'

'He knew which side his bread was buttered. I'm a wealthy man, Inspector. He could see that the long-term benefits would outweigh anything I offered him now. Travel writer! What sort of job is that? Money coming in in dribs and drabs and never a secure income from one year to the next! Oh no, he knew that if he married Tess I'd never see her go short, he'd have a meal ticket for life. Of course he refused.'

'Nevertheless,' said Thanet, 'you must see that all this builds up into a strong case against you.'

'Then all I can say, Inspector, as I said before, is prove it. And you never will. Not ever. Because it didn't happen.'

Thanet could see he wasn't going to get anywhere. He stood up.

'Hang on, not so fast,' said Sylvester.

Thanet raised his eyebrows.

'Before you go, we've got some unfinished business to deal with.'

233

'What?' said Marion.

'That woman upstairs, that's what.' Sylvester sounded savage. He stood up.

His wife clutched at his trouser leg. 'What are you going to do?'

'See she gets what she deserves, of course.'

'What do you mean exactly, Ralph?'

'Well, first I'm going to make damn sure she knows it's all out in the open now and there's no point in her trying to put anything over on you ever again, and then I'm going to tell her, with the Inspector and the Sergeant as witnesses, that we're going to take great pleasure in prosecuting her. We have got grounds, haven't we, Inspector?'

Thanet nodded. 'No doubt about that. I assume you have records of the payments you've made, somewhere, Mrs Sylvester?'

'Yes. But I don't want to! Bring it to Court, I mean.'

'Why not?' Sylvester sat down beside her again with a thump. 'You can't mean that, surely, darl, not after all she's put you through!'

'But that's just the point, don't you see? I've had enough, I really have. And to think of it all coming out in Court . . .' She shuddered. 'I couldn't bear it. I really couldn't.'

'It would all be done very discreetly, Mrs Sylvester,' said Thanet. 'In cases of blackmail we take great trouble to protect the victim, otherwise nobody would ever bring a prosecution.'

'No! All I want to do now is put it behind me! Please, Ralph. And have you thought what it would do to Tess? If it went to Court, there's no way we could keep it from her.'

Sylvester smote his forehead. 'Idiot! Damn and blast, I

hadn't thought of that! You're right, darl, of course you are. OK. If that's the way you want it, then that's the way it'll be. But you do agree that she'll have to go out on her ear, don't you? Now? Today?'

Marion nodded.

'Then humour me in this. It goes against the grain to let her off so lightly, and I'd like to put the frighteners on her, make her realise that she's only getting off by the skin of her teeth. So I want to confront her with it now, in front of the police.'

'OK, Ralph. It's up to you.'

'You're happy about that?' He gave her a searching look. She nodded again.

'Right. And you don't mind waiting, Inspector?'

'Not in the least. Quite the contrary, in fact.'

'Good.' Sylvester jumped up and marched purposefully to the door. 'Mrs Mallis?' he bellowed.

Thanet had noticed a large handbell on the table in the hall near the telephone and Sylvester went out and rang it vigorously. 'Mrs Mallis!' he shouted again. Then, more quietly, 'It's all right, Roper, there's nothing wrong. Sorry to have disturbed you.'

Roper had obviously come out on to the landing to see what all the noise was about.

Sylvester came back into the room. 'She's coming,' he said.

A moment later Barbara Mallis entered and stood just inside the door, hands folded meekly in front of her, the picture of an obedient servant. 'You rang?' she said sweetly, sarcastically. Sylvester had rung the bell so loudly it had probably been heard by the Fieldings down by the front gate.

'I certainly did.' Sylvester had taken up a stance on the hearthrug, hands clasped behind his back, chin down.

235

There was a pent-up ferocity in him, as if he were restraining himself with difficulty. He reminded Thanet of a bull about to charge and that made him wonder: had this latent violence erupted during an encounter with Max on Saturday night?

Now that she had had time to absorb the atmosphere in the room Barbara Mallis obviously sensed the tension and hostility. Her eyes flickered from Sylvester, to his wife, to Thanet, to Lineham and back to Sylvester again. She shifted uneasily and subtly her attitude underwent a change. Her eyes became guarded and she frowned. 'Why? What's the matter?'

'How you have the nerve to stand there and ask me that, I simply do not know!' said Sylvester. 'What the bloody hell do you think is the matter?'

Her aggression flared up in response to his. 'How should I know?'

'Blackmail, that's what's the matter! It's been going on for years, I gather.'

Barbara Mallis shot Marion a look of pure venom. 'I don't know what you're talking about.'

'Oh,' breathed Marion. 'You wicked woman. You really are a wicked, wicked woman.'

'It's interesting,' said Thanet, 'that only a short time ago Sergeant Lineham and I were querying the fact that you seemed to have so much money to throw around. Now we know where you got it from, don't we? You do realise, of course, that blackmail is a criminal offence?'

Barbara Mallis gave Marion another vicious look. 'Amazing what stories some people will dream up to make themselves the centre of attention,' she said, obviously deciding that whatever happened there would be no future for her in the Sylvester household. 'Especially bored middle-aged housewives without enough to do.'

'How dare you!' shouted Sylvester. 'I won't have you insulting my wife like that!'

Marion stood up alongside him and put a restraining hand on his arm. 'Shh, Ralph. Don't let her get to you.' She looked at the housekeeper and lifted her chin. 'Middle-aged I may be, but at least my story can be backed up by proof.'

'Proof? What proof? I always ...' Barbara Mallis's mouth closed like a trap over the dangerous words which had almost escaped her lips.

'You always what, Mrs Mallis?' said Thanet politely. 'Always insisted on payment in cash? Is that what you were about to say?' He glanced at Marion Sylvester for confirmation.

She nodded. 'But I kept a record. Always.'

Barbara Mallis's lips tightened.

'And of course,' said Lineham, unable to resist joining in, 'we can always check your bank statements. Unless you actually kept the money under your mattress or in the wardrobe – where we'd still find some of it, I imagine – you must have paid at least some of it into the bank.'

She said nothing, but the shaft had gone home. The muscles along her jawline bulged as her teeth clenched. Then, unexpectedly, she laughed, an unpleasant, jeering sound. 'Haven't you forgotten something?'

'What?' said Sylvester.

'Your precious daughter. Tess. Have you told her, too? No. I can see you haven't. Such a pity if she were to find out, wouldn't it be?'

'Right!' said Sylvester. 'That's it!' He turned to his wife. 'We've got to do it!'

Marion shook her head. 'No.'

'But, darl ...'

237

'No!' She looked at Barbara Mallis. 'I think you ought to know that we *had* decided not to prosecute.'

The housekeeper's eyes narrowed.

'Partly,' said Marion, 'because I was too much of a coward to face all this coming out in Court. But also because if it did there would be no way to prevent Tess from knowing. And she's been hurt enough. So let me tell you this. If you breathe so much as one word – no, even drop the merest, slightest hint to Tess, then I shan't hesitate to go ahead and take you to Court, however difficult I may find it. That I promise you.'

'I second that,' said Sylvester. 'And meanwhile, you can pack your bags and get out of our house. I give you one hour, no more.'

Barbara Mallis smiled. 'My contract says one month's notice. Or pay in lieu of.'

'Don't push me,' said Sylvester between clenched teeth. 'One hour. And count yourself lucky.'

She shrugged. 'Ah well, it was worth a try.' And she walked jauntily out of the room.

'What a poisonous woman!' said Lineham, expressing the feelings of all present.

'Good riddance!' said Marion. 'Oh Ralph, it's such a relief, I can't tell you! I'd never have believed that something good could come out of all this!'

'We're not out of the woods yet, darl,' said Sylvester grimly. 'Remember what the Inspector said. Somehow we've got to prove I wasn't involved in what happened to Max.'

'We will.' Marion smiled radiantly up at him. 'It'll be all right, you'll see.'

Back in the car Thanet said, 'I wish I shared her confidence. For my money, Sylvester is still at the top of the list. But it's difficult to see where to go from here.

Tell you what. The team working on the suspects' alibi checks should be finished by now. If the reports are all in perhaps it's time that we had a session putting them under a microscope.'

'But DC Penry is doing all that on the computer. It's ideal for that sort of job.'

'All right. So we'll talk to Penry, see if he's come up with anything.'

'And if he hasn't?'

'We'll see.'

Lineham groaned. 'I know what that means. And there was I thinking that was it for today, I could go home and put my feet up.'

'Come on Mike, that's not like you, where's your enthusiasm, your dedication! Personally I know I won't rest tonight until I feel satisfied that we've been over all the ground we've covered so far and haven't missed anything.'

Back at the office DC Penry was unequivocal. 'I've just finished, sir. Every piece of information with reference to the alibis is now on file. It's all collated and I've asked the computer every possible question I can think of, without positive results.'

'I wish you wouldn't talk about that machine as if it were a person,' said Thanet. The next generation of policemen would no doubt take computers for granted but personally he didn't like them, never had and never would. He conceded that they could be useful in certain cases but their major disadvantage in his view was that they were only as efficient as the person who operated them; if you didn't ask the right question you wouldn't get the right answer.

'Come on, Mike,' he said now. 'Let's see what the human computers can do.'

239

Lineham rolled his eyes at Penry but followed Thanet up to the office.

'Right,' said Thanet. 'I'll take Hartley, Gerald and Anthea, as they were together around supper time, and you take the Sylvesters.'

'Including Tess?'

'Including Tess. Just in case she'd had enough of his flirting and decided to have it out with him.'

'And left him to drown?'

'Mike, just get on with it, will you? And remember, we're looking for discrepancies, no matter how small, no matter how apparently unimportant.'

They settled down to work. Bentley and his team had done an excellent job, thought Thanet. He had been the perfect choice for the job. Patient, thorough, painstaking, he had made sure that all witnesses had been interviewed, even if one of his team had had to go back several times to catch them in. The reports had then all been assembled in logical order.

First came the statement of the suspects. Some time had obviously been spent with each of them, dredging through his or her memory. Checking quickly, Thanet counted that Anthea claimed to have seen or spoken to twenty-six people who might have remembered seeing her on her way to, in or on her way back from the upstairs bathroom which had been made available to female guests. Hartley had come up with eighteen names and Gerald, who had remained behind in the queue and then returned to their table, with fifteen. On each suspect's statement these names had been listed in the claimed chronological order, with approximate times beside each one.

The witnesses' statements had then also been assembled in the same chronological order. Some of them remembered seeing or speaking to Anthea/Hartley/Gerald at the times they claimed, some did not, but then that was scarcely surprising; there were a lot of people milling about and just because someone didn't happen to have noticed you at the same time as you noticed them, it didn't mean you weren't there. Anthea had actually been separated from the other two longest, Thanet noted, having left them at 9.40 and returned about 10, but again this was not unduly surprising; women always tended to take a long time in the bathroom, presumably because they were seizing the opportunity to comb their hair or repair their make-up. Hartley had been away for between ten and fifteen minutes, having left just after Anthea and returned five minutes before her – a period therefore during which both he and Gerald would theoretically have had the opportunity to slip along to the pool house. Amongst those who backed up their statements were Barbara Mallis, who had seen Anthea coming down the stairs; Fielding, who had been looking for Carey at the time but had noticed Hartley coming out of the dining room; and Marion Sylvester and Jeopard's aunt, Louisa Burke, who had noticed Gerald returning to his table just before Hartley (Gerald claimed to have been chatting in the queue for ten minutes, but the witnesses interviewed about this were vague about the length of time they had had to wait to collect their plates of food).

Thanet sat back and sighed.

Lineham looked up. 'You haven't found anything, sir?'

Thanet shook his head. 'Have you?'

'Not a thing.'

'The big problem is the timing, isn't it. We're talking about such a short period, only twenty minutes at the most, and practically everyone says they couldn't be sure of the exact time. Why should they, after all? It was a party, no one was clock-watching. Most of them relate what they did or who they spoke to to certain events.' Thanet shuffled through the statements, picking out phrases and reading them aloud: ' "After we were told supper was ready"; "Before I collected the first course"; "Not long before Ralph asked me if I'd seen Max"; "After I'd been to the loo".' He tossed the papers on to his desk in disgust.

'I know. Bentley's done his best but this chronological order is pretty useless really. Most of it is according to what the suspects have told us.'

Thanet shuffled the reports together. 'Right,' he said. 'That's it for tonight. I don't know about you, but my brain feels as though it's stuffed with cotton wool. Let's sleep on it.'

If we can, he thought gloomily as he drove home.

Matters improved, however, when he got there. Joan came to greet him, all smiles.

'You look cheerful,' he said, giving her a half-hearted kiss.

'Which is more than could be said of you. Case not going well?'

Thanet sighed and shook his head.

'Well, this'll make you feel better. Ben's decided to go to university! He's putting Bristol as his first choice.'

'Good! Excellent!' Joan was right. The news had lifted his spirits. 'Is he in?'

'No. Come on, have something to eat. That'll cheer you up even more.'

And once again she was right. By the time he'd consumed beef casserole with dumplings and settled down to watch television with his pipe drawing well, he was feeling a new man. Forget the case, he told himself. Tomorrow is another day.

It was an effort but he managed it, sitting mindlessly

through a documentary about AIDS in the Far East, followed by a play which was so boring he fell asleep.

It wasn't until he was getting into bed that he realised: as so often happened, while his conscious mind was switched off his subconscious had been working away regardless. The conviction sprang into his brain full-blown: some time today he had read, seen, heard something which he should have picked up and hadn't.

'What's the matter?' said Joan, noticing his sudden immobility.

He shook his head as if to clear it. 'I'm not sure.'

'You're feeling all right?' she said, in alarm.

'Yes, yes, I'm fine. But I've just realised that I've missed something.'

'What?'

'If I only knew!'

'Sleep on it,' said Joan. 'You've often said it's the best way.'

'Easier said than done.'

'In that case . . .' she said, rolling over to face him, putting her arms around him and lifting her face to his kiss.

Thanet wasn't going to argue with that. He responded with enthusiasm.

TWENTY-ONE

After their lovemaking Thanet went out like a light and didn't wake up until the alarm went off next morning. He was in the bathroom shaving when it hit him. Of course! That was what had been bothering him last night!

The revelation had unsteadied his hand and a bright red globule of blood oozed out where he had nicked his chin. Automatically he dabbed at it with a tissue and reached for his styptic stick, his mind busy with this new discovery. Could it have any significance? The more he thought about it the more his initial excitement faded. It was probably a genuine mistake on the part of the witness and even if it wasn't, it was difficult to see its relevance. Still, it was precisely the type of discrepancy he and Lineham had been looking for last night, and as such would have to be followed up.

Of course, his memory could be playing tricks on him and he might not be remembering the statement accurately. Anxious to get to the office and find out, he speeded up his early-morning routine. He was eating a piece of toast standing up when Joan came into the kitchen. She glanced at the bare table. 'No breakfast?'

Because he never knew whether or when he would get

lunch Thanet invariably ate a good breakfast. In the early days of their marriage it had been cornflakes followed by bacon and egg, white toast, butter and marmalade. Only the marmalade had survived Joan's campaign for healthy eating, the rest having gradually been replaced by bran flakes or muesli mixed with fresh or stewed fruit and yoghurt, followed by wholemeal toast and polyunsaturated margarine. Bacon and egg were now saved as a rare treat for high days and holidays.

He shook his head. 'Something I want to check.' He kissed her, shoved the last piece of toast into his mouth and left.

He arrived at work before Lineham and was riffling through the reports, looking for the statement he wanted, when the sergeant arrived.

'Morning sir. What's up?' said Lineham, registering Thanet's air of purpose.

'Remembered something this morning, and I just want to check. Ah, here it is.' Thanet began to read. A moment later he stabbed triumphantly at the paper with his forefinger. 'I thought so. Look.' He turned the statement around and passed it across to Lineham. 'Read that.'

Lineham did so. And read it again. Then he looked up, puzzled. 'So?'

Thanet leaned back in his chair. 'I'm glad you missed it too. I was beginning to think I was slipping. But before I went to bed last night I began to think there was something I'd overlooked – you know, you just get that feeling sometimes. Then this morning I realised what it was.'

'I wish I knew what you were talking about.' Lineham glanced down at the paper he was holding. 'I still can't see that there's anything to get excited about here.'

'Well, I agree that there may be nothing in it. It could

245

just be a slip of the tongue. Or perhaps a misunderstanding on Bentley's part.'

'Sir!' Lineham put the paper down and folded his arms belligerently. 'If you don't tell me what you're going on about . . .'

'All right, all right.' Thanet picked up the sheet of paper. 'This is one of the statements taken to check Hartley's alibi, right?'

'Yes. Fielding's.'

'Quite. Now if you remember, Hartley says he was on his way out of the dining room when he saw Fielding.'

'Yes. Fielding was in the house looking for Carey . . . Oh.' Lineham stopped.

'Ah. You've got it.'

'Yes, I think so. It's the timing, isn't it? Fielding confirms what Hartley says. But Hartley claims to have left the dining room to go to the loo immediately after Anthea, at twenty to ten. And he was back in the dining room getting his supper, as I recall, by five to ten. Whereas it wasn't until five to ten that Roper went down to Fielding's bungalow to ask him to help look for Carey. So . . .'

'Exactly. What was Fielding doing in the house at twenty to ten?'

'I don't think we ought to get too excited about this. He could have gone in for any one of a number of legitimate reasons. One of the guests might have left the lights on, on his car. Or dropped something in the drive outside. Or –'

'Yes, yes,' said Thanet testily. 'I'm well aware that there *could* be a perfectly reasonable explanation. But in that case, why didn't Fielding tell us he'd been into the house earlier? I did specifically ask him, if you remember,

246

and he said no, he hadn't been in until he went to look for Carey. He was quite definite about it.'

'If it was a trivial errand, perhaps it just slipped his mind.'

'Well there's only one way to find out. We'll have to ask him. What I don't understand is how we could both have missed this until now. I suppose it must be because it was Hartley's statement we were checking and we were looking at the other statements only in the light of whether or not they confirmed his. It just goes to show, though, how things can be missed. In fact, I'm just wondering if we'd better start again, go through all the other statements looking at them from a different point of view.'

Lineham groaned. 'Not now, surely. Not after that session yesterday.'

'Well, perhaps not. But if we get stuck again . . . Anyway, what about you? Did you have any bright ideas in the night?'

Lineham shook his head. 'Only that I think we ought to take a closer look at the three young people, Anthea, Gerald and Hartley. They've all got strong motives and we've only interviewed them once so far. Perhaps we've been concentrating too hard on Sylvester.'

'I was thinking the same thing. Right. That's what we'll do today, then. But we'll check with Fielding first, get that sorted out.'

It was another bright March day with a brisk breeze and cotton-wool clouds chasing each other across the sky. The spring sunshine was having its effect, Thanet thought: each time they drove out to the Sylvesters' house, the haze of fresh green foliage on the hedgerows seemed to be more intense.

On the way Lineham said, 'You still haven't told me

247

how you got on with the chiropractor. Louise was asking me last night.'

Thanet told him, doing his best to describe the treatment. 'It was amazing!' he said. 'My brain was telling my arm to stay up but it simply wasn't obeying!'

'Incredible! Anyway, what sort of an effect has it had?'

Thanet moved experimentally in his seat, testing for aches and pains. 'At first there was an unbelievable difference. When I came out of there I felt as though I was walking on air. But I've got a nasty feeling the joint has slipped out of position again – probably yesterday, when I sat down with a thump, remember? I muttered about it at the time. Still, she said that would probably happen, to begin with. I'll just have to be more careful.'

'But she thinks she might be able to get it to stay back in position permanently?'

'She's not promising, but she's willing to try.'

'That would be great! After all this time!'

'I wish I'd gone years ago. To be frank, I wasn't expecting the treatment to do any good. I only went because Joan kept on nagging at me.'

'I bet she was pleased.'

'I told her, I was only too delighted to have been proved wrong! She –' Thanet broke off. They were nearing the Sylvester house and ahead of them in the lane, a couple of hundred yards short of the gateway, was a woman pushing a wheelchair. 'Mrs Fielding and her daughter, I should think.'

Lineham had slowed down and was signalling left. The woman had pulled in to the side, waiting for them to pass, and Thanet glimpsed Linda Fielding's face for the first time. It was covered with unsightly blotches.

'Poor girl,' said Lineham. 'It must be terrible for her parents.'

248

Thanet said nothing, didn't even hear what the sergeant had said. He was experiencing that unique moment in every murder case he had ever solved, when suddenly the relevant pieces of information come together, assume their true importance and reveal a solution so clear, so obvious that he wondered how he could possibly have missed seeing it before.

But no, in this case he was wrong, he must be.

'Sir?' said Lineham.

Thanet became aware that the car was parked, the engine switched off, and that he was staring fixedly through the windscreen. He turned a dazed face towards Lineham.

Knowing him so well, the sergeant saw at a glance what had happened. 'You've got it!' he said.

Thanet nodded, slowly. 'Perhaps. I'm not sure. But if so, I only wish I hadn't.'

'Well?' said Lineham. Then, as Thanet did not immediately respond. 'Don't tell me you're going to hold out on me?'

'No. I'm still trying to absorb it, that's all.'

'So?'

Thanet told him.

Lineham listened with rapt attention. His reaction was gratifying. When Thanet had finished he said, 'Beats me how you ever worked that one out. And I agree, it's just possible you could be right. But if so, how on earth are we ever going to prove it?'

'To be frank, I'm not sure I want to. But I suppose we have to try.'

They got out of the car and walked back down the drive. By now Mrs Fielding was pushing the wheelchair up the path to the front door of the bungalow and as Thanet and Lineham came up behind them the two women looked around apprehensively. Thanet was familiar with the expression 'a shadow of her former self' but felt he had never truly appreciated what it meant until he took his first proper look at the face of Linda Fielding. Superimposed upon the hollow cheeks and sunken eyes he envisaged the plump, healthy features of the girl in the tennis photograph, and his stomach twisted in sympathy as he smiled at her and introduced himself. 'I'm sorry to trouble you. I wanted a word with Mr Fielding.'

There were no answering smiles. The two women exchanged nervous glances and Mrs Fielding laid a hand on Linda's shoulder as she said, 'I'll see if he's in.'

Fielding must have heard voices and a moment later he opened the door, his welcoming look for his wife and daughter fading when he saw the two policemen.

'Could we have a word, sir?'

Fielding gave a grudging nod.

Thanet and Lineham waited while the Fieldings manoeuvred the wheelchair through the doorway, a difficult procedure as there was only an inch or so of clearance. In the hall Mrs Fielding hesitated.

'You and Linda go in the kitchen,' said Fielding. 'I won't be long.'

'Why don't we go into the kitchen?' said Thanet. 'I'm sure Miss Fielding would be more comfortable in the sitting room.'

Mrs Fielding gave him a grateful smile and removed the rug from Linda's knees. Then, with the clumsiness of those unused to such skills, she and her husband each tucked an arm under one of their daughter's and lifted her to her feet. Her slow, shuffling progress across the hall to the sitting room was painful to watch. The doorway was too narrow to admit the wheelchair, Thanet realised.

A moment or two later Fielding returned and led them into a spotlessly clean small square kitchen equipped with an old-fashioned range of cupboards, a stone sink and a drop-leaf formica-topped table with three chairs. In the inner wall was a serving hatch which was slightly open, Thanet noticed. Did this mean that Mrs Fielding and Linda would be able to overhear their conversation?

'D'you want to sit down?' said Fielding ungraciously.

'Thank you.'

Lineham was to begin the questioning and now he said, 'We just wanted to go over what you said in your statement, Mr Fielding.' He took out the photocopy he had made and handed it to Fielding. 'Perhaps you'd just glance through it.'

Fielding took a spectacle case out of his pocket and put on some steel-rimmed reading glasses. When he'd finished reading he passed the paper back to Lineham without comment.

Lineham tapped it. 'You say here that you saw Hartley Jeopard coming out of the dining room while you were looking for Carey.'

'That's right, yes.'

Lineham was shaking his head. 'That doesn't make sense.'

Fielding frowned. 'Why not?'

'Because Hartley Jeopard came out of the dining room at just after twenty to ten. He was back in the supper queue by five to ten and then remained at his table until the alarm was raised at 10.35, when his brother's body was found. Whereas you told us you didn't go into the house until after Roper came down to tell you Carey was missing, at five to ten. So how could you have seen Hartley at twenty to?'

Silence. Fielding was still frowning. He was beginning to sweat, too, Thanet noticed.

Lineham waited for a few moments and then said, 'Can you explain this, sir?'

Fielding was shaking his head. 'No. I can't. I must have been mistaken. Perhaps I didn't see him.'

'Yes, you did. Because he certainly saw you. Which is why you were questioned closely about this in the first place.'

Another silence. Then Fielding said slowly. 'Well I just don't understand it. It's a real puzzle, isn't it? I suppose I must have gone in on some errand or another. But if so, I can't remember what.' He stood up. 'I tell you what, I'll have a think about it and let you know.'

Lineham glanced at Thanet, who shook his head and said, 'I'm sorry, Mr Fielding, we can't leave it like that. You see, there's something else.'

'Something else?' Fielding glanced from Thanet to Lineham, as if wondering from which direction the blow would fall. He subsided slowly back on to his chair as if his legs would no longer bear his weight.

'Yes.'

Lineham was as puzzled as Fielding, Thanet could tell, though he was hiding it well.

Thanet hesitated, torn. Now was the moment of decision. He could go on, or he could simply shake his head and say, 'Never mind, it's of no importance,' and leave it at that. The inner man counselled compassion, but the policeman in him urged him on. The years of devotion to duty, the ingrained habit of a working life, would not allow him to falter now. If he did, he knew his conscience would give him no rest. It was after all not up to him, not up to any individual to be judge and jury, only to oil the wheels of justice. He took out his notebook, tore off a sheet of paper and handed it to Fielding, together with a biro. 'I'd like you to write something for me, please.'

The Adam's apple in Fielding's throat moved as he swallowed, nervously. 'What?'

'Write, "Meet me at 9.45 in the pool house."'

Fielding swallowed again. His weatherbeaten skin had gone the colour of uncooked pastry and his hand shook as he began to write. 'What was that? "Meet me . . ."'

'". . . at 9.45 in the pool house."' Thanet watched the biro travel laboriously across the page. Fielding's hand was shaking like that of someone with Parkinson's disease. At times like this Thanet wished he was anything but a policeman.

Fielding pushed the paper across the table.

'Thank you.' Picking it up only by the extreme tip of one corner, Thanet studied it. 'Yes.' He glanced at Lineham. 'I think we have all we need here. Have you got the sheet we tore off the telephone notepad at the house, to compare?' He was confident that by now Lineham had understood what he was doing.

'I'll get it. It's in the car.' Lineham stood up.

But Fielding was shaking his head. 'Don't bother. What's the point?' He dropped his head into his hands, clutching at it with one hand on each side as if to try to contain his despair.

Lineham raised his eyebrows at Thanet and Thanet signalled, *Wait*.

Head still bent, Fielding shook it and mumbled. 'It's obvious you know what happened.'

Neither of the policemen moved or spoke. This still wasn't enough.

Then, at last, Fielding straightened up. His eyes were bleak and his shoulders sagged, as if weighed down by sorrow. 'But it was an accident, I swear.'

Thanet realised he had been holding his breath. He nodded at Lineham, who gave the caution.

He had been right in thinking the two women in the next room had been able to overhear the conversation. While Lineham was still speaking the hatch was pushed up to its full extent and Mrs Fielding appeared. She waited until he had finished and then said quietly, and with a sad dignity, 'I think you all ought to come in here now.' Then, to her husband, 'Linda and me want to be with you.'

Fielding looked at Thanet, who assented, and in silence the three men filed next door.

Linda was sitting in an upright armchair near the hearth, where a fire burned brightly. Without her coat it was even more obvious how frail, almost skeletal, she was. More of the unsightly blotches disfigured her neck and the backs of her hands. As her father entered she gave him a loving smile and patted the end of the sofa beside her. 'Come and sit here, Dad.'

He did as she asked and Mrs Fielding sat down next to him. Wife and daughter each took one of his hands and held it. The message was clear: *divided, we fall.*

'We knew it would have to come out in the end,' said Mrs Fielding. Her eyes flickered to Linda. 'But we hoped it wouldn't be just yet.' In contrast with the slight frame of her husband and the fragility of her daughter she looked solid, substantial, as if she was prepared to use up every last ounce of strength she possessed to shore up her disintegrating family.

'And it really was an accident,' said Linda. She smiled at her father and squeezed his hand. 'Dad wouldn't hurt a fly.'

'But you did leave him to drown,' said Thanet, looking at Fielding.

254

Fielding was shaking his head. 'I still don't understand how that happened. He could swim like a fish, I've seen him, a thousand times.'

'We thought he must have banged his head on the side and knocked himself out as he went in,' said Linda. 'It's the only possible explanation.'

'You don't think Ron would have just walked out if he'd *known* Max was unconscious?' said Mrs Fielding.

Thanet looked at Fielding and their eyes met, each reading what could not openly be said.

I can't guarantee that.

I wouldn't condemn you if you had.

'Perhaps you'd better tell us what happened,' said Thanet quietly.

TWENTY-TWO

Suddenly, as if a dam had burst, the Fieldings were all speaking at once.

'I only wanted to talk to him.'

'Ron didn't mean him no harm.'

'It's all my fault,' said Linda. And, to the consternation of everyone present, dissolved into tears.

In a flurry of concern Fielding fished a handkerchief out of his pocket and thrust it into Linda's hand and Mrs Fielding got up, squatted down in front of her daughter and put her arms around her. 'Hush, lovey. That's not true. It simply isn't true.' She glanced over her shoulder at Thanet and her eyes were hard. 'If it was anyone's fault, it was his. Max's.'

'I assume it happened on the night he took Linda to the College Ball?' said Thanet.

Linda had regained her self-control and now she wiped her eyes, blew her nose and nodded.

Her mother gave her one last hug and returned to her seat. 'The pig!' she said. 'He spiked her drink and then took advantage of her. She's not used to alcohol, we don't hardly ever touch it in this house. She thought she was drinking orange juice and never knew no better until she woke up in his bed next morning. She never told us at

256

the time, of course. I knew she was upset, but I thought it was just because he never asked her out again. So when she got this, this . . .' She shook her head.

It had to be spelt out. 'It's AIDS, isn't it,' said Thanet.

They all looked down, as if they were ashamed to admit it.

'I feel so dirty all the time,' said Linda. 'I don't know if you can understand that.'

'Understand, yes. Agree, no. As your mother says, it wasn't – isn't, your fault.'

'Intellectually I know that,' said Linda, unconsciously reminding him that unlike her parents she was university-educated. 'But emotionally it's a different matter. I think I could have found any other illness easier to bear.'

'That's why we haven't told anyone,' said her mother. 'No one around here knows what's really the matter with her. They know Linda's ill, of course, but I think they all believe it's cancer.'

'Yes, they do. At least, that's what Mrs Sylvester told me.' Thanet looked at Linda. 'And there was absolutely no doubt that Jeopard was responsible?'

'There was never anyone else,' she said. 'If it weren't for him I'd be a phenomenon. A twenty-five-year-old virgin in the nineties!'

'Linda!' said her mother, shocked by such plain speaking. This wasn't the kind of household in which sex would ever have been discussed openly, Thanet guessed.

'Mum, it's all right! I'd guess the Inspector's pretty unshockable by now. Am I right?'

'I admire the fact that you're able to joke about it,' said Thanet. 'I would find it hard to consider the situation even remotely funny.'

'If I didn't, I'd go mad at the unfairness of it all.'

'So when did you learn the diagnosis?' said Thanet.

'Not until the first lesions started to appear.' Linda looked at the blotches on her hands. 'Until then no one knew what was the matter with me. My doctor, rightly or wrongly, had never thought of testing for the AIDS virus.'

'He knew you, that's why,' said her mother. 'Knew you were a decent girl, not the type to pick up something like that.' She looked at Thanet. 'Linda's right. That's what's so awful about it. It's so unfair. It's not even as if she agreed to go to bed with Max. Then you could say that she asked for it. But Linda was innocent! Innocent!'

Her husband was nodding agreement and he patted her hand. 'No point in upsetting yourself all over again, Mother.'

'But look where it's got us!' she cried. 'Look what he's done to our family! There's Linda so ill and now you, in all this trouble. He was a wicked, wicked man and that's the truth of it. How could he do such a thing, to a girl like Linda?'

What was there to say? 'So Jeopard must have been HIV positive,' said Thanet. 'And never developed full-blown AIDS.'

'They said it can take years for that to happen and there are cases when it never does,' said Fielding. 'You can be a carrier all that time and never know it. Terrible, isn't it? We think he probably picked it up in foreign parts. We've seen programmes about it, on the telly. Those little girls in Thailand and such like ... He was always off on his travels and the Lord alone knows what he was up to when he was away, if he could do this to a girl like our Linda.'

'But what I don't understand is why you left it until the day of the engagement party to tackle him about it,' said Thanet.

'Because we didn't know until that morning who the man was, who was responsible!' said Fielding. 'Linda would never tell us.'

'When we found out it was AIDS,' said Linda, 'I couldn't believe it at first. I mean, I'd never had a serious boyfriend. But when they told me it can take years to develop, after being infected, I realised it must have been Max. There was just no other explanation. I didn't tell Mum and Dad it was him, though. It was bad enough for them to know what was wrong with me, that I was going to die, I just felt it would be even worse if they realised they knew the man who had infected me. Better, I thought, for them to have this shadowy, anonymous person to hate than someone they could put a name and face to. But I was worried in case Max didn't know he was HIV positive – worried, that is, about all the other women he might have infected or still could infect, without even being aware of it. I could have written to him, I suppose, but somehow I wanted to do it face to face. It was wrong of me, I suppose, but I wanted to say to him, look, look what you have done to me. I wanted to punish him, make him feel guilty, acknowledge the consequences of what to him must have seemed a bit of harmless fun.'

'Harmless!' said her mother. 'Harmless!'

'Hush, Mother,' said her husband. 'Let Linda explain.'

Mrs Fielding clamped her lips together and glared, but subsided.

'That's what I feel most guilty about,' said Linda. 'If I hadn't wanted revenge, my petty little revenge, and I'd contented myself with writing a letter, then Dad wouldn't be in this position now. The excuse I gave myself for not doing so was that I wanted to ask Max about Tess. And it's true that I was worried about her, naturally.'

And not only Tess, did you but know it, thought

Thanet grimly. There was Marion Sylvester, Anthea, Rosinha and perhaps even her unborn baby, apart from countless other women Jeopard might have infected in his promiscuous way through life.

'I was pretty sure he must have slept with her, and every time I saw her it was a relief that she was still looking healthy, but this was something I wanted to ask him about, for my own peace of mind. I felt I couldn't trust him to reply, if I asked him about this in a letter.

'My other excuse, of course, was that I was feeling pretty rotten. It's been a ghastly few months, one way and the other, and I've had to conserve all my energies just to cope with day-to-day existence. But I hadn't forgotten about contacting Max. I knew it was becoming urgent, and when I went into the Hospice at the beginning of last week I realised it would have to be sooner rather than later. The next serious infection might well be the last. So I'd pretty much decided that when I came home I was going to stop hoping to tell him in person and write to him instead, and you can imagine how I felt when I did get home on Saturday morning, saw those balloons tied to the gatepost and learned why they were there. Until then I'd no idea that Tess had broken off her engagement to Gerald and was getting engaged to Max.'

'It didn't occur to us to tell her while she was in the Hospice,' said Fielding. 'To be honest, we didn't even think about it. All we were concerned about was how she was getting on, whether or not she'd be able to come home again and if so, how soon.'

'We could tell she was upset when we told her about the engagement,' said her mother. 'But she wouldn't say why. Not until the afternoon.'

'I had to think,' said Linda. 'I didn't want to have to talk to Tess about it, you see. Picking up the virus is a bit

260

like Russian Roulette, I gather, and I was just unlucky, especially as it had only happened the once. Rather like girls who are unfortunate enough to get pregnant their first time, I suppose. Anyway, if Tess was all right I didn't want to worry her – I mean, it could give her nightmares for years, and all for nothing. So I decided the only thing to do was to stop prevaricating and talk to Max then, that day, preferably before the party. I knew that if I missed the chance I might not get another for months – perhaps not at all, and besides, what I really wanted was to get him to agree to call the engagement off, for Tess's sake, before it was officially made public. I thought, if he really loved her, he'd do it.'

'Not Max! Not if it didn't suit his book!' said Mrs Fielding grimly. 'In my opinion he always looked out for number one, first and last, never mind anyone else.'

'But I had to try, Mum, you must see that. If he refused, I was prepared to take pretty desperate measures to make him agree, threaten to tell Tess, to begin with, and then, if he still wouldn't listen, threaten to get Dad to wheel me up to the party and make a public announcement.'

Thanet could imagine what courage that would have taken and what a furore it would have created.

'Anyway, the point was, I didn't know when Max was coming down from London, so I got Dad to find out, casually, from Tess. I was hoping that if he came down early, in the afternoon, perhaps, I might manage to get a message to him, to come and see me.' She gave a wry smile. 'I thought if he saw me like this he'd realise what he'd be saving Tess from if he agreed to give her up. But unfortunately we discovered he wouldn't be arriving until the same time as everybody else. So at that point I decided that there was only one thing to do. I couldn't

261

hope to go up to the house myself and manage to get a word with him in private, it would be too difficult to arrange, so I'd have to ask Dad to do it for me.'

'That was when she told us,' said Fielding. 'That Max was the one.'

'You must have been absolutely furious with him,' said Lineham.

'Oh, I was,' said Fielding. 'No point in denying it. We both were, weren't we, Mother?'

His wife nodded. 'Can you blame us?'

'But by the evening I'd calmed down,' said Fielding, 'and I agreed to do as Linda asked, chiefly because I could see how much it was worrying her but also because I'm fond of Tess. She's a lovely girl, isn't she, Mother, and we've seen her grown up from a toddler. I couldn't bear to think of this happening to her, too.' He glanced at Linda, raised her hand to his lips and kissed it in a strangely courtly gesture.

He was, Thanet thought, a truly gentle man. What could Jeopard have said or done to goad him beyond endurance?

Linda smiled at her father. Then she turned to Thanet with a serious look. 'So you see, it really was all my fault. If I hadn't insisted . . .'

'Shh,' said Fielding 'Don't start that again, lovey. We agreed. There's no point in trying to say who's to blame and who isn't. Your mother's right. When it comes down to it, Max brought it on himself and no one can say different.'

'So what happened, exactly, on Saturday evening?' said Lineham.

'Well, I was directing the car parking,' said Fielding. 'So it was easy for me to look out for him. But when he arrived he was in a hurry, as usual, and when I asked him if I could have a word he just brushed me off and said, yes, sure, later, and went racing off. So I decided the only thing to do was write him a note and get one of the waitresses to hand it to him. I was very busy for a while, the guests were arriving thick and fast, so I didn't have a chance until later. When I did, I nipped into the house and scribbled a message on the pad by the telephone in the hall. Well, you know about that, don't you.'

'You didn't sign it.' Thanet made this a statement, not a question. He didn't want Fielding to guess that the words he had asked him to write down had simply been an inspired guess.

'No, I didn't, deliberate, like. All the while I was parking the cars I was thinking what to say, and I decided to keep it short and simple and not to sign it so that he'd be, well, sort of intrigued. I just said something like, meet me in the pool house at 9.45, on a matter of life and death.' Fielding lifted his chin in defiance. 'Well, it was, wasn't it?'

Only too true, thought Thanet.

'I thought that would bring him, if anything would. And I was right. It did. When I got to the pool house he was already there, waiting for me.'

Thanet's imagination was setting the scene: darkness pressing against the windows; light reflecting off the water; Max, elegant and debonair in his expensive suede trousers and silk shirt; and Fielding, a complete contrast in his old cord trousers and tweed jacket.

'Fielding? What do you want?'
'I told you earlier, I wanted a word with you.'
'Well I can't speak to you now. I'm expecting someone.'
'That's me.'

263

'What do you mean? You mean, you wrote this?'

'Yes, I did.'

'Of all the bloody nerve! What the hell do you think you're up to? A matter of life and death indeed!'

'But that's true. It is. Linda's death. My daughter's. And yours, too, probably.'

'That stopped him in his tracks,' said Fielding with satisfaction. 'He was halfway to the door by then.'

'What the devil are you talking about? What do you mean, mine? Look here, are you threatening me?'

'Not in the way you think. If you do die you'll have only yourself to blame.'

'You're out of your mind, man. Raving. Let me pass.'

'Not until you hear what I have to say. Linda is dying. Dying, do you hear me? Of AIDS. And you are the only man who's ever slept with her.'

'What?'

'I said, Linda is dying of AIDS, and you're the only man who's ever slept with her. You know what that means, don't you? You're HIV positive and you've got a time-bomb ticking away inside you.'

'I don't believe you!'

'It's true. Just come and take a look at Linda and you'll see how true it is. She's in a wheelchair now, did you know that? She can hardly stand up unaided and she's spent all this week in the Hospice. The next infection she picks up will probably carry her off. And make no mistake about it, you're the one who's responsible. You, and no one else.'

'*I just don't believe that. Look at me! I'm perfectly fit and healthy.*'

'*You may seem so, now. But just wait and see. And believe me, nothing gives me greater satisfaction than knowing that from now on for the rest of your life you're going to wake up every morning afraid to look in the mirror, for fear of seeing that first lesion. Your death warrant.*'

'*She's lying! She must be!*'

'*Don't you dare call my Linda a liar! She's worth a hundred of you any day. What sort of a man spikes a young girl's drink and then seduces her?*'

'*Oh, that's what she told you, is it? Well, let me tell you, she was willing. Not just willing, panting for it, d'you hear me? Your precious daughter couldn't wait to –*'

'*That's not true!*'

'And that,' said Fielding sadly, 'was when I pushed him. He was standing near the edge of the pool saying all these terrible things about Linda and I just couldn't bear it, I just wanted to shut him up. So I gave him one great shove and walked out. I admit I was beside myself, but I swear, Inspector, that I didn't mean to kill him. I had no idea he'd hit his head on the side as he went in and I didn't look back. I just heard this almighty splash and thought, *that'll ruin your fancy clothes. How are you going to explain that away?* Then I came back home.'

'He told us what had happened,' said Linda. 'We were waiting for him, to see how he'd got on. And we all had a good laugh about it! We couldn't believe it, later, when Dad came back and told us Max had been found dead in the pool.'

Thanet shook his head gravely. 'Why didn't you tell us all this straight away?'

'Because of Linda!' said Fielding. 'If I had, everyone would have had to know why Max and me were having the argument in the first place! This terrible thing with Linda is *private*, Inspector. We haven't got much longer together and we wanted to be able to spend that time quietly, by ourselves. It takes every last ounce of energy we've got to face up to this situation day by day. We couldn't bear the prospect of all the rumpus, all the publicity. Surely you can understand that?'

'Oh yes,' said Thanet sympathetically. 'Only too well.'

'Yes,' said Linda. 'I believe you do. But there's not much hope of keeping it quiet now, is there? We must just bear it as well as we can.'

'What will happen to Ron?' said Mrs Fielding fearfully.

'Mr Fielding will have to accompany us back to Head-quarters,' said Thanet. 'He will be formally charged, and have to stay there until he comes up before the Magistrates. But if we can hurry that up I think it highly probable that in these rather special circumstances he'll be released on bail. So he should be home again in a day or two.' *And you'll still be able to spend Linda's last weeks together.*

'Really?' Linda smiled, for the first time.

She was looking exhausted, he realised, was barely able to remain upright in her chair.

He was glad that he had been able to give the stricken little family at least some small grain of hope and consolation.

TWENTY-THREE

'It's a relief to get away from the office,' said Thanet, peering into the mirror. 'What do you think, love? This tie or that one?'

It was Saturday night and they were getting ready for the Dracos' party.

Joan considered, head on one side. 'The spotted one, I think.'

'You don't think it's a bit conservative for a celebration?'

Joan paused in applying her lipstick. 'If that's how you feel, why not go for something really wild? Like the one Ben gave you for Christmas?'

This was a concoction of fluorescent swirls, guaranteed to cause comment. So far Thanet had worn it only once, on Ben's birthday.

'Why not?' he said. 'It's pretty representative of my state of mind. The last few days have been a nightmare. I feel as though I've been living in a state of siege.' He took the tie out and started to put it on.

'Luke, you're not really going to wear it?'

'Why not? It was you who suggested it.'

'But I wasn't serious!'

'But I am.' Thanet finished tying the knot and stood back to study the effect. 'There. What d'you think?'

Joan closed her eyes. 'Dazzling.'

'Good!'

'What d'you mean, a state of siege? The press?'

'Partly. Though it's nothing to what the Fieldings have had to put up with.'

It had been impossible to keep Fielding's arrest quiet. It had been such an unexpected and astonishing development that the media had been on to it like a pack of hounds and the clamour for more information had been deafening. Fortunately Draco had proved unexpectedly cooperative. Perhaps his own experience through the years of his wife's illness had given him a special sympathy for the Fieldings' plight, and he had allocated Thanet extra men to protect the little family from unwarranted intrusion by the media.

'But apart from that, everyone involved in the case has been pestering me for an explanation of what happened, and the problem is, my hands are tied until it's officially confirmed that Jeopard was HIV positive.'

'Until you get the results of the test back, you mean?'

'That's right, yes.'

'And when will that be?'

'The sample wasn't sent off until Wednesday – the test isn't a routine part of a post-mortem – and it takes a week, apparently, so it'll be several more days yet.'

'But you are certain about it, aren't you? That he was HIV positive, I mean?'

'Oh yes. There's no doubt in my mind that Linda Fielding is telling the truth, poor girl. If you'd seen her, Joan . . . Every time I think of her I imagine how I'd feel if it were Bridget in that condition.'

'Well, let's hope and pray that Bridget marries a man who's never been in contact with the virus, and that she has the sense meanwhile never to have unprotected intercourse. Heaven knows she's had the message dinned into her often enough.'

'The other thing that's worrying me is all the other women who were involved with Jeopard. They all seem well at the moment, but I can tell you I'm really dreading breaking the news to them. And again, that can't be done until we have official confirmation. At the moment, as I say, everyone remotely connected with the case is completely bewildered by Fielding's arrest and can't understand why we won't give them a proper explanation. Jeopard's mother, especially, has been bombarding us with phone calls and visits and is furious that I keep fending her off. Well, you can't blame her, can you? If it had been my son, I'd feel entitled to an explanation too. But it does make life rather difficult for me.'

'I'm just off now.' Ben appeared at the door. 'Wow! Great tie, Dad!'

'Thought it was about time I gave it another airing. Where are you going tonight?'

'Disco at the Blue Moon.'

'Well, have a good time.' With difficulty Thanet refrained from adding, 'But be careful.' He'd said it often enough in the past. If Ben hadn't got the message by now he never would.

'Ditto.' And he was gone, whistling.

Thanet and Joan exchanged indulgent smiles.

'What d'you think?' she said, standing up to display her dress, which was a new one, bought especially for the occasion. It was in a fluid smoky-blue silk which deepened the colour of her eyes, emphasised the curves of breasts, waist and hips and swirled around her calves as she moved.

'Give us a twirl.'

She obliged.

'Mmm, delicious.' He put his arms around her and nibbled her neck. 'You look good enough to eat.'

'But not now!' she said, giving him a quick hug before easing herself away. 'I couldn't face doing my make-up all over again.'

'As if I would suggest it!'

Outside Joan shivered. 'I'm glad I put my thicker coat on.'

For no apparent reason the temperature had plummeted. Although dusk was falling, over to the west the sky was still stained with the remnants of what must have been a spectacular sunset – mandarin-gold, shell-pink and apricot.

'I think there'll be a frost tonight,' said Thanet.

Inside the car Joan huddled into her coat and said, 'But I still don't understand how you came to suspect Fielding in the first place. I mean, he really didn't seem to have anything to do with the case, so far as I can gather, apart from being a part of the Sylvesters' household.'

'I know. That was what was so misleading. It simply didn't occur to me that he might be involved. But once I realised, of course, the whole thing fell into place. The clues were all there, I just hadn't appreciated their significance.' He switched the heater on. 'I think the engine should be beginning to warm up by now.'

Joan waved her hand in front of the air grill. 'Yes, I can feel it.'

'Well, I knew quite early on that Linda had been one of Max and Tess's crowd. But I tended to dismiss her, partly because she doesn't seem to have been involved with them for quite some time now, partly because she wasn't at the party, and partly because Marion Sylvester had told me that Linda had really only been on the fringe of the group, she hadn't been nearly as closely involved as the others.'

'Why was that?'

'Chiefly, I think, because her background was so different – not in the social sense, the Sylvesters certainly aren't snobs by any means – but because her parents were getting on a bit when she was born and I gather that, as so often happens with only children of older parents, Linda was much more staid and reserved than her contemporaries. But as she was in the same class as Tess and Anthea at school and also because she happened to be right there, on the doorstep, she was often asked to make up a four at tennis. So she certainly knew the others fairly well, even if she'd never been close to any of them.'

'She sounds the last person Max Jeopard would take to a College Ball, from what you've told me about him.'

'In normal circumstances, I agree. But Jeopard had counted on taking Tess, you see. As I told you, when he went up to Oxford she followed him, took her secretarial course there and then stayed on, took a job there, to be near him. I suspect he wished she hadn't, that as Ralph Sylvester said, he'd probably have preferred to be footloose and fancy-free during his university days, but even so there was no real excuse for the fact that he didn't tell Tess until the end of his final term that the day after the College Ball he'd be leaving on a year-long trip to China. He must have been planning it for ages, all the travel arrangements were made. She was so upset and so furious with him that she broke it off, said she never wanted to see him again.'

'I'm not surprised! So only a few days before the Ball he found himself without a partner.'

'Exactly. And the problem was that because the Ball was being held after the end of term all the girls he knew well either had partners and were staying on especially for it, or had already gone home. So he had to think of someone who might be available at the last minute.'

'I.e. Linda.'

'Yes. She was in her first year at Bristol and might be free, not being the type to be caught up in a social whirl. Oxford terms are shorter than most other universities, so he knew she'd still be there. I should think he also counted on the fact that she would swallow her pride at being asked only at the last minute and agree to come. The Oxford College Balls really are rather special and I suppose most girls would jump at the chance. Apart from which, Anthea's mother told me she thought that as a teenager Linda had secretly had a crush on Max and if that was so I imagine Max was aware of it.'

'And she accepted the invitation.'

'She did. To her bitter regret in view of what happened. She was, of course, being the innocent she was, the perfect victim to have that sort of trick played on her.'

'What a truly despicable thing to do.'

'I know. And that it should have such disastrous and far-reaching consequences, all these years later . . .'

'Poor girl.'

'You should see her, Joan. She's such a pathetic sight. I've never actually met anyone who was really ill with AIDS before. But the moment I set eyes on her I realised what was the matter with her. The Fieldings had kept it quiet, you see. It's awful, they feel so ashamed about it. Even the Sylvesters still think that she has cancer, which is what they'd told me. And if I hadn't seen that film on AIDS I don't suppose I would have questioned it. You know the one I mean, we saw it last year.'

272

'The one in which the wife discovers her husband is an active homosexual and has been having unprotected intercourse with her for years, you mean?'

'That's right, yes. You remember the bit where she watches a documentary on AIDS?'

'Oh, I see!' said Joan. 'The lesions.'

'Exactly. Linda has them on her face and neck as well as her hands. I gather from Doc Mallard that they are usually even more widespread on the trunk. But they are instantly recognisable, believe me. And when I saw them, well, everything suddenly came together – the fact that Max was promiscuous, had done a lot of foreign travel, had taken Linda to a College Ball where things can often get out of hand, that Linda's illness was sufficiently serious to have reduced a strapping, healthy girl to a frail-looking creature in a wheelchair . . . From there it was only a hop, skip and a jump to suspecting her father. We were already on our way to interview him because he had been seen in the house much earlier than he claimed . . . It all just fitted.'

'Yes, I see. But how on earth did you get him to admit it? From what you're saying I gather there wasn't a shred of evidence against him?'

Thanet shook his head. 'No, there wasn't. So I played a trick on him and I'm not proud of it, I must admit. I still feel ambivalent about it. I've come up against this before in cases where I feel I'd really rather not make an arrest at all.'

'What are you suggesting? That you shouldn't have pursued the matter, that you should have just left it?'

'Perhaps. It would have bought them a little time, you see, enough for Linda to have spent her last days in peace with her parents. After her death I'm pretty sure Fielding would have owned up. He's not the sort of man who could live indefinitely with something like that on his conscience.'

'And what would you have done in the meantime? Would you have told Draco?'

'I shouldn't think so. He'd probably have insisted on having Fielding in for questioning and the whole object of the exercise would have been defeated.'

'So you'd have gone through the motions of continuing the investigation. And a number of innocent people would have been left in uncertainty for an indefinite period of time.'

'Not long, I shouldn't think.'

'All the same, I don't think you would have been very comfortable with the situation.'

'No, I'm not pretending I would. But to be honest, Joan, I can't pretend my motives in manipulating a confession were pure. I have a nasty feeling that I had to go on, I had to find out, for my own satisfaction. And to show everybody what a clever person I am. Apparently to have failed to solve the case would have made a big dent in my vanity.'

'But even if that's true, and I suspect that because you feel sorry for the Fieldings you're going too far the other way in questioning your motives, you've said over and over again that it's not for you to judge in such matters. Your job is to find out the truth and then hand it over to others to decide what to do with the culprit.'

'I know. But it's not always an easy course to follow.'

'Well, I don't really see that you had any choice. I feel you did the right thing. So stop agonising about it and tell me how you did it.'

'I suppose you're right.' Thanet was silent for a few moments, thinking, and then gave Joan a smile and said, 'Yes. Of course you are. Well, what happened was that

Mike and I played a little charade. You remember the note I told you about?'

'The one that was handed to Max at the party, which you hadn't been able to trace?'

'Yes. We knew it hadn't been in an envelope, we checked, so we guessed that someone had written it on impulse. Now, obviously, very few people carry notepaper around with them, especially to a party, so Mike came up with the idea that it might have been written on the telephone pad in the hall. One of the disadvantages of all these crime series on television is that the general public has learned too much about our techniques for catching criminals. But in this case, it was an advantage. By now most people know that we can lift from a message pad the impressions made on it by words written on a sheet that's been torn off.'

Joan was nodding. 'I'm sure you're right.'

'Yes. Well, the problem was that I'd slipped up there. It didn't occur to me – until Mike suggested it, as I say – that we should have examined the telephone pad earlier. By the time we took it away, it had been used a number of times in between, and forensic have confirmed that the important top sheet was long gone. But, and this was the point, Fielding didn't know that. I also banked on the fact that if the note had been been written on impulse for some reason – as in fact it was, because Max refused to talk to Fielding when he first requested it, on Max's arrival – then the writer wouldn't have thought of disguising his handwriting.'

'You're saying that if someone is planning to write an anonymous letter he'd probably use capital letters, whereas if he scribbles something off in a hurry he won't bother?'

'Exactly. So I tricked Fielding into thinking we had

275

that top sheet, the one on which his handwriting would have been indented, by getting him to write down what I guessed the message would have been, and pretending we were going to compare it.'

They had arrived at the Dracos' house, or at least as near to it as they were likely to get. The Superintendent lived in a select cul-de-sac of five large modern houses and the influx of cars spilled out into the road leading to it. Thanet pulled into the kerb and switched off the engine.

Joan made no move to get out, however. Her curiosity still wasn't entirely satisfied. 'But how did you know what to tell him to write?'

'Pure guesswork. In fact, the whole thing was a gamble. As I said, at that point, apart from the fact that Fielding was clearly under stress during the interview – and let's face it, a lot of perfectly innocent people react badly to being interviewed by the police – we didn't have a shred of proof. But again, he didn't know that.'

'And you guessed correctly!'

'Luck.'

'Stop being modest.'

'I always am, you know that!'

Joan laughed. 'I'm glad to see you're back on form. Anyway, it worked.'

'It did. Though as I say, I could almost wish it hadn't.'

'What happened to the note itself? You said you hadn't been able to find it. Did Fielding take it away with him?'

'Unlikely as it seems, yes, he did, though he didn't realise he had until the next day, when he found it in his pocket. Apparently, when he arrived in the pool house Jeopard was actually holding it in his hand, looking at it, and during their conversation thrust it at him, right into his face, to ask if he was claiming to have written it.

276

Fielding thinks he must have taken it, as one does if someone shoves something at you like that, and was then so engrossed in the conversation that he put it in his pocket without realising it.'

'So you've seen it?'

'No. He burned it.'

'Poor man.'

'Yes. I really do believe that he didn't look back when he walked out, and had no idea Max was knocked out when he fell into the water. When Fielding got home they actually laughed together about him pushing Max into the pool, you know. I really can't believe they'd have done that if Fielding knew what had happened.'

'Well,' said Joan, opening her door, 'let's hope he gets off lightly. Somehow I think he will.'

'I agree,' said Thanet, getting out of the car. Lightly in one way, perhaps. But the gardener and his wife would no doubt spend the rest of their days mourning the daughter they would soon so tragically lose. And what of the others – all three Sylvesters, Anthea, Rosinha, who was still with the Jeopards, perhaps even the baby? What if they too were HIV positive? How must it be, to live with the threat of AIDS poised like the sword of Damocles above one's head, always to be watching, waiting, wondering when or if it would descend? With a considerable effort he pushed them to the back of his mind. Tonight was Angharad's night and he must do nothing to dampen the mood of celebration. 'Come on,' he said, taking Joan's arm. 'Let's try now to forget about the case and enjoy ourselves.'

'A vain hope, I should think, in view of the company we'll be keeping.'

Thanet shook his head. 'Shop talk has been banned for tonight.'

As they turned the corner into the cul-de-sac the Dracos' house came into view. With light blazing from every window the jubilant message came over loud and clear. *We made it! We came through!*

The front door had been left ajar and Thanet rang the bell before pushing it open. Inside they were enveloped by light, warmth and the hubbub of a successful party well under way.

'Luke!' shouted Draco, who never used Thanet's Christian name at work. He was resplendent in bow tie and plum-coloured velvet smoking jacket. 'And Joan!' He kissed her on both cheeks with enthusiasm. 'You look absolutely ravishing!' he said, his Welsh accent even more pronounced than usual. 'Lucky men, you and me, Luke, aren't we, boyo! Let me take your coats.' He handed them to a girl in black dress and white apron, obviously hired for the occasion. 'Put these away for me, will you, *cariad*?'

Behind his back, Thanet and Joan exchanged indulgent smiles. 'He's well away!' whispered Thanet as they followed him into the sitting room.

And here they all were, the familiar faces he saw every day, cares and anxieties smoothed away, transformed by the atmosphere of rejoicing: Lineham and Louise, Doc Mallard and his wife Helen, Tody and Boon and their wives and many, many more, mingling with the Dracos' other friends.

And, above all, there was Angharad, in celebration of whose continuing survival this party was being held. Thanet had always thought she was one of the most beautiful women he had ever seen; had found it difficult to believe, when he first met her, that Draco, that near-ugly little Welshman, could have won such a prize. But he had quickly realised that their devotion to each other was equally matched, had castigated himself for so superficial a judgement, and during the years of her illness had often wondered what would happen to Draco if Angharad should die. Now, looking at her tonight, it was difficult to believe that this radiant woman had ever lost that wondrous cloud of copper-coloured hair, had ever looked as though she was holding on to life only by her fingernails.

He only wished that there was even the remotest possibility of Linda Fielding making a similar recovery.

'What's the matter?' whispered Joan, observant as ever.

He shook his head. 'Nothing.'

'Great tie!' said Lineham. 'Why don't you wear it to work?'

'Be careful!' said Thanet. 'I might.'

'That would raise the Super's eyebrows!' said Lineham. They all laughed.

After supper they all raised their glasses in response to Draco's birthday toast to Angharad.

'And now,' he said, with the gleeful air of a conjuror about to produce an especially large rabbit out of his hat, 'we come to the *pièce de résistance* of the evening. If you'd all move across to the windows on that side . . .'

They did as they were asked, and an expectant hush fell.

Suddenly the lights went out as at the far end of the garden a match flared. With a fizzing of light, the letter A sprang at them out of the night and then, in swift succession, NGHARAD.

There were oohs and aahs. Angharad exclaimed in delight and clapped her hands. Someone began to sing, 'Happy birthday to you, happy birthday to you,' and they all joined in as rockets exploded in a myriad stars and her name hung emblazoned across the darkness.

Once again Thanet made an effort to push the thought of the Fieldings and all the others out of his mind. Tonight, he thought, it would have to be enough to know that at least one story had had a happy ending.

Printed in the United States
By Bookmasters